CHRISTMAS SURPRISES AT THE DOOR

Fifth Novel in the
Door County Quilts Series

ANN HAZELWOOD

C&T PUBLISHING
Another Maker Inspired!

Text copyright © 2022 by Ann Hazelwood
Photography and artwork copyright © 2022 by C&T Publishing, Inc.

Publisher: Amy Barrett-Daffin
Creative Director: Gailen Runge
Acquisitions Editor: Roxane Cerda
Executive Book Editor: Karen Davis of Gill Editorial Services
Copyeditor: Karly Wallace
Associate Editor: Jennifer Warren
Cover Designer: Michael Buckingham
Book Designer: April Mostek
Production Coordinator: Zinnia Heinzmann
Cover illustrations by Amy Friend and Michael Buckingham
Cover photography by David Prahl / Shutterstock.com
Portrait photography owned by Michael Schlueter

Published by C&T Publishing, Inc., P.O. Box 1456, Lafayette, CA 94549

Library of Congress Control Number: 2022910086

Printed in the USA
10 9 8 7 6 5 4 3 2 1

Dedication and Thanks

After writing more than thirty books over the years, I continue to dedicate my books to the many who have influenced me in some way. Two sources have been a constant support for me:

My husband, Keith Hazelwood, has been there to help me in numerous ways, whether it's heavy lifting, travel companionship when traveling, extra chores around the house, or just being my best cheerleader as I keep writing. To this day he's never read one of my books, but he appreciates what I do. How's that for love?

My readers, who consist of family, friends, and strangers from many parts of the world. You've supported me with your loyalty and your lovely comments. How could I not dedicate this last book in the Door County series to you?

Love to all of you,
—*Ann Hazelwood*

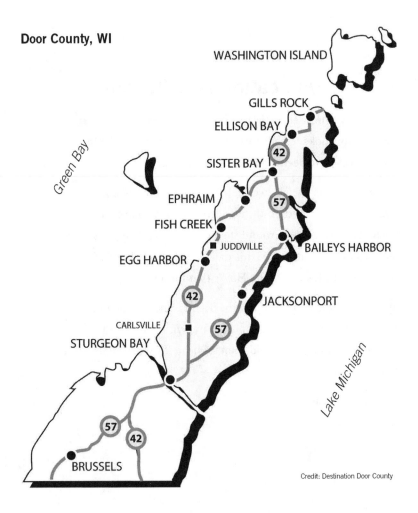

Door County, WI

WASHINGTON ISLAND

GILLS ROCK
ELLISON BAY

Green Bay

42

SISTER BAY

EPHRAIM

57

FISH CREEK

JUDDVILLE

EGG HARBOR

BAILEYS HARBOR

42

JACKSONPORT

CARLSVILLE

57

STURGEON BAY

Lake Michigan

57

42

BRUSSELS

Credit: Destination Door County

WHO ARE THE QUILTERS OF THE DOOR?

CHER CLAMPTON, 56, grew up and attended school with Claire Stewart in Perryville, Missouri. After divorcing her husband, Cher moved from Green Bay to a small cabin in Fish Creek, Wisconsin. When her mother, Hilda, became ill, Cher returned to Perryville to take care of her, and Claire took up residence in her cabin. Cher happily moved back to Door County and rejoined the quilt club after her mother passed.

GRETA GREENSBURG is Swedish, in her sixties, and one of the charter members of the club. She led the group with an iron fist for the first several years, holding firm in keeping to the tradition of only nine members who are diverse in their quilting styles. That is, until Cher and Claire stirred things up. Greta makes quick and easy quilts and is one of the few members in the club who machine quilts.

MARTA BACHMAN is German. She's 58 and lives in Baileys Harbor. She took over as president of the quilt club after Greta stepped down. Her family owns a large orchard and dairy farm. Marta makes traditional quilts by hand. She typically has a large quilt frame set up in her home.

AVA MARIE CHANDLER is 55 and loves any kind of music. She served in the Army, where she sang for anyone who would listen to her. She's blonde, vivacious, and likes to make quilts that tell a story. She loves her alcohol, so no one knows when her flamboyant behavior will erupt. When she left her husband, she moved in with Frances, who needed some help after her stroke.

FRANCES McCRAKEN is the eldest member of the group at 79 years old. She loves spending time in the local cemetery where her late husband is buried. She lives in the historic Corner House in Sturgeon Bay with Ava and has a pristine antique quilt collection that she inherited. The quilts she makes use old blocks to make new designs.

LEE SUE CHAN is Filipina and is married to a cardiologist. The couple live in an ornate home in Ephraim. She is 49 years old and belongs to the Moravian church, also in Ephraim. Lee is an art quilter who loves flowers and landscapes. She is an award-winning quilter who is known for her fine hand appliqué.

OLIVIA WILLIAMS is Black and lives in an apartment over the Novel Bay Booksellers in Sturgeon Bay. She is 41, single, and likes to tout the styles of the Gee's Bend quilts as well as quilts from the South. She is quiet in nature, but the quilts she makes are scrappy, bright, and bold.

RACHAEL McCARTHY, 51, lives on a farm between Egg Harbor and Fish Creek with her new husband Harry. They run a successful barn quilt business and sell Christmas trees in season. Rachael makes the business unique by giving each customer a small wall quilt to match their purchased barn quilt.

GINGER GREENSBURG, a 40-year-old redhead, is Greta's niece. Recently divorced, she owns a shop in Sister Bay where she sells vintage and antique items. She resides upstairs and has two children. While she works in the shop, Ginger likes to make quilted crafts to sell, and she repurposes old quilt tops.

AMY BURRIS, 41, owns the Jacksonport Cottage in Jacksonport, Wisconsin, where she also lives with her husband. She sells Amish quilts and other items made by the Amish.

ANNA MARIE MEYER, 46, is the niece and goddaughter of Marta. She's single and recently moved to Baileys Harbor from Ludwigsburg, Germany. She does dimensional quilting and is a fabulous baker. She lives above her bakery, Anna's Bake Shop.

CLAIRE STEWART, 56, is single and the main character of the series. She became a member of the quilting club when her friend Cher moved back to Missouri to take care of her mother. Claire was eager to leave Missouri and moved into Cher's cabin in Fish Creek. Greta and the quilt club made a rare exception to let Claire replace Cher until Cher moved back to Door County. Claire, a blonde who is showing some gray streaks, is a quilter and watercolor artist who sells her artwork in galleries and on her website. Claire's brother and mother live in Missouri.

Chapter 1

"Ouch!" I shouted as a large apple landed squarely on top of my head.

"Oh, Claire!" Cher said, worried. "Who said the apple doesn't fall far from the tree? Are you okay?"

"Yeah, I think so," I said, rubbing the sore spot on my head.

"I guess I should have warned you about that. Many of the apples are ready to fall without notice, so be careful," Marta told us. Marta and her husband have an orchard on their farm in Baileys Harbor and had graciously welcomed the Quilters of the Door members to join her for a day of picking.

"My bucket's already full," Ginger claimed. "I'm heading back to the house."

"Mine, too!" said Ava as she climbed down from a short ladder. "Oh, I wish Frances could see all of us doing this. I know she'd love to be here today."

"I took a lot of photos so we could show her," Olivia noted. "I never dreamed in a million years that I'd ever go apple picking. Marta, I don't know how you do everything here.

Just dealing with all the apples seems like it would be a full-time job."

"Our hired hand and my grandson Billy take care of most of the orchard when the time is right," Marta explained. "Now, I don't think Kelly and Billy are getting much picking done from the sound of their laughter and silliness."

I had to chuckle because she was right. It was good, innocent fun to witness. Kelly and Billy were the same age. They'd met during our first outdoor quilt show and hit it off immediately.

"Isn't it great to be young and flirtatious?" I reminisced. "Billy is going to miss dear Kelly when she goes off to college."

"Marta, will Billy be going to college next year?" Rachael asked with interest.

"No, I'm afraid he's committed to being a farmer like his grandpa," Marta explained. "Billy has followed him around since he was a youngster. He always told my husband he'd take over the farm one day."

"What about his dad?" Cher asked.

"His dad, Harold, only helps at harvest time, but he likes his job at the MFA, which means he's still involved with farming in a different capacity."

"I think it's great that Billy already knows what he wants to do when he grows up. It takes most of us a lot longer to figure that out, if we ever do," Rachael noted.

"Ladies, I don't want to wear you out. Let's complete our day with a rest under the shade tree by the house," Marta announced. "I've got apple pie, coffee, and lemonade for you."

"Oh, that sounds wonderful," Lee said as she picked her last apple. "I can't wait to show my hubby the fruits of my labor." We chuckled at her pun.

"Don't you just love the Honeycrisp apples?" Amy asked. "I guess I'm just a good Wisconsinite through and through."

"Nothing wrong with that," Marta replied.

We followed Marta to the tree that provided enough shade for all of us. We'd had such an enjoyable time when Marta previously invited us over for a quilting/lunch day. When our summer quilt show wrapped up, she invited the group to come apple picking. She'd told us there would be plenty of apples for all of us, and we could go home with the bagful we picked. Most of us had never picked our own apples before.

"How's your head, Claire?" Marta asked.

"I guess I'm not as hard-headed as I've been told I am," I joked. "I can feel a tender bump on my head already. The apple must have fallen from pretty high up there to hit as hard as it did."

"I'm sorry that happened to you," Marta said. "It'll feel better in a day or two. Now, you ladies help yourselves and enjoy this nice breeze coming through."

She'd covered their long picnic table with red-and-white checkered tablecloths, and scattered about were nice wooden lawn chairs. Every one of our club members was there except for Frances and Greta. Frances had had a stroke not long ago and lamented that she still wasn't comfortable being away from the house for extended periods. And Greta was still in a snit about our last quilt show. I wondered if she would stay away from the club permanently because of it. That would be okay with me.

"This pie is so delicious!" Amy complimented. "Did you make these pies, Marta, or did you, Anna?"

"I can't take credit for them," Anna quickly responded. "Aunt Marta makes the very best pies."

"Thanks, Anna," Marta blushed. "It's just because I've been baking them all my life."

"I'm no baker, but I can tell this pie crust is from an experienced baker," I added. "For me, it's all about the pie crust. We're lucky to have good apples here in Door County. And cherries. All summer long, Cher and I have made it a point to eat as many cherries as possible. We take our duty very seriously!"

Lots of giggling followed. "It's hard not to overindulge with apples and cherries here. And you know what they say about an apple a day keeping the doctor away," Olivia joked.

"Yes, indeed," Marta agreed. "I always tell my family that a bad apple can spoil the whole bunch."

"So true, Marta," I nodded. "And Grayson once told me I was the apple of his eye."

"Oh, aren't we getting clever here?" Cher asked. "Years ago, my dad would tell me, "Now, don't go upsetting the apple cart!"

"I bet you didn't listen, did you?" I joked.

"Did any of you take an apple for your teacher?" Ginger asked.

"Yes, but can you imagine kids doing that today?" I replied.

"No way," Rachael agreed. "Remember when we learned in grade school that A was for apple?"

Ava chimed in, "My, my. Don't we sound like a bunch of old ladies? I think we're dating ourselves with all this apple talk!" We burst into laughter.

Chapter 2

Rachael reminded everyone that the Leaf Peepers would be arriving any day now. Leaf Peepers was the name the locals gave to all those who traveled to Door County to take pictures of the fall foliage. She hoped that the Peepers would see the sign she and her husband Harry had put up earlier this year on Highway 42 advertising their Christmas tree farm. They used to sell just trees on the farm, but I had talked them into expanding their merchandise, and they'd be offering pumpkins and hay bales for the fall season.

Marta explained that in the next week she'd be making apple butter and applesauce.

"I'll try to remember to bring some apple strudel to the next quilt meeting," Anna noted.

"Oh, that would be wonderful," said Cher. "Why do quilters always have to connect food to quilts?" Everyone chuckled.

"Isn't that the truth?" Ginger agreed. "I guess we're a hungry group!"

"I should have been helping Carl today at the shop, but I just couldn't miss this special day," Cher confessed. "By the way, Claire, we could use another *Quilted Leaves* wall quilt for this time of year."

"I've started one of those, and I have a *Quilted Snow* marked, so I'll do my best," I answered.

"So, are you doing more quilting than painting these days?" Olivia asked me.

"The last painting I did was of Julie's Park Cafe & Motel. Since then, I've just been quilting," I explained. "I've started working on a tie quilt for my brother Michael. I decided it's going to be a wall quilt of three bookshelves. He's a writer with his first book in print now, so I thought he'd like that idea."

"Of course, he would!" Marta cheered. "I can't wait to see it when you're finished. I have a big fall project ahead with a quilt ready to go in the frame. It's been a busy summer, so I'm ready to settle inside on the rocking chair and quilt."

"I bet you are! I'm sure there's always something to keep your hands busy around here," Rachael added.

"After I get those apples taken care of, I'll be working on a log cabin quilt for my niece," Marta told us. "If I stick to it, she'll have it for Christmas."

"That was such fun when all of us quilted around your frame when we were here the last time," I reminisced.

"Well, ladies, I'll let you know when I'm all set up and ready to quilt," Marta noted happily.

Amy chimed in, "I'm having a booth at the fall festival this year in Sister Bay."

"Oh, I don't want to miss that this year," I replied. "Hopefully, I won't be too busy with the barn's gift shop."

"You're doing a beautiful job with the gift shop," Rachael told me. "I love Halloween and autumn, but I never thought I could do anything other than Christmas at the barn till you came along." I blushed at the compliment.

"Your pumpkin party will be the perfect time to introduce other holiday gifts to the gift shop," I replied.

"Harry is being really generous with all our new plans," Rachael noted. "We'll see how long that lasts!" We all chuckled. "He's probably wondering where I am as we speak. I'd better get on home."

"See what happens when you get married?" Cher teased with a wink.

"She's a happy newlywed trying to please a good man," I defended.

"Oh, how I wish I could have been at that wedding," Ava said.

"You had your hands full, Ava, with that nasty husband of yours," Rachael noted as she shook her head. "I sure hope things work out for you."

"Thank you," Ava said with a smile. "Frances has been a lifesaver for me. Really, she's been the mother I never had. We even started a quilt together recently. We'll bring it to show-and-tell one day."

"We'd love to see it," Rachael answered.

"Oh, this has been such a therapeutic day," Olivia said, sighing. "Maybe I need to start looking for a good farmer to marry. Or, on second thought, maybe not. I don't know if I want to work as hard as Marta does!" We all chuckled.

Rachael said she could hear Harry's stomach growling from right here on the orchard, several miles from their farm. She was the first to leave, and we all reluctantly waved goodbye.

"So, are you going to make your beau Grayson an apple pie from that bucket of yours?" Cher asked me with a grin.

"I know you're trying to be cute, but no one's ever accused me of being Susie Homemaker. I really don't know yet what I'll do with them. I'll think of something," I answered. "Maybe Kelly will take some apples to her sweet daddy. Speaking of Kelly, has anyone seen her and Billy?"

Chapter 3

"They were headed to the barn," Marta answered. "Billy has a rope hung in there and can swing pretty far. It's where I find him most of the time."

"I'm sure that's a new experience for Kelly," Cher noted. "Do you really think the two of them have a romantic attachment, or are they just good friends?"

"I think Billy looks at her romantically, but I'm not sure Kelly thinks of him the same way," I surmised.

"Time will tell. Speaking of romance, when did you see Grayson last?" Cher asked me directly.

"Well, Grayson, Kelly, and I went to Sister Bay Bowl last weekend, which was pretty fun. My bowling is on par with my cooking, but we had a fun time anyway."

"So, does this confirm that Kelly approves of you?"

"Yes, I believe so. This weekend, there's a going-away party for her at Grayson's house, but I decided not to go."

"Why's that?"

"I just don't want to paint a wrong impression. I want the party to be about her and Grayson."

The others in the group nodded.

"You're crazy, Claire Bear," Cher said, shaking her head.

It was hard to explain to everyone that just because Grayson and I had gotten back together recently, we weren't going to drive away into the sunset and get married after Kelly went to school. When Grayson and I talked about what happened on New Year's, he explained that he thought he'd lose me if he didn't propose when he did. He knew I valued Kelly's relationship with me, and he was afraid she'd screw it up. I wish he'd addressed the topic with me before going to the trouble of planning an extravagant dinner complete with a carriage ride and a ring, but so it goes. It had certainly taken a while for either of us to make the first move to fix things. But after our long talk, we both made a pact to relax and see where time would take us. So far, it was working. I hadn't gone into all that detail with my quilt group until now, but I knew I was among friends. They seemed to understand and gave words of encouragement.

"Well, ladies, I've got to get back to the shop to relieve my helper today," Amy said. "This has been the best day. Thanks for everything, Marta. I'm going to make my grandmother's apple crisp recipe tomorrow with some of my haul."

"I need to get back to Frances," Ava said. "I took some great photos today that I'll share with the group. Olivia, I can take you home if you want a ride."

"We should probably all be on our way," I said with reservation. "We don't want to wear out our welcome."

"You ladies come back anytime," Marta told us affectionately. "I can tell you enjoyed yourselves, and I'm happy to share our apples. I'll let you know when I get that quilt in the frame."

"Please do!" Cher replied.

We each hugged Marta goodbye and walked to our cars to leave. The afternoon at Marta's had been delightful. There was no talk of the last outdoor quilt show that had ended on a rainy, disastrous note, and there was no quilt program to rush through like at the monthly meetings at the library. The farm setting had been relaxing for all of us.

The drive back was pretty along Highway 57. The day had been full, but I didn't want it to end. Arriving back at my little cabin, Cher almost seemed regretful about moving from there.

"I see the early leaves are falling from the maple tree. I always hated when that happened because it's the first sign that summer is over."

"I know. I do love fall, but it points to what's ahead. That first snow is still a killer for me."

"I'm going by Ericka's tonight. I promised her and George I'd pick up a pizza from Husby's."

"That's sweet of you. How's she doing?"

"Terrible really. I don't know how else to describe her condition. Now she needs oxygen, so she's even more reluctant to leave the house."

"Poor Ericka. That must be awful for her considering how independent she was before cancer took over."

"George and I try to pretend everything's normal, but since she knows she can never go back to work, she thinks her life is over. She's really depressed and sleeps most of the day."

"I find it so hard to think of her that way. Cancer's a terrible thing. She's lucky to have her brother to take care of her. What if you or I get it someday, Cher?"

"I think of that a lot since my mom died from it."

"I'm sure you do. Do you want to come in for a bit?"

"No, but thanks."

"Well, give Ericka my love. If she'll see me, I'd like to visit sometime."

"I'll tell her. Today has been a wonderful day, but I'm afraid it won't end well for me."

"We need to remind ourselves to be thankful for the life we have, Cher Bear."

"Indeed, Claire Bear."

We gave each other a hug. Lifelong friends. There's nothing like them. I went inside to find my cat Puff waiting for me. Suddenly, I became distracted by a large UPS truck pulling into my drive. Soon the delivery driver walked my way with a narrow, flat package under his arm.

Chapter 4

"Ms. Stewart?" I nodded. "Please sign here."

As soon as I closed the door, I began racking my brain trying to remember if I'd ordered anything. Nothing came to mind. I found my scissors and cut along the tape lines of the box. In the middle of all the foam peanuts was what appeared to be a painting enveloped in bubble wrap. A card dropped out, and I saw the gift was from Foster. The note read, *A night I'll never forget. Love Foster.* This can't be. I removed the plastic packaging to unveil the picture. It took me a bit to take in what I was looking at.

It was a rough sketch of me looking into the sunset on Foster's private beach at the Blacksmith Inn. We'd shared dinner there one evening, and while he was grilling our halibut, I was enjoying the sunset. I remember him coming up behind me saying something sweet. The only color on the painting was the fiery sunset. The painting was incredibly lovely, and it brought a smile to my face.

Foster was a true romantic. If Grayson hadn't come into Alexander's restaurant that night to take me home after our last quilt show, I might still be dating Foster Collins, the famous painter. It was so sweet of him to send this. He was a client friend of Grayson's I'd dated for a while when Grayson and I had split up. He must know I'm not completely over him, or he'd never have sent this sentimental gift. Now what? I had to thank him somehow. I taped his sweet card on the back of this 14- ×16-inch gift that could be worth a lot of money someday. I'd never be able to afford to buy one of Foster's paintings. They're sold for thousands of dollars.

I poured myself a glass of wine and heated the last of my leftover pasta for dinner. I took it to the porch so I could enjoy more of today's early fall breeze. I knew my days on the porch would end soon and glass windows would cover my screens.

I sat there with a smile on my face thinking of Foster and our sunset dinner that he'd captured so well. After I finished eating, I decided I had to give him a call to thank him.

"Foster," he answered bluntly.

"It's me, Claire. I just received an amazing surprise today from a wonderful artist I know."

"Did you, my dear," he responded calmly. "I hope you were pleased."

"More than pleased. I don't know how you managed to do this."

"You've been vivid in my mind since the day I met you, Claire Stewart. When I was grilling our dinner, I looked over at you, staring at the night sky. My heart was full of hope, wondering if you would be mine someday, but it was not meant to be."

"Oh, Foster. I don't know what to say."

"That's okay. I have memories of our time together, and I wanted you to have something to share that moment."

"This is one of the sweetest things anyone has ever done for me."

"I'm so glad you feel that way. I knew that once Grayson came back into your life, I'd lose you. You're lucky to have each other."

"I can't predict the future. No one can. I hope you and I can always be friends. I've learned a lot from you as an artist. I haven't been painting much these days, but I'm sure something will inspire me to pick up the brush again."

"Perhaps you'd like a few private lessons from an old pro like me sometime?"

"Really? You can't be serious! You've never taught before, have you?"

"No, but when I notice talent such as yours, I see so much potential. I'll leave that offer on the table, free of charge."

"Don't tempt me, Mr. Collins," I teased. "I couldn't possibly take advantage of you like that."

"You know how to reach me. I appreciate your call, Claire."

"Thank you again, Foster. I'll cherish your painting forever."

I hung up feeling blessed to know him. He was famous, kind, and handsome. And even though he was older than me, I found much to like about him. I felt bad about accusing him of being a womanizer in the past. Actually, he was shy in a lot of ways.

I went up to bed feeling emotionally drained. Hearing from Foster helped get my mind off of Ericka. I had much to be thankful for today.

Puff took a while to get comfortable. Perhaps she had things on her mind, too. What would I do without this inherited cat that gave me unconditional, nightly snuggles?

Chapter 5

When I woke up the next morning, I began thinking about what my day had in store. I'd committed to helping Rachael after lunch.

Puff was already waiting for me downstairs, so I quickly fed her before taking my coffee and toast to the porch. The air was brisk but refreshing as I drank my coffee. My cell was ringing in the kitchen.

"It's your mom, honey," she said sweetly. "How are you?"

"I'm good, Mom. It's always nice to hear your voice in the morning. I'm having a chilly breakfast on my porch."

"I knew it was going to be cold there today. I checked your weather on the five o'clock news."

"What's new in my hometown of Perryville, Missouri?"

"Well, the gumball tree is gone. That's what's new for me."

"Really? My goodness. That tree's been there my entire life."

"The tree company was here cutting it all day yesterday. Bill took me for a long drive so I wouldn't have to watch the mess of it all."

"Where'd you drive?"

"We went down around East Perry. Remember how beautiful it is around those rolling hills? He has relatives who still live around there. We loved seeing all the churches, graveyards, and manicured farms."

"Oh, I do remember. I went to school with some folks from around there."

"Do you remember Dr. Paulson's old house right in the town of Borna, Claire?"

"Yes, I think so. It's quite large, right?"

"Well, yes. Now it's all refurbished, and it's called Josephine's Guest House. Bill said he remembers going to Dr. Paulson when he was little."

"Wow."

"We also stopped for coffee at that little building that used to be the bank in Altenburg. It's now a coffee shop. Would you believe they serve that good German coffee cake we love?"

"Oh, Mom. That sounds like such a perfect day. It's nice to know those women down there still make that coffee cake."

"It was delicious, too. Not only do those church ladies cook and bake well, but they make a lot of quilts, too."

"Yes, I know!"

"I was so tired after our long day out that I didn't even look in the backyard till this morning. It sure looks different without that big tree. I have to say, they did an excellent job cleaning up. Now some of my flowers will get better sun."

"We can thank Michael for getting that tree taken care of."

"Yes, he was so kind to arrange all that after my birthday party."

"I had a good day yesterday, too. Marta invited the quilt club to her farm to pick apples."

She chuckled. "*You* picked apples?"

"Believe it or not, I did. Now I just need to figure out what to do with them. She let us keep any we picked."

"Well, I bet Grayson would like an apple pie if you felt up to it. I never met a man who didn't love a woman who baked for him."

"Good to know, Mom. My apple pie would never be as good as yours, though. And I don't know when I'd get around to it. This afternoon I'm working at Rachael's so we can get the gift shop open. They're having a pumpkin party to sell pumpkins and fall things. That's where I come in."

"That'll be fun, knowing you. And how are the newlyweds doing?"

"Rachael and Harry work nonstop, it seems. They did manage to take a honeymoon, but they cut it pretty short. They have to plan way ahead for their Christmas tree season."

"Oh, where does the time go? I need to rest now, honey, but if I had those apples, I'd make you a pie." I smiled at the thought.

"I know you would, Mom."

I hung up with a pang of homesickness and went up to shower.

When I came back downstairs, I noticed Brenda pulling into my drive. I hadn't seen her in a while. She was either coming or going to her job at the White Gull Inn, most likely. I opened the porch door to greet her.

"Come on in, stranger," I greeted.

"I'm on my way to my shift at the inn, but I wanted to stop in and say hello. I hear you're going out to the farm to work in the gift shop today. I wish I could help you, but I have to make a living."

I nodded. "Yes, you do! How's Kent?"

"He's great! He wanted me to go with him and his girls to The Farm last weekend. Have you ever been there?"

"No, but isn't that place just for kids?"

"It's for everyone actually. I really enjoyed it. The weather was perfect, and the girls were able to feed the baby goats and cows. It's like a real farm. It's very well laid out with gardens of vegetables and flowers. I could have stayed there all day. They even had some pumpkins for sale already. I'd never have gone without Kent's invite."

"That sounds fun. How old are the girls now?"

"Lizzy is five, and Lucy is seven, I believe. They had a ball."

"Brenda, you seem to be spending a lot of time with Kent these days," I teased.

"It's nothing serious, really. We just have fun together."

"Whatever it is, it agrees with all of you."

She blushed. "Well, girl, I'd best be going. The White Gull Inn is calling my name. Have fun at the barn today."

"I will. Thanks for stopping by."

As soon as she left, I put in a load of laundry and then left for Rachael's.

Chapter 6

I couldn't believe all I was seeing when I approached Rachael's farm. Hay bales and pumpkins were stacked everywhere. The newly constructed gazebo built for their wedding had corn shucks around it, and my new fall garlands for sale were accenting it nicely. When I'd ordered them, I didn't think about using them on the gazebo, but Rachael was great at marketing.

"Hey, guys!" I said as I entered the barn. "I can't believe this place. I love what you did with the gazebo!"

"You ordered some nifty stuff, so I put it to good use," Rachael said behind the counter. "Another box came this morning, but I saved it for you to open. Help yourself to some of Harry's chili if you haven't had lunch. That guy's either thinking of food, cooking it, or eating it all the live-long day."

"Well, it's so nice to have a man around the house," I sang from an old tune. "I hope you made him something good from the apples you brought home."

"No time," she said, shaking her head. "But we're grilling pork steaks tonight, so I'm going to bake some of the apples or make a quick cobbler."

"Yum," I responded. "I'd gain so much weight if I was around Harry all day."

"He says food is love," Rachael said with a chuckle.

"Well, I couldn't agree more. Where is he?"

"The last I saw of him, he and Kent were out back trying to put some scarecrows together. He wants to put them out front with a sign for the pumpkin party directions."

"You've thought of everything. And what are you working on now?"

"It's a barn quilt for a really good customer. She purchased about six of these quilts. They're all the same size, just with different patterns. I think she's putting them all along her backyard fence."

"Wow! And are you still trying to make a wall quilt to match each barn quilt you sell?"

"I'm glad you asked. Harry came up with the idea that if people don't want the wall quilt, I can give them a discount on the barn quilt. Many have agreed to the discounts, and it sure saves me time."

"What would we do without Harry?" I chuckled.

"He continues to surprise me, Claire," Rachael said, shaking her head.

The afternoon went quickly. Without interruptions from customers, we were able to get a lot done. The box I opened was all Christmas decor and ornaments. I knew if we got folks inside the barn, they'd snatch these goodies right up.

In the middle of the afternoon, I took a break to eat a bowl of chili. I couldn't resist the aroma any longer. When I finished, I went outside to pick out some pumpkins for myself. I grabbed one for Ericka just in case I went by to see her. I arranged them in the backseat of my car, and when I tried to pay Rachael, she wouldn't have it. She called them perks of my job.

"Where did you find these darling barn ornaments?" Rachael asked as she looked closer at the box I was unpacking. "They're perfect for us to sell."

"Aren't they? There are six different kinds of barns, so I thought we could offer people a discount if they ordered all six."

"Who wouldn't go for that? Great idea, Claire."

"I do love spending other people's money," I joked. "Ornaments sell early in the season, so I bet these will go quickly. I'm going to use that small artificial tree to display them until we can get a live one."

"I have to admit that having some Halloween things to sell is a clever idea. Harry wasn't so sure about it till I told him it brings me joy."

"Well, Harry wants you to be happy, that's for sure. Now, tell me about the pumpkin party and what time you want me here, Rachael."

"I'd like you here as early as possible. Kent is in charge of the hayrides for the kids after he gets everything set up. Harry wants to push the hay bales, so that's his focus. I think Anna may come and sell apple strudel and pumpkin pie slices. Kent is setting up a spot for her."

"That'll be a big hit. I just hope she doesn't run out of inventory like she did at the Tannenbaum party."

Chapter 7

It had been a full day. I was feeling the good kind of tired from having accomplished a lot.

My phone rang as soon as I stepped out of my Subaru.

"Hey, sweetheart. How was your day?" Grayson greeted.

"Productive and exhausting. I just got home from Rachael's. We finally have everything ready in the gift shop. How about you? Good day?"

"It was fairly easy. I made some maintenance calls to make sure guys were on the job."

"And were they?"

"Oh, yeah. I've got a good crew right now. We're busy, as many are docking their boats for the season and want work done."

"I see."

"I thought I'd stop by to see you or take you to dinner. I think they're still serving outdoors at Barringer's, which is close by. How about it?"

"Sure, if you'll give me some time to change."

"You're worth the wait."

Grayson's invitation was lovely, but I'd have been just as happy skipping dinner and crashing for the night. I guess I'm getting old.

After we hung up, I set my pumpkins on the porch. I noticed Tom, the gardener, already doing fall cleanup for the Bittners next door. I gave him a friendly wave. My cabin looked so pretty with all the flowers I'd planted for the summer. I hated the thought of them disappearing come winter. My first winter here in Door County had been quite brutal.

In no time, I heard Grayson pull up. I hadn't seen him for some time, and it seemed to me that he'd accumulated a few more gray hairs to go with his dark strands. I loved it, but I'd bet he wasn't too happy about it.

He greeted me by the door with a kiss on the cheek, as he frequently did.

"Would you like to have a drink before we go?" I asked.

"I think I'll pass. Do you object to walking there? It's quite a pleasant evening."

"I agree. I'll grab a jacket."

Barringer's was a fantastic steak and seafood restaurant off of Main Street. It had its start as an ice cream shop more than a hundred years ago. I loved the black-and-white interior in the dining room, but I had a feeling Grayson had the patio in mind. We found a table outside and gave our drink orders. Grayson took both my hands before he spoke.

"I've missed you, Claire. I'm going through all kinds of emotions these days. I drive Kelly to school tomorrow. She can't wait to go and experience all that college has to offer. And, of course, tonight she's out with her friends she's leaving behind. You wouldn't believe all the stuff she's taking with her."

I chuckled but tried to appear sympathetic. "I know this is hard on you, Grayson. The two of you have had only each other since Marsha's death, but now you have to let that little girl take the next step in her life. Just keep in mind that even though she's smart and independent, she'll always need her dad."

"Letting her go is easier said than done, though. She'll always be on my mind. I won't be able to stop wondering where she is and what she's doing even when she's gone."

"I can understand that. It'll take some getting used to, but your busy schedule will help take your mind off her absence."

"I really hope so, Claire. I'm going to need all the help I can get."

We perused the menu. Grayson ordered a lobster roll, and I ordered the house chopped salad. My salad turned out to be a work of art that I hated to mess up by taking a bite. But I ate it anyway, and it was absolutely delicious. Before long, folks started stopping by to say hello to him. That often happened when we were out. As the owner of Sails Again, Grayson was well known throughout the community.

"You're certainly popular around here, Mr. Wills."

"Well, I'm not as famous as Foster Collins."

I didn't know how to respond to that. "Perhaps, but you're famous in a different way. I think you'd have to be connected to the art world to know Mr. Collins."

Grayson grinned. "Is that what attracted you to him, Claire?"

I looked deep into his eyes. "Actually, I believe so. I'd always been impressed with his work and was pleased when it started showing up at Carl's gallery. It was Carl who introduced me to him."

"So, do I have anything to worry about with this famous artist?"

I chuckled at his worry and shook my head. "There's only one Grayson Wills."

Just then the server brought our food. Thank goodness that subject was over. Talking about Foster with Grayson was touchy.

As we ate our meal, the air turned much cooler, and Grayson could tell I was uncomfortable. We rose to leave, and Grayson put his arms around me as we walked home. He said he and Kelly were leaving early in the morning, so he needed to get back.

"Please tell Kelly I wish her luck at school and I hope she'll be taking the quilt I made for her."

"Oh, I'm sure she will, Claire. She really loves it."

We hugged and kissed before I went inside the cabin alone. I watched him leave and knew his life would change forever after tomorrow. Kelly was his baby, and she was leaving the nest.

Chapter 8

After breakfast the next day, I went to my office/sewing room to begin cutting up Michael's ties for his quilt. I'd watched a video on how to proceed, but I found his narrow ties to be really challenging.

I couldn't help but wonder what occasion or circumstances Dad had purchased or worn each tie for. Some of my dad's ties were familiar to me from this collection Michael gave me, and I wondered if I'd been the one to give those to him. Michael probably rarely wears ties anymore in his newspaper business.

The colors of these were mostly subdued, as you'd expect from older ties. I needed enough color in each tie to stand out on the black background I planned to use. I also wanted to break up the books on the shelf to add more interest. Perhaps I could insert a fabric photo, which would make the quilt even more personal. If I didn't have the right photos, I knew Mom would. I was so completely immersed and excited about the project that I jumped when my cell phone rang.

"Claire, it's Brenda."

"Hey, what's up?"

"I'm at work, and I wanted to grab some tickets for the last fish boil of the season. Would you like to go? I thought I'd take six of them for Grayson, you, Rachael, Harry, and then Kent and me. What do you think? It's my treat!"

"Oh, Brenda, that really sounds like fun! How generous of you!"

"Well, it's one of the perks here, so I hope it works out. I hope I didn't interrupt your painting."

"No, I was just working with Michael's ties. I'm going to make him a quilt."

"How awesome! I can't wait to see what you come up with."

"Well, it's turning out to be a little more challenging than I thought it would be."

"I'll let you go. I'm pleased you're up for going to the fish boil."

"Thanks again, Brenda."

I continued working with the ties till around three o'clock, when I got a call from Cher.

"Come to the front door! I have something for you."

I jumped up from the floor, wondering why I hadn't heard her knock.

"Look what I baked for you!" she said, holding up what looked like an apple pie.

"You didn't!"

"I made two of them: one for Ericka and George, and one for you. Since I didn't bake one for myself, how about you fix us some coffee so I can taste it?"

I burst into laughter. "I like your style, Cher. And I support your idea because I skipped lunch today. Come on in."

As I made coffee and pulled out a couple plates, I asked Cher how she learned how to make pie.

"I inherited Mom's old cookbook that's messy, stained, and torn because she used it so much. I found a recipe for pie and figured it was the one she used to follow."

"Oh, how special, Cher."

As soon as the coffee was ready, I cut each of us a piece of pie. The crust looked perfect.

We each took our first bite and just smiled.

"It's heavenly, Cher Bear."

"Seriously?"

"Yes. I bet if Anna were here, she'd say the same thing. Thanks for thinking of me."

"I'm just happy you were willing to share it with me."

"Did you already deliver Ericka's pie?"

"Yes. George answered the door and took it. Ericka was napping, so I didn't go in. He said she's usually up all night, so he's glad when she sleeps during the day."

"That poor dear. Is she eating?"

"Yes, much better than before since she's not taking chemo. I just wish I could do something to lift her spirits. It's like she's given up. If only she could do something to occupy her hands. That was never Ericka, though. She was always promoting a cause if she wasn't working."

"Yeah, I remember when I'd just moved here she was trying to get me to sign a petition to stop a development. I felt bad I didn't sign it for her, but I was so new to the area that I really didn't feel I should voice my opinion on something I knew nothing about. She was so big on environmental causes then. She may not feel up to fighting anything these days."

"What hurt Ericka more than anything was when the clinic strongly suggested she leave, rather than letting it be her own decision. I'm naïve. I really thought she'd be able to keep working."

"How did the two of you meet?"

"I really can't remember. Maybe I met George first when he did some repair work for me, and then he introduced me to her. Oh, by the way, I work at the gallery tomorrow. I meant to tell you that Foster stopped by the other day."

"And?"

"Well, he's quite sorry that you're back with Grayson."

Chapter 9

I took a deep breath. "I have something to show you."

I went to get the painting Foster had given me. I didn't know where to hang it, so I'd temporarily put it behind the couch. I held it up for her to see.

"What's this?"

"Who do you think that is in the painting?"

She paused. "It's you, right?"

"It is. Foster did this for me. He had it delivered to me as a surprise, so I now own a Foster Collins painting."

"Girl, this is pretty cool. When did he paint this?"

"I don't know exactly, but he took my picture on one of our dates, and he painted off of that. He was grilling our halibut for dinner when I was looking out into the sunset."

"Oh my, Claire. You truly have someone who admires you. He's so sensitive and romantic, don't you think?"

"Oh, indeed he is. He made my heart putter more than once, but he wasn't Grayson."

"Of course not. So how's the man in the red scarf who holds your heart?" I chuckled remembering that red scarf of Grayson's that made me first take notice of him.

"He's fine. He may not feel so great today, though, because he drove Kelly to college."

"Aww. Poor guy. That will definitely be hard on him. But having Kelly out of the picture for a while will be better for your relationship, I suppose."

"I'm not so sure. I'm afraid she'll always be on his mind."

"Well, he sure has a lot to do as president of the chamber of commerce. Are you going to the next meeting at the Fireside?"

"I'm not sure. You know I went there one night with Foster for dinner."

"Hmm, I'm not sure I knew that. Well, Claire Bear, I must be off. The pie was certainly delicious if I must say so myself." I chuckled at her honesty. "I'm leaving the rest here with you, though. You can share it with Grayson, but don't lie and tell him you made it, you hear?"

I grinned. "I promise, I won't. I think I'll just end up eating Marta's apples by themselves without doing anything more than washing them. They're just so good."

I gave Cher a hug of thanks for the pie and conversation, and off she went. That pie she brought served not only as my lunch, but also as my dinner.

I returned to Michael's ties and began ironing the strips I'd cut. Puff sat there watching every move I made and got in my way once or twice as cats love to do. Once again, time escaped me. At eight o'clock, I heard a text alert.

[Grayson]
I've completed the dirty deed. My daughter has gone away to college, and I'm sad. Seeing her happy

helped, but my life will never be the same, and neither will hers.

[Claire]
I'm glad she seemed happy at least. You need to hang on to that. If you need a hug, I'm here.

I didn't hear back from him, which made me a bit sad. He was still driving, most likely, and not in the mood for a chat. He'd probably go home and shed a tear or two in Kelly's room. I had to remind myself that he was also likely thinking of Kelly's mother Marsha today. She certainly still held a big piece of his heart with all their history together.

I put away some of my mess from the tie project. I was ready to retire early.

After I got into bed, I was hoping for a good movie on Turner Classic Movies. *From Here to Eternity* was showing, and I wasn't in the mood for that. I reached for the book *Lady in Waiting* from my bedside table. I loved anything English and was always intrigued with royalty. I found it hard to concentrate on the story since Grayson was hurting over Kelly. I ended up falling asleep.

Chapter 10

I chose to pass on the chamber of commerce meeting even though I knew Grayson would be looking for me. I needed to focus right now on doing things to earn a living for myself. I finished another whole cloth piece for Carl, but I made the best money from my paintings.

I'd have to rethink my idea of the quilt buildings I was painting. Would people still want a reminder of the last quilt show I did that ended so poorly? I did hope so. The participation of the shops on the hill had inspired me. It would be nice to have a simple representation of the quilts on display there. I could call it *The Quilted Shops on the Hill*. The idea was taking off and pulling me out of the painting slump I'd been in. Maybe I could start by doing some kind of sketch today. I still had plenty of time to finish Michael's tie quilt for Christmas. My phone began ringing. It was Cher.

"Where are you? I thought you were coming to the chamber's breakfast this morning."

"I decided I had too much work to do. I don't have a cushy job like my friend does at a famous gallery. Speaking of which, I thought you had to work today."

"Well, I'm here at the chamber with Carl, and this breakfast will end before the gallery opens."

"Have you talked to Grayson yet?"

"No, but he keeps looking around for you."

"That's good for him. It'll keep him guessing."

"You're bad, Claire Bear. I guess I won't see you until the quilt club meeting tomorrow."

"I wouldn't miss it. You can fill me in on everything then."

I filled my coffee cup and went out to the porch, hoping to reacquaint myself with that artist from The Quilted Palette. I breathed in the fresh air slowly as if all my inspiration depended on it. The blank canvas stared at me, waiting. What size should this painting be, and how detailed? I knew colors needed to catch the eye. Drat. There goes my cell again interrupting my creativity.

"Claire, it's Cher again. While I have a few minutes, I wanted to share with you who I met at the chamber meeting. Her name is Laurie Rosenthal, and she owns Trinkets on Main Street."

"Oh, I love that shop."

"Well, I got to talking to her, and it turns out that she's from St. Louis. She has a sister living there who's an artist, and her sister Lily owns a shop in Augusta in the wine country where we'd go now and then. A third sister lives in Green Bay. Anyway, the sisters come here to visit Laurie once a year. Isn't that a small world?"

"Sure is."

"I never run into Missouri people who actually live here. They're always tourists. Laurie is really likable, and she's single and around our age, I think. I told her about you, and she wants to meet you."

"Oh? Did she say whether she has any quilters in her family?"

"She does. The sister Loretta, who's a nurse, quilts. And Lily must be a quilt collector because her shop is called Lily Girl's Quilts and Antiques."

"Oh, how interesting. Her shop must not have been there when we went, or I definitely would have made a stop. I love the name of her store."

"Anyway, sorry to bother you again, but I wanted to be sure to tell you all this before I got too busy and forgot. Maybe you can stop and introduce yourself to Laurie sometime."

"I will for sure. We can always use another old maid in Fish Creek to have fun with," I joked.

"Wash your mouth out, Claire Bear! We're not old yet! Say, what are you so busy working on right now that you had to skip the chamber this morning?"

"Oh, I'm trying to get started on something to represent the shops on the hill for the quilt show."

"That sounds challenging. How would you do that without picking out just one shop?"

"I'm trying to figure that out. I want to encourage those shops to have their own quilt show if ours completely fizzles. They really shined at the last one."

"You're always thinking, Claire Bear. But for the record, I haven't given up on our show just yet."

"So, did you get to talk to Grayson at the meeting?"

"No. He took off right after the meeting."

"Yeah, he did that the last time, too. Well, thanks for the tip on the Missouri girl, Cher. I'll try to meet her soon. See you tomorrow."

Chapter 11

It felt good to put on a sweatshirt again. The current climate is just what our tourists want when they come to Door County. Some trees have started dropping leaves, and the colors are starting to show their brilliance.

I ate a quick banana for breakfast. Anna would be bringing apple strudel for the quilt club meeting this morning.

This would be our first meeting since July's quilt show. Marta had canceled the August one in favor of picking apples on her farm. The break was nice. It gave us an opportunity to enjoy some social time together, and it gave me space to gather my thoughts about the rained-out show.

It would be interesting to see whether Greta would return to meetings after her disgust with the show. She'd made it a point to offend nearly everyone who had anything to do with it.

I pulled in the parking lot and walked in with Ginger.

"How are things going for you?" I asked her with concern. "We didn't get to visit much at the farm."

"I'm so busy right now at the shop, but I just can't afford to hire anyone. Now, I'm not complaining about the busyness of the shop ..." She grinned.

"That's good to hear, Ginger. I hate to ask, but is your divorce final now?"

She nodded. "Yes, it went fairly smoothly. Oh, don't look now, but I just saw Greta get out of her car."

"Wonders never cease!" I said, shaking my head.

Anna and Marta had arrived before us and were all set up with their coffee and strudel. I grabbed the seat next to Rachael, and when Cher arrived a few minutes later, she took the seat on the other side of me. I had a bestie on both sides.

Greta quietly helped herself to the strudel and coffee without talking to any of us.

The best surprise was seeing Frances and Ava walk in right before the meeting was to begin. Frances was using a cane.

Marta got our attention for the meeting to start without the hard gavel banging that Greta used to do when she was our leader.

"Good morning, apple pickers," Marta greeted as we smiled. "Look who we have here this morning! Welcome back, quilt sister Frances!" Everyone clapped, and some whispered their greetings to her.

"I can't tell you how nice it is to be back," Frances replied, blushing. "I missed all of you, and I'm pleased to say that I'm feeling much better. I credit my sweet caretaker Ava for that."

Ava smiled at the applause that followed. "I'm proud of her progress, and I absolutely love living with this lady. It's also been interesting to learn my way around Sturgeon Bay."

"Well, we've all missed you, and we're happy this arrangement is working out for both of you." Marta continued, "Now, let's thank Anna for this delicious strudel. She said she'd share the recipe if some of you are still wondering what to do with the apples you picked at our orchard."

"Danke," Anna said, smiling.

"I thought we'd begin today's meeting with a recap of the quilt show," Marta announced, looking at me instead of Cher. My knees were shaking.

Chapter 12

"As you all know, we had another beautiful show, but we also had some challenges," I began. The room went dead silent. "The show went off without a hitch till around two o'clock when the rain started. At that point we implemented our contingency plan. Thanks to Marta and others for their help in protecting the quilts." I made the mistake of looking at Greta, who was fuming. "We ran into a few glitches, but we resolved those later, thank goodness. I really don't want to focus on what went wrong because we have many folks to thank and congratulate. If you haven't heard, Marta won third prize in our Quilted Cherries challenge, and Lee won first! Congratulations to both of you!" Several clapped to show their approval. "The cherry tree quilt that Lee let us display was truly the hit of the show. With our cherry theme for this show, it was almost as if Lee had quilted it just for the occasion. Thank you, Lee. I also want to thank the volunteers, including all of you, plus so many more who lent us their quilts. It takes a village, as they say. Oh, and the cherry pie contest for this show was a big hit, especially with the husbands." Everyone nodded and chuckled. "Seaquist Orchards was happy with its sales and wants to come back even bigger next year. We heard no complaints from any of the sponsors; they were gracious and understood our lack of control over the rain. Cher and I have yet to decide whether to pursue another outdoor quilt show next year. It's too soon to make that call. We'll have to see what the town board says about it, too, so just stay tuned."

"Well, I doubt if the board will let the show happen again," Greta said smugly.

"We'll have to see, Greta, but the decision will likely be ours to make." She shook her head in disgust.

"Well, I sure hope this show goes on," Rachael said in defense. "Your helpers were great, and as a vendor, we couldn't have been more pleased."

"The quilt shop did well, too," Olivia agreed.

"My shop also had good sales," Amy added. "I never make that much on a Saturday."

"I'll make it a point to address the board on your behalf, Claire," Marta followed. "I was proud to be part of this event. Everyone did their best, so whatever decision you girls make, we'll support you." I thought Greta was going to stand up and oppose, but she didn't.

"Okay, ladies, we need to move on," Marta reminded. "Today I asked Ava and Frances to share their joint project with us. Even though they haven't finished their project, they can show us their progress. Ava is going to tell us about it, and then we'll see what everyone else has brought today for show-and-tell."

"Thanks, Marta," Ava began. "First let me begin by telling you how much fun we're having quilting something together. Isn't that what it's all about? Now, you all know I'm more of an embellishment quilter, and Frances is more of a traditionalist. Well, our current project started one night when I took one of her quilt blocks and put my own touches on it."

"I watched her work and couldn't believe it," Frances joked.

Ava added, "One thing just led to another, like we quilters tend to do. That's when we decided it would be fun to do a project together."

"As most of you know, I love history, and Door County has much to tell," Frances explained. "I figured some quilt patterns could help tell that story, and Ava's embellishments could make the blocks really come alive. Today we brought just one block with us so you could get an idea of where we're going with this."

Ava held up a simple pieced house block that she said represented the Noble House. I loved it. Ava had embellished a small quilt hanging from the porch, like we did for the quilt show.

"I like that you included the gazebo in the background," Ginger noted.

"I love the quilt on the house as a reminder of our quilt show," I added. "This idea of yours is simply wonderful!"

"Keep up the excellent work," Marta encouraged. "I can't wait to see more blocks. Now, did anyone else bring a show-and-tell today?"

Ginger stood up. "I have something. I know all of you were convinced that my wall quilt that fell onto the ground was ruined at the show, but I brought it today to show you how beautiful it turned out thanks to Claire. She took it home to work her magic, and I couldn't be more pleased.

You would've never known that this quilt had been dragged through the mud." Everyone marveled at it.

Amy stood up next and showed us an Amish miniature quilt in the Tumbling block pattern that one of her consignors at her shop had made.

"Mrs. Mueller likes working with small pieces, and ladies, this is not paper-pieced," Ginger explained. "I always ask her how she does it, and she just blushes like it's no big deal."

"Is that for sale?" Lee asked. Amy nodded.

"Yes, see me after the meeting if you're interested," Amy told her and grinned.

"Anyone else?"

Anna rose from her chair. "I don't think I've shown you this little tissue box cover I made that's supposed to replicate my bake shop. What do you think?" Everyone clapped.

Anna's talent for detail was incredible. Everyone wanted her to pass it around so they could see it closer.

"Thank you, ladies," Marta said. "We have time for one more."

"Mine is more of a tell," Olivia said, standing up with a handful of marking pens in her hand. "We got in these new pens, and I'd like to know what quilters think about them. I brought all of you a free one to try." The group responded with glee.

"How nice of you, Olivia," Marta said before she asked for a motion to adjourn. Greta quickly gave the motion and then bolted out the door. Cher and I looked at each other and shook our heads.

"I can't believe she actually came," Cher commented. "It's not her club anymore."

"Yeah, thanks to us!" I replied.

Chapter 13

"Lunch?" Cher asked as we left.

"I'd better not," I answered. "I've got to quit playing and start paying."

"Paying?"

"My bills."

"So, my friend Claire is a poet now, too?"

"Maybe I should be. It probably pays more."

"I think I'll stop by Ericka's since you're passing on lunch."

"Why don't you take her some of Anna's strudel?"

"Good thought. Anna's still here, and I'm sure she wouldn't mind. I'll see you later, Claire."

"Tell Ericka I said hello."

"Will do!"

Because of the generous portion of apple strudel I'd devoured at the meeting, I had no desire for lunch. As I was pulling into my driveway, Cotsy Bittner was getting out of her car next door. She came over when she saw me.

"How are you?" I greeted.

"We're good! Claire, is it my imagination, or have I seen Grayson coming around again?" She teased.

"I'm happy to confirm it wasn't your imagination. Grayson and I had a meeting of the minds, so to speak. All is well right now."

"Oh, I'm so happy for the two of you. Dan and I were so bothered by what happened to you. We like you both so very much."

"That's so sweet, Cotsy. It helps to have the support from folks like you."

She smiled. "We still haven't decided when to leave for Florida. It's easier to have Christmas here in the snow than try to make the beach look Christmassy."

"Well, then I hope you leave after Christmas. The holidays are stressful enough without trying to create an effect elsewhere that comes so naturally here."

"Dan gets anxious with the cold. He's all about the warm weather and the beach."

"I can't say I blame him. My first winter here was brutal. I thought it would *never* end."

"Like it or not, winter will be here before you know it. I'm so glad I got to talk to you, Claire."

"You know where to find me!"

I headed inside and tried to focus on my painting of the shops on the hill. The challenge was the layout. The shops were in a U-shape instead of a straight row, so the front of some shops was obscured. I kept sketching and reworking. Without a good sketch, I couldn't move on to painting.

My day flew by. Before I knew it, cars were driving by to see the sunset on Sunset Beach. The last time I was there for a sunset was with Foster. I poured myself a glass of wine and realized the strudel had worn off and I was hungry. A frozen pizza would have to do.

The cabin became chilly, but it was way too soon to turn on the furnace. Did I dare have my first fire for the season? Puff headed in the direction of my fireplace as if she could read my mind. While the pizza was cooking, I decided to build a fire. Thanks to Tom, I had plenty of firewood. He kept my firepit ready, too, by gathering any of my fallen branches and dropping them near the pit for me to use as kindling.

I had no phone calls or texts to return, so I leisurely enjoyed my pizza as I listened to the crackling of the fire and stared at its flames. The fire mesmerized my thoughts, and I began to get sleepy. I extinguished the flames and headed upstairs for the evening.

Forgetting my tiredness, I turned on the TV, which was always on TCM. To my delight, my favorite movie, *Casablanca*, was playing. They were singing, "It Had to Be You," and I thought of Grayson. Ingrid Bergman and Humphrey Bogart were at their best in this film. Their facial expressions showed such passion. I'd seen the movie so many times that I almost knew which line would be next. And I loved the song lyrics. "You must remember this: A kiss is still a kiss, a sigh is just a sigh...." My tears began forming. The ending with Bogart sending Ingrid on her way with her husband got to me every time. He loved her so much that he said goodbye. Ingrid's noisy escape plane took off, and I turned out the light thinking how Ingrid must have felt.

I fell asleep and had my first *Casablanca* dream. I was singing to Grayson and playing the piano when Greta came in to interrupt me. In her stern voice, she said she was shutting the place down, and I should leave before the Germans came. Needless to say, I awoke in a cold sweat.

Chapter 14

If I made an early coffee stop at the Blue Horse this morning, I'd probably see Grayson. It was worth a shot.

I put on jeans and my jean jacket and then gave Puff her breakfast and fresh water before heading out.

My first stop was the post office to pick up my mail. I left my car in that lot and walked to the coffee shop. I smiled when I spotted Grayson's SUV.

As usual, there was a long line of customers waiting to be seated at the Blue Horse, so I decided to get my order to go. Grayson often worked while he was here, so I'd just drop by his table to say hi.

I looked toward the porch, and my heart sank. He was having coffee with Jeanne, his secretary.

I'd have been happy to have gone unnoticed, but he saw me place my order.

"Claire, over here," he called out.

I was sure Jeanne wasn't pleased about me joining them. I'd met her at the company's Christmas party last year, and she was very cold to me. There was no question she wanted to be more than Grayson's assistant. Even Grayson realized it.

I nodded and smiled at them and then walked to their table when my order was ready.

"Good morning, Ms. Stewart," Jeanne greeted me as if I were a business associate.

"Good morning, you guys," I greeted them casually. "It looks like you're getting some work done pretty early today."

Jeanne chuckled. "Not really. I'm nursing him along since Kelly's away at school now. I've been in that position with my daughter, so I understand his pain." Like I didn't, of course.

"Well, I'll let the two of you get back to therapy," I said sarcastically.

"Claire, won't you join us?" Grayson pleaded.

"No, I got my order to go, and I have a busy day ahead, but thanks," I responded politely.

"Oh, that's too bad," Jeanne said, shaking her head as if she really cared.

"I'll give you a call," Grayson nodded and smiled. I knew he could read my mind.

"Have a good day!" I said as I departed.

Grayson was in a bad spot. I knew he had no personal interest in Jeanne, but he told me often how much she did for him. He was in a vulnerable place emotionally at the moment, and she could easily steal him from me.

As I drove back to the cabin, I happened to see a lady putting out lawn ornaments in front of Trinkets. This must be the woman from Missouri whom Cher met at the chamber meeting. I had time, so I pulled over to introduce myself. It was still early, so I was able to park right in front.

"Are you by chance Laurie Rosenthal?" I asked while approaching the cute gate in front of the yard.

"Why, yes I am," she smiled and nodded. "Do I know you?"

"No, but you met my friend Cher at the chamber of commerce meeting. I wasn't able to attend, but she said you had a friendly conversation about your Missouri origins." I put out my hand and said, "Hi, I'm Claire Stewart."

She shook my hand. "Hi, Claire. It's nice to meet you. Sure, I remember Cher. I'm actually surprised we hadn't met before."

"I've admired your shop. I'm an artist and quilter and still feel somewhat new to Door County. Cher and I grew up in Perryville. You lived in St. Louis before moving here? And your sister Lily has an antique and quilt shop in Augusta? I frequently visited the wine country in that area."

"Yes to both. Have you ever been to the quilt shop there?" I shook my head. "Well, it's as cute as it can be in this bright yellow old house where a doctor used to live."

"I'd love to see it, as I also sell quilts I've made."

"Yeah, my family is pretty talented, with the exception of me. I just buy pretty things," she giggled. "My sister Lynn has a gallery in the Hill area of St. Louis. My other sister, Loretta, lives in Green Bay. She's a nurse, but she quilts in her free time. We also have a half-sister, Ellen, whom we just recently discovered."

"You do have a talented family. Are you another Door County single like we are?"

"I am, and that's pretty much the way things are gonna stay," she laughed.

"There's nothing wrong with that. There are times it's a relief to be single."

"Amen to that. I'd be happy to join you and Cher sometime. Here's my card."

"Sure!"

"My family will be coming to Green Bay again this year, which means they'll spend time in Door County. I like to think I'm the draw, but I think it's more likely the shopping. Maybe you'll have a chance to meet them."

"I'd love that. Oh, and Cher and I frequently go to Bayside Tavern for drinks on Saturdays. Maybe you could join us sometime."

Her eyes lit up. "Yes! I'm free any time after five o'clock when I close the shop."

"Great! We'll do that soon. It sure was nice to meet you, Laurie," I said as I left the shop.

Chapter 15

I left feeling like I may have just met a good friend. Why hadn't I met Laurie before? Her mom sure must like the letter *L*: Laurie, Lily, Loretta, and Lynn. I'm glad I took time to stop at Trinkets today. It got my mind off of seeing Jeanne and Grayson.

I returned to my easel once I was home. I stared at my current project and hoped it would paint itself. I waited, but I had no such luck. Maybe I should take Foster up on his free class offer.

I wondered if Grayson would call me like he said he would. He finally did around two o'clock.

"Hi, Claire. It was good to see you this morning. How's your work going?"

"Good. How about yours and Jeanne's?"

He chuckled. "Okay, I know that didn't look good, but I couldn't refuse her invitation after all she does for me. She acts like she's really concerned about Kelly leaving."

"Why would she be?"

"I can't say for sure, but there aren't many secrets in that office."

"I know. I'm just teasing you. You've got to admit, she relished that I saw the two of you together."

"You're probably right about that. I have to be so careful what I say around her. If I give her the least little compliment, she seems to read into it. That's a bit troubling."

"It is. By the way, next weekend Brenda got us complimentary tickets to the last fish boil at the White Gull Inn. She also invited Harry, Rachael, and Kent."

"Nice! I haven't been to a fish boil in quite some time."

"Does that mean you'll join us?"

"Sure! It'll be fun. So, Kent and Brenda are still hanging in there?"

"Yes. Odd, isn't it?"

"Whatever works, I suppose. His children are pretty young, aren't they?"

"Yes. Five and seven. Kent invites her to be with them more and more. They all just went to The Farm."

"That's such a great place for families. Now, back to us. How about a coffee date tomorrow around eight o'clock? Maybe that will cancel out what happened today."

I chuckled. "Okay, I accept."

We hung up, and I thought about what a sweet man Grayson Wills was.

I returned to my painting and decided to go in another direction than I'd originally intended, which happened frequently. Around seven o'clock, I stopped and covered it up. I went to the kitchen to pour some wine, and Cher called. I knew from her voice she was upset.

"What's wrong?" I could hear her try to catch her breath.

"Is it Ericka?"

"Yes. She looks like death all over. Her breathing is so heavy, and she won't leave the house. I don't know if she even wants me around."

"Is she telling you everything? Maybe there's something else going on."

"That's possible, but I don't think she'd keep anything from George."

"I feel bad for her and everyone concerned. All I can do is pray. On a good note, today I met Laurie Rosenthal. I suggested the three of us meet up at Bayside sometime."

"Oh, good!"

"I'm having coffee with Grayson tomorrow morning. I think he's a bit embarrassed that I saw him there with his secretary yesterday."

"Uh oh."

"We both know she has her eyes on him personally as well as professionally. She's protective of him, and I'm a woman who threatens her future with him."

"I'm sure she loved it when you and Grayson were apart for some time."

"No question."

"Claire, thanks for helping me keep my mind off of Ericka for a while."

"Why don't you try to talk her into letting you drive her out to the pumpkin party on Saturday?"

"I doubt if she'd agree. Plus I'm scheduled to work at the gallery."

"Oh, darn! I'm so anxious for you to see everything I've done to the gift shop."

"I'll get there eventually. Enjoy your coffee date."

"I love you, Cher Bear! Try not to worry so much."

"I love you too, Claire Bear."

I needed to say more prayers for my friends. It was no wonder sleep often eluded me.

Chapter 16

Fairly well rested, I got up extra early the next day with the pumpkin party on my mind. It was still so very dark outside, which made me feel like I was wandering around in the middle of the night. Fall was here and taking us into winter.

When I came down to join Puff for breakfast, I was already dressed for the day in my jeans and bright orange shirt that I only wore this time of year. Its color helped me prepare for the season. Knowing Anna would be at the farm this morning with her strudel and pumpkin pie, I skipped breakfast and prepared to take my coffee to go.

I got to Rachael's around six thirty, and she was pleased I'd thought to arrive early. She had all sorts of things to tell me about, such as what all would be taking place outdoors for the pumpkin festival.

Harry had hay bales delivered, and some were for sale. They made a great entrance as I approached the farm this morning. There were all sizes and shapes of pumpkins, so Rachael showed me the price list. Gathered corn husks were scattered inside and out. Someone had been doing a lot of work.

I straightened things up and patiently waited till Anna arrived with her goodies. Harry had created a little space for her to set up shop and a few tables and chairs where folks could sit and enjoy their coffee or cider. Rachael said Anna would be coming alone, that Marta was working for her in the shop. We went out to greet her and help where we could.

"Oh, these tiny pumpkins would be cute around Anna's space," I suggested to Rachael. "I'll also take a few to display in the gift shop."

"I just hope folks don't help themselves and not pay for them. Hey, guess what? I've already sold two barn ornament sets to the neighbor down the street!"

"That's great! I love how you decorated the gazebo, by the way."

"Can you imagine how lovely it will be at Christmastime?"

"Yes, I can. This is all very warm and clever now, but nothing beats your Christmas tree farm. I know how you love Halloween, though, so enjoy."

"Did you smell the chili Harry made for us today? I hope you don't get tired of it, but it's an easy meal to have on hand for these cooler days."

"I never make it for myself, so it sounds good."

"I also have cornbread in the back room, so help yourself. After eating this strudel, though, I may not have any room for chili."

Rachael left to tend to other things, and I noticed Anna already engaging with folks wanting something sweet from her table.

"Your strudel was delicious, Anna," I told her. She nodded and grinned, as she always does.

Chapter 17

It seemed like everything Harry and Rachael did turned to gold. Cars started piling in, and in no time, I heard complaints about not having enough parking. It seemed everyone wanted to stay longer. Rachael stayed mostly outside, and I managed to hold down the gift shop. Before Anna's pumpkin pie sold out, she was nice enough to bring me a slice to eat later.

The pumpkin party was turning out to have many more kids in attendance than we ever saw for Christmas tree shopping at the farm. They were enjoying picking out their very own pumpkins small, medium, and large. Kent had scrapped the pumpkin carving idea and come up with short hayrides on the wagon instead. He had a nice circular route that took kids all around the farm.

Folks seemed pleased with the addition of fall and Halloween merchandise. Maybe a little too pleased. The shelved items were now in disarray, and hay that had been dragged in from outside covered the floor. I was getting nervous watching the kids handle the ornaments. I was hoping Brenda would show up to help me. Rachael was too busy outdoors to even check on what was happening in the gift shop.

Rachael finally came in around three o'clock, and we both took a break to eat a bowl of chili and a piece of cornbread. I was starving.

"I'm so sorry I didn't get in here sooner," Rachael said with regret. "I hope you managed okay."

"Well, from the looks of the place, I didn't manage it very well. Look at this mess."

"I love it, mess and all! I even saw someone leaving with the big witch I've had my eye on. What have we created here?"

I chuckled. "Sales were good outside as well, I hope."

"Oh, yes! The hayrides were a big surprise to us. Kent's still going round and round. I think he wants to stop at four o'clock."

"Where's Brenda?"

"Unfortunately, she had to work. Anna could have used her help, too. Anna sold out of her baked goods, so she's packing up. Did I see a barn quilt go out the door? And did any of the quilt club gals show up?"

"Yes, we sold one barn quilt. I didn't see anyone from our quilting group. I was hoping Cher would make it out and bring Ericka, but it sounds as if Ericka is way too sick and doesn't leave the house anymore. Cher is really taking her illness hard."

"I'm sure she is. Loved ones feel so powerless when they can't do anything to help. Cher has truly been a great friend for her. When you live alone, you have to depend on so many others." I sadly nodded, knowing that would be me at some point.

Rachael took over the sales tally for the day as I began to tidy up the place. I started sweeping the concrete floor, amazed at how much people had tracked in. I also made a mental note of what people had bought so I could decide whether or not to reorder. In the corner was one broken ornament. Likely someone had hidden it there so they wouldn't have to buy it. I guess I should be thankful it didn't cut someone. Perhaps selling breakable ornaments wasn't my smartest idea. The retail response today had been really positive. I guess retail was in my blood.

Brenda had just arrived and was helping Kent close out his hayrides.

"Where's Harry?" Rachael asked with concern.

"He's been everywhere," Kent answered. "The last time I saw him, he was talking to the pumpkin man about today's sales. I think they were deciding which pumpkins would go out to the pasture."

"Oh, the pasture?" I asked. No one heard me.

"I'm ready for a beer," Kent said. "Anyone else?"

"I'm in. What about you, Claire?"

I nodded. A beer after all this hustling sounded good. "Kent, I didn't see the girls today. Were they here?"

Kent nodded. "Oh yeah. Their other grandpa brought them out for the hayride, but they left after that. Sorry you didn't get to see them."

We all took a break and sat around the table in the back room. It was fun hearing everyone's take of the day. The consensus was that everyone wanted to repeat it next year. While Rachael and I discussed the reorder strategy, Kent and Harry talked about Christmas tree deliveries. It was seven o'clock before I left the farm. I took my slice of pumpkin pie and a few more pumpkins to decorate with. Rachael said if I didn't take them, they'd go to waste.

Chapter 18

I drove as far as Egg Harbor and wondered what Grayson was up to. I didn't especially need to see him, but a conversation would be nice. I bet he wondered what the party was like today.

It was eight o'clock when I pulled into my driveway. I decided on the location for my newest pumpkins and then started nibbling on my pie. Shortly after that, I called Grayson.

"Oh, hi, Claire. What's up?"

"I'm beat after a full day at the pumpkin party."

"I bet you are. Was it successful?"

"It was. I'm sure finding out what's involved with running a gift shop. How was your day?"

He paused. "Well, Jeanne and I are still working on something for next week, so it's been a long day for both of us, I guess."

"Oh, I guess I never realized you worked in the office at night."

"It always depended on Kelly and what her schedule was. Now I don't feel as guilty when I have to stay here. I talked with her today, and she seems happy with everything but mentioned missing me."

"Aww, that's sweet. Well, I'll let you two love birds get back to your work," I said jokingly.

"Cute. Thanks for thinking of me. I'll see you tomorrow."

"Goodnight, sweetheart," I said before hanging up.

Our phone conversation certainly didn't go as I'd planned. I could almost see Jeanne smiling right through the phone at Grayson's report of the two of them working late. Cher called soon after I hung up.

"Yes, Cher Bear. What's going on?" I answered.

"What time is the Episcopal church service in the morning? Would you please come with me tomorrow?" she asked rather seriously. I thought about my coffee date with Grayson.

"Why, sure. Do you think you could bring Ericka?"

"I already asked, and her answer was no, but I'll keep trying."

"Tell her I said she should go. We could take her to lunch afterward. She's still eating some, I hope."

"She doesn't seem to be. She didn't touch the strudel I brought home from club."

"That's not good. Why don't you come over around nine forty-five, and we'll walk to church together?"

"Thanks, my friend," she said as she hung up.

I decided to send a quick text to Grayson canceling our coffee date tomorrow. Chances are he'd be relieved. I didn't get a response, so he was still involved with what's-her-name.

As I thought about Cher's request, I wondered who needed more help right now. Was it Cher or Ericka? I went to the kitchen and made myself a cup of hot tea and finished my pie. There was always a copy of the *Pulse* newspaper on the table. I glanced at it to get my mind off of Ericka.

Puff jumped on my lap to snuggle. I was gone for a long time today, and she needed some attention.

We went upstairs for the evening, and I switched on TCM. *Singing in the Rain* was on. It was a little too happy and lighthearted for my current mood, so I shut it off.

I turned on the bedside lamp and pulled out a tablet to make a list of my thoughts for the gift shop. The list ended up being rather long. Shortly afterward, I turned in for the night.

Chapter 19

Sunday was such a beautiful day, and it was nice to know I had church with Cher to look forward to. I could only hope that Ericka would agree to join us.

I took my time eating breakfast. Mom called while I sipped my coffee.

"Good morning, Mama dearest," I greeted. She chuckled. "Aren't you usually at the early church service at this time?"

"Yes, you're right, but I'm dealing with some sniffles and just wasn't up to it this morning. I ran into Carole yesterday and mentioned feeling ill. She was kind enough to bring me some chicken noodle soup last night, so I'm sure that will help."

"How sweet of her. I'm sorry you're feeling sick. Please rest when you can."

"I will. Bill said if I'm not better by Monday, he'll insist I call the doctor."

"Good advice. I'm actually attending church this morning with Cher. We're going to that cute little Episcopal church by my house."

"How nice! I remember it well. How's Grayson, dear?"

"Oh, he's been a bit sad lately since Kelly left for college, but he'll get used to it."

"Yes, he will. I'm so glad you kids made up and are back together again." I chuckled at the thought of Mom still considering my brother Michael and me kids.

"I am, too. Keep me posted on your health, okay?"

"I will, sweetie. I love you."

"I love you, too."

I felt so grateful to have friends near Mom who kept an eye on her. I'd say a prayer for her in church.

I quickly changed out of my pajamas after hanging up with Mom. When nine forty-five came around, Cher showed up alone.

"Are you ready?" Cher asked with a sweet smile.

"I am. Let me put Puff in her chair and grab my jacket."

The morning was quite chilly, but the sun was out, and I was with my bestie. We walked hand in hand like we had when we were little. Cher needed emotional support, and I wanted to be there for her. I didn't ask about Ericka.

Church of the Atonement was the oldest church in Fish Creek. The historic building was even listed on the National Registry of Historic Places. We read on their sign that Bishop John Henry Hobart Brown conducted the first sermon at the church in 1877. I couldn't imagine all the stories held here. It only held about sixty-five folks at the most. People considered it a mission church since it had visiting bishops and priests.

The weather was too cool for it this morning, but the last time I was here, the church served hot coffee in their little courtyard.

Just like my last visit, a woman bishop conducted the service. The pews filled quickly, and I don't think everyone got a seat. Tourists were always welcome to attend, so it was tricky predicting how many people would show up.

I could tell Cher was stressed. Her voice even seemed shaky. As we sat there praying, I couldn't even look at her. I knew tears were streaming down her cheeks.

When the service concluded, I wondered if Cher would ask the bishop to call on Ericka. Instead, Cher simply shook the bishop's hand and complimented her on her sermon.

"Let's treat ourselves to lunch at the White Gull Inn, shall we?" Cher suggested. "Brenda might be working."

"Sure! That sounds great!"

We entered the restaurant and remained silent till the server approached us. Our order was simple. We both wanted iced tea and whitefish chowder.

"That was such a lovely sermon," I said to get Cher's reaction.

She nodded. "I wish Ericka could have heard it."

"Hey guys! Brenda greeted as she came toward us from the kitchen.

"Are you working, right now?" I asked her.

"Actually, I'm just getting off the early breakfast shift," she explained. "You must be part of the after-church crowd."

"We are," Cher reported. "We're both feeling a bit down because of Ericka's failing health. We'd hoped she'd be well enough to attend with us."

"Oh, I'm so sorry," Brenda responded. "It's got to be tough for her and for you. Say, Claire, are you all rested from the pumpkin party?"

"That was really something, wasn't it?" I responded. "I couldn't believe all the people!"

"Rachael will never have time to quilt at this rate," Cher claimed.

"Brenda, how come you've never expressed interest in joining the Quilters of the Door?" I asked.

She snickered. "Oh, I've heard enough to know I'd never fit in with your group. I do so little quilting. I like to vary my crafts."

"Well, if you ever change your mind, let us know," I reminded. "You'd fit in just fine."

"Thanks anyway," Brenda said with a smile as she began to leave. "I need to get ready for a barbecue Kent is having at his place tonight."

"You go, girl," Cher cheered.

"Now, you know we're just good friends," Brenda insisted. "Well, I've got to run. See you later."

"How does she get by with being a cougar?" Cher joked after Brenda was gone.

"How would I know? But she's quite good at it, and I'm happy for her. I do worry a bit about how attached Kent's girls are getting to her. That could be a problem if they break up."

"Everything we do can be a problem, girlfriend," Cher responded sarcastically. I nodded in agreement.

We finished our lunch and decided to pass on dessert. Cher was quiet as we departed, which told me she was still feeling down. All I could do was hug her.

Chapter 20

Once inside the cabin, I checked my phone. I'd missed a call from Michael. Why would he call? I was always the one to reach out to him. I sat at the kitchen table and called him immediately. I was a bit worried something was wrong.

"Sorry to have missed you, Michael. I was at brunch and didn't see your call until now. Is everything okay?"

"I think so. I just talked to Mom, and I do wonder how serious this cold of hers really is. She brushed off my idea of going to the doctor."

"Carole took her some soup, which should help, but I assure you, Bill is on it and will make her go to the doctor if she doesn't get better soon."

"I do have Bill's number, so I may give him a call. If I learn anything, I'll let you know. She keeps pressing for the two of us to come home Thanksgiving. How are things there?"

"I know. She's mentioned Thanksgiving to me, too. Right now Cher and I are dealing with Ericka's illness, so we're a bit down."

"How sad. We just lost someone here in the office to cancer this past week. Young guy. Maybe forty."

"I'm sorry to hear that, Michael. How's Jon? Did his mother improve? And how did the trip to Las Vegas go?"

"Jon's mom has improved a lot. The trip was good and actually productive. I have to say, Jon can't stop talking about our trip to Door County, Sis. You hooked him."

"Well, how about coming for Christmas? It'll be white, cold, and beautiful here then."

"I'm sure. If I can bring Mom, we'll be there. I won't leave her with no family for the holiday."

"I understand. I'd really love for you to meet Grayson."

"Will he have his red scarf? I may not recognize him if he doesn't."

"Very funny, Michael. If it's Christmas, Grayson may very well have on his red scarf."

He chuckled. "Well, I'd better get back to cleaning up some papers around here."

"Thanks so much for calling, Michael. I needed your call today. I love you, brother."

"Anytime, Sis. I love you, too."

I hung up and broke into tears. Life felt overwhelming at the moment. I laid my head on the table and let loose of all my emotions that had been building up. Thoughts circled of Ericka and Mom. I said a little prayer and decided that with Michael on my mind, I'd work on his tie quilt today. Touching those ties brought me back to family, and family's what I needed today. Poor Ericka wasn't so lucky.

Looking at my first row of sewn books for the bookcase, I could finally start to visualize how clever this quilt could be. Maybe I could embroider titles on the book spines. I'm sure Michael would love to see the title of the book he wrote on one of them.

Eventually I went downstairs and poured myself a glass of wine. From the porch, I watched a flurry of leaves blowing something fierce. Fall was arriving before my eyes. The season was usually sad for me as a child because it meant not walking around barefoot and needing to break in new shoes for school. It also meant snow would be coming, and I never liked snow unless it meant a day off from school. The only joys of fall for me then were the bright colors of nature.

I looked around. I really needed to get busy replacing the screens on the porch with storm windows. Puff was going to miss the breeze out here that blew her fur around. At least her favorite spot on the chair would still have a sunny spot if the sun decided to show itself.

Chapter 21

I had to hang on to the thought of fall passing quickly into Christmas. It was so much preparation for one day, but it always seemed worth it. Thank goodness for my fireplace. It was my go-to place to unwind almost every evening.

I was deep in thought when my cell rang. Foster was someone I wasn't expecting to hear from.

"Am I catching you at a free moment?" he asked hesitantly.

I smiled. "I was in such a moment of solitude that your call surprised me. I'm sitting here on the porch coming to the realization that I can't do anything to stop fall from coming. I know winter is around the corner."

"As I sit here on the beach having a cocktail, I'm not sure I can control much either. The sunset tonight was magnificent. I can't help but think of the beautiful lady I once shared this with." I didn't know how to respond.

"You're very sweet to think of me," I responded simply. "I haven't made my first fire yet despite how chilly the cabin is beginning to feel. It's somewhat like not wanting to drink that first cocktail before five o'clock."

He chuckled. "Well, they say it's five o'clock somewhere, my dear. I'm grilling a piece of swordfish tonight on the grill. With the addition of beet salad, I'll have a meal fit for royalty."

"Beet salad?"

"Oh, yes. You should try it sometime. It's healthy, quick, and delicious. And what are you having for dinner, Claire?"

"Red wine."

"I see. Now, you know you could easily have what I'm having without lifting a finger."

"Will you stop tempting me, Foster?"

"Probably not. If Grayson wasn't such a fine man, I'd be putting my heart and soul into winning you back."

"Oh, Foster, you're a charmer."

"Well, I don't like the idea of you sitting there drinking wine alone. You can't make me a bad guy for wanting to shower you with attention and pleasure."

"You need to forget about me, Foster. Haven't you seen any other women lately?"

"I have to admit, I haven't. Once you've found someone who's pure and sweet, you hesitate to try something different. Sometimes it's better to be alone than with someone who's not to your liking."

"Boy, do I agree with that. That's how I felt when I moved here. I can be perfectly happy by myself."

"I'd say that's a sign of a well-balanced and happy person."

"Well, Foster, you've awakened my appetite with your dinner menu, so I'd better find myself something to eat around here."

"Good idea. Then refill your glass of wine and make a toast to your friend on the beach."

"I will. Thanks for calling. Enjoy your dinner."

I had to admit, getting this phone call from Foster lifted my spirits. It was nice that he thought of me. I wondered what Grayson was up to now. I didn't want to consider that he might be working late again with Jeanne.

Chapter 22

Sitting at the kitchen table the next morning, I received an email from Brenda reminding me about tonight's fish boil. I hoped Grayson saw her message and remembered. I decided to send him a text about it.

[Claire]
Hey, Mr. Wills. I'm expecting you this evening for the fish boil. Should I just meet you there?

Seconds later he replied.

[Grayson]
I'm looking forward to it, Miss Stewart, but this gentleman prefers to pick up his date at five forty-five if that suits you.

[Claire]
Miss Stewart would love that. Don't forget that Harry, Rachael, Kent, and Brenda will join us.

[Grayson]
I haven't. See you tonight!

Mission accomplished. I quickly dressed for the day so I could get to the post office. I also needed to check on Ericka's condition. With Cher working at the gallery today, I'd just stop by there after picking up my mail.

I swung Puff into my arms to kiss her goodbye and then set her on her chair that was now on my very chilly porch. Somehow I didn't think she'd mind the crisp air.

At the post office, I said hello to all the morning regulars who checked their mail about the same time I normally did. After that, I went into the tourism area to pick up the latest edition of the *Pulse* to take home.

Before I stopped to see Cher, I went to Fish Creek Market to have them make a couple of sandwiches for me. I also remembered to grab some cat food for Puff. The couple running the little mini market were so pleasant. They worked hard to supply all the incidentals that the tourists and nearby residents needed.

When I arrived at Carl's gallery, Cher was helping a customer. I saw no sign of Carl. I looked around at all their unique merchandise to find something I could send to Linda for her upcoming birthday. I looked through the 8×10 prints and found one of Bayside Tavern. I smiled, knowing she was quite fond of the place. When Cher was free from her customer, I asked if she could put a frame to it for me.

"Sure, we have some this size in the back if you're not too picky. Maybe I should get one of those Bayside ball caps for her."

"That's a great idea, Cher. Um, I hate to ask about Ericka, but is there anything new?"

"I just talked to her before my shift, and she said she was in bed all day yesterday. If it's that bad, she's going to need twenty-four-hour care soon. George checks on her daily, but that's not the same. No one's making her eat, so who knows how much nutrition she's getting."

"Maybe you can suggest to George that he get someone to help with that."

"I plan to. Is this all you need, Claire? Oh, one more thing. Let me see if there's a paycheck for you on Carl's desk."

"Thanks. I appreciate that."

Cher returned and shook her head.

"Thanks for the frame and having it wrapped to send."

"You're very welcome. How's your mom? Any better?"

"I need to call her later. I'm relying too much on getting news from Michael, Linda, and Carole."

I left for home feeling I'd accomplished something. I couldn't wait to have one of the deli sandwiches from the market.

After my delicious lunch, I went upstairs to decide what to wear for my big date. Of course, the fish boil would be casual, so I'd need a sweater of some kind. I loved seeing Grayson dressed casually, as it happened so rarely.

I spent the afternoon sewing a bit of Michael's quilt and watering my flowers, which made the day go by quickly. I took a shower and jumped into the navy cords and pink chenille sweater I'd selected.

There was a threat of rain for the evening, but I hoped it wouldn't happen until we were all inside the White Gull Inn for dinner. Grayson arrived on time wearing a red and gray sweater that brought out his eyes and hair. We grinned at each other before we kissed.

"Should we go ahead?" he asked as he helped me with my coat.

"Yes, I know Brenda will be there early. Kent will likely carpool with Harry and Rachael."

Chapter 23

We walked to the inn hand in hand. We didn't have far to walk, but I couldn't believe all the traffic. Door County was at its highest tourist peak, it seemed.

Brenda greeted us happily and took us to a large table out back on the patio. She informed us that another couple would be sitting with our group. Grayson went to the outside bar to order us cocktails. As always, Rachael, Harry, and Kent were running a bit late.

While the boil master started his gigantic fire, the other couple Brenda had mentioned joined us at the table.

"Hello," the man began. "We're Kate and Cole Alexander."

"Please join us," Grayson responded graciously. "I'm Grayson Wills, and this is my good friend Claire Stewart."

"Nice to meet you both," I chimed in. "Our other friends haven't arrived yet. Are you by chance locals, or are you tourists to the area?"

"Oh, I assumed everyone around here was a tourist," Cole joked. "My wife and I have been here before, but we're from Borna, Missouri. I don't expect you've heard of it, but it's in the eastern part of Missouri. How about you?"

"I'm actually a native and live close by," Grayson explained, but my pretty friend here is also from Missouri." Their eyes lit up.

"Yes, I'm from Perryville, so I know exactly where you're from," I nodded with a smile. "I just moved here a couple of years ago."

"What a small world!" Kate responded. "We're familiar with Perryville. We have a guest house in Borna that I operate, and Cole here is in real estate development."

"Oh, really? What's the name of your guest house?" I inquired.

"Josephine's Guest House," Kate answered with pride. "It's in an old house that used to belong to a Dr. Paulson. He lived there with his wife Josephine, whom I named the guest house after."

"Oh, I'm familiar with that place," I added. "It's a lovely house."

"The house sits on some acreage, so when Cole and I married, we built a new house on the same property," Kate explained.

"Interesting," Grayson chimed in.

"Now, what my wife isn't telling you is that Josephine still occupies the house in spirit only," Cole said with a grin.

"Oh, I've read about those kinds of guest houses!" I said with a chuckle.

"Look! Here comes our friends we want you to meet," I said, as I happily greeted Harry, Rachael, and Kent. "Hey, guys. We just met Kate and Cole from Borna, Missouri. They're joining us this evening."

"Well, none of us are from Missouri, but any friends of these folks are friends of ours," Harry responded with his trademark hearty laugh. "Can I buy all of you a drink?"

"Thanks, Harry, but we're good," Grayson replied.

"Sorry, guys," Brenda said as she joined us. "We got a little busy, and I had to help them out."

I introduced Brenda to Cole and Kate just as the boil master began to explain his process of fixing our dinner.

It was a process I'd heard before, but it seemed to be the boil master's job to tell it in an entertaining manner for all the folks who were experiencing a boil for the first time. Grayson asked Cole and Kate if they'd ever been to a boil before tonight. They said no just as the big flames erupted and the boil master added salt to the boiling water.

Kate and Cole were an attractive couple, and for not being newly married, they were very affectionate toward each other. Brenda couldn't keep her eyes off Kent, who was watching the boil with interest. Harry, too, seemed mesmerized by the boil master. I wondered if he was thinking of adding a fish boil to the farm's activity. Poor Rachael if he was.

After all the hoopla of combining the fish and potatoes, the boil master announced that we were to file into the restaurant to eat his delicious meal. We could sit anywhere we liked, and someone would take our drink orders before our meal arrived. Anyone who didn't want fish could substitute it for chicken. Frankly, I was ready to try the alternative to the white fish, but I didn't.

"Kate and Cole, please join us at the same table to continue our conversation," Grayson graciously offered. They nodded with approval.

"Why, sure!" Harry added. "The more the merrier."

Chapter 24

Brenda led us to a table for eight, and the merriment began. I sat next to Kate and found her most delightful.

"So, tell me more about the artwork you do, Claire," Kate asked with interest.

"I paint and quilt, you might say," I replied after I gave the server my drink order.

She smiled. "East Perry County has so many quilters. I try to help out with quilting at my church once in a while, but I don't have much time. I think the church lady quilters are better off without me, really. Plus, I'm busy baking blueberry muffins for my guests, which the guest house is known for."

"Ooh, I bet they're delicious! Having a popular food item is always a draw."

"I'm originally from South Haven, Michigan. I moved to Borna after my first husband died. I'd intended to sell the property but ended up staying."

"Moving to a new area is certainly a big change."

Kate nodded. "It is. Fortunately, I had a next-door neighbor who came over and introduced herself, and that really helped. I don't know what I would've done without Ellie. She's still my best friend."

"I had a similar experience when I moved to Fish Creek. And how did you and Cole meet?"

"Well, he had this red jeep for sale, and basically, the rest is history," she chuckled.

"Well, there must be something about red. One morning I was having coffee at the local coffee house when a man in a red scarf got my attention, and you know the rest of the story." She burst into laughter as the others looked our way.

"I love it! So, are you two engaged?"

"No, you might say we're still a work in progress."

"Hey, you two over there," Harry said to get our attention. "Are you taking time to enjoy your dinner, or are you just going to jabber and let your meal get cold?"

I laughed. "We're doing a pretty good job of both!"

"Don't mind him." Rachael answered. "You know Harry just wanted your attention. He has to be the life of the party."

"Rachael, how do you and Harry know Claire and Grayson?" Kate asked innocently.

"Claire and I belong to the same quilt club, so that's how we met. But after a while, I was lucky enough to talk her into helping us at the Christmas tree farm that Harry and I have."

"Christmas tree farm?" Kate repeated as her face lit up. "I love seeing them on the Hallmark Channel. They're so romantic!" Rachael chuckled out loud.

"Claire, Cole is quite a golfer it seems," Grayson revealed. "Since there are so few nice days left, I asked him to join me on the course while the golf club is still open."

"How nice!" I responded.

"Well, while the guys are golfing, maybe the two of us can have lunch," Kate suggested, looking directly at me.

"You're on!" I agreed.

"When are you going back to Perryville for a visit?" Kate asked.

"I'm not sure," I said with hesitation. "It may be Thanksgiving. My mom isn't feeling well these days, so I'll be heading home before too long."

"Well, if you ever need a place to stay, you're welcome to stay at our guest house."

"Oh, Kate, that's nice of you to offer. I'm just not sure when I'll get there."

"Ready for cherry pie and ice cream?" the server interrupted.

"I'm always ready for that!" I was the first to say. "When in Door County, cherry pie is a necessity. Since Brenda works here, she's always tempting me with the inn's wonderful food."

"Did you enjoy the dinner?" Brenda asked Kate.

"My, yes!" Kate answered. "But having dinner with Missouri folks makes it even better. I told Cole I'd love to come back here for Christmas, but the look on his face said I'd better forget about it."

"Yes, and you could visit the Christmas tree farm," Rachael reminded her.

"Folks, this was quite fun," Harry said as he stood up from the table. "Now I'd like to go somewhere and buy everyone a nightcap."

"Thanks very much, Harry," Cole was the first to respond. "We're staying here at the inn, so I think we'll call it a night. We've had a busy day."

"I agree," Kate nodded. "Claire and I will get to visit again at lunch. Rachael, you and Brenda are welcome to join us if you'd like." They smiled but didn't respond.

"Okay, folks, it was nice to have met you," I added as everyone made their way to leave. "Kate, I'll meet you at the Whistling Swan tomorrow at noon."

"And Cole, I'll meet you tomorrow on the green," Grayson said with excitement.

"I'll look forward to that," Cole nodded.

Everyone said their goodbyes with hugs as if we were long-time friends. I hated for the evening to end. The rain had even held off, making it a perfect night.

Grayson and I walked back to the cabin, but this time his arm was around me to keep me warm. The evening had brought a chill with it.

"I loved this night with my sweetheart," Grayson said with affection as he gave me a kiss.

Chapter 25

The next day I nearly forgot I was to meet up with Kate for lunch while our guys went golfing. Since Brenda and Rachael declined to join us, I'd be able to visit more intimately with Kate. As I was dressing, Mom called.

"Feeling any better, Mom?" I asked, concerned.

"I suppose it's just old age, as the doc tells me all the time. So, how are things with you?"

"You're not going to believe who Grayson and I met last night at a fish boil at the White Gull Inn!"

"Well, I couldn't say."

"Remember when you said you and Bill drove down to East Perry and noticed that Dr. Paulson's house and office is now a guest house?"

"Yes."

"Well, the owners are Kate and Cole Alexander, and they're here in Door County vacationing. They built a new home for themselves on the property near the guest house."

"Well, that's something! I believe the sign said Josephine's Guest House, but she's not Josephine?"

"That's the place, but Doc Paulson's wife's name was Josephine. That's who it's named after."

"Now that you say that, it's all coming back. I'd never met her."

"Well, to hear Kate and Cole tell it, Josephine is still alive and well as a spirit in the house."

"Oh dear!"

"We were there with Rachael, Harry, Brenda, and Kent, and we all got along famously. Grayson even invited Cole to play golf with him today while they're in town. And I asked Kate to have lunch with me so we could visit more."

"So, is she a relative of the Paulsons?"

"No. She's actually from Michigan. She said her inheritance of the property was a long story. Her intention was to sell it, but she fell in love with Borna and the community. That's where she met her husband."

"It sounds like you have a lot to talk about. I'm glad you met some new friends. Bill's coming to supper tonight, so I'm planning to put a pot roast in the oven soon."

"Oh, now you're making me homesick." She chuckled.

We hung up, and I smiled knowing Mom would be spending time with Bill instead of being alone. Mom made the best gravy for that pot roast. I wish I had paid more attention to her cooking all these years.

I dressed and then prepared Linda's present for mailing at the post office.

It was pretty chilly out, but the sun was shining, so I decided to walk the couple of blocks. The street was bustling with tourists, and most were carrying shopping bags. That was good to see. I'm sure Cher and Carl were busy at the gallery today.

I arrived at the Whistling Swan to find Kate already sitting at a table.

"I asked for a table inside. I hope you don't mind," she quickly explained.

"No, it's perfect. I love the decor here."

"Yes, Cole and I almost ended up staying here, but I loved the rooms better at the inn."

"So, did you have the decadent cherry stuffed French toast for breakfast this morning?"

"No, but the thought of it sure tempted me. My omelet was tasty. You're so lucky to have all these wonderful restaurants nearby. As you know, where we are, there's nothing but a spot of bar food here and there." I chuckled. I loved her smile.

"It's so nice of you to take time for me today, Claire. You didn't have to do this. I could have entertained myself on this street."

"I don't get to entertain folks from Missouri very often, so this is a treat for me. I talked to my mom in Perryville this morning, and she couldn't believe you were here. She'd just taken a drive a week ago and told me she passed your guest house." Kate smiled.

"For not being a native of Missouri, I've gotten to know so many wonderful people, not to mention all the tourists. I'm still trying to find out information on the doctor and his wife so I can pass it on to others."

We ordered our meals, and then I couldn't help but ask Kate if she knew a Dr. Austen Page in Perryville.

Chapter 26

"I can't say I do. Why?"

"He's a pediatrician in Perryville, and I lived with him for five years."

"I bet that's a story," Kate joked.

"It is, and I won't bore you with it, but when I left him quite unexpectedly, I moved into my friend Cher's cabin here in Fish Creek. She moved to Perryville to take care of her mom but has since moved back."

"Oh my. How convenient."

"Moving to Fish Creek was the best thing I've ever done. I do miss my mom, however. She's eighty-five, and I don't know how much more time I'll have with her."

"Would she ever consider moving here?"

"Never! Perryville's her home, and I'd never do that to her."

"Well, if we ever get you and Grayson to Borna, I want you to bring your mom with you."

"I appreciate that. Could her boyfriend come as well?"

"Boyfriend?"

I chuckled. "Yes, they're both widows but were good friends as couples. Bill, her friend, said he remembers going to Dr. Paulson when he was young."

"Well, of course, he must come! I love to bake, and I mentioned to you last night that I'm known for my blueberry muffins. I was really into baking before opening the guest house. There was a time I thought about opening a little bake shop, but I was too busy."

"I love anything blueberry."

"South Haven, where I grew up, is known as the blueberry capital of the world, so everything's about blueberries, just like cherries reign supreme in Door County."

"I wish I enjoyed cooking and baking, but I had the perfect mom who did it all for me, you might say."

"Then be glad you're single. Cole loves to eat!" I chuckled.

"Thanks for the tip. Not to change the subject, but I wanted you to know there's a very nice Missouri business owner here on Main Street I just recently met. Trinkets is the name of her shop. It's the one with all the colorful yard ornaments outside."

"Oh, yes. I remember passing that. I can't wait to go there."

"Laurie, the owner, has sisters who will be coming here at Christmas. I guess one of them lives in Green Bay. Another sister, Lily, lives in the Augusta wine country area. Do you ever go there?"

"Oh, yes. It reminds me a lot of East Perry County with all the winding roads and beautiful countryside. We love the wineries, of course. Especially Mt. Pleasant."

"Well, this sister who lives in Augusta has a quilt and antique shop called Lily Girl's Quilts and Antiques. Isn't that adorable? She briefly mentioned having a half-sister, Ellen, but I don't know where she lives."

"The wine country is doing a much better job of promoting tourism than we are in East Perry. We have a lot of old-timer Germans who want things to stay the same and are very leery of any new development. We do have a popular Lutheran Heritage Center and Museum that attracts a lot of folks. They've just expanded, and they do a beautiful job of rotating exhibits."

"Mom told me that the old Altenburg bank is now a coffee shop, so that says something."

Kate nodded and laughed. "Yes, a friend of mine owns that now. It's quite popular. Claire, you really do need to visit again."

"I think I will."

Our lunch lasted longer than I expected, but it was so enjoyable. I didn't want to keep Kate too much longer because I knew she wanted to shop while Cole was busy golfing.

We hugged each other goodbye and promised to stay in touch. She asked me to pass on a message to Grayson about how much Cole appreciated his offer to play golf.

I glanced at my easel when I got back to the cabin and just didn't feel inspired. I guess I'd work more on Michael's quilt, which was turning out to be fun and challenging. I couldn't have idle hands.

Chapter 27

Later that evening, Grayson called.

"So, my dear, how was your lunch today with Kate?"

"Oh, we had such an enjoyable time together. I really like her. How was your golf day?"

"Cole is a great golfer. He put me to shame, but it sounds like he gets to play much more than I do. We also got to talking about real estate. He asked me a lot about the market here in Door County. It sounds as if he's done well with his investments."

"Well, that sounds interesting. I think they're going home tomorrow. Kate left me for some Christmas shopping without Cole."

"Just like a woman, right?"

He chuckled. "Right. You just can't shop the same way with someone else even when they mean well."

"You sound like you have experience."

"You're correct!"

Grayson chuckled. "Oh, I heard from Kelly today."

"And?"

"She didn't say anything about missing me this time. She has her eye on joining a sorority, and I'm not sure I like that idea."

"I'm sure she'll make a good case if she decides to. When will she be home again?"

"She hinted it may not be till Thanksgiving. I want her to come home as often as possible. If some young guy starts asking her out, she won't want to give up her weekends to come home."

"I'm glad you realize that's a possibility. Starting college isn't just about all the classes if you recall."

"Speak for yourself, Miss Stewart," he kidded. "I bet you broke some hearts in your college years, didn't you?"

"I don't know about that, but I did spend way too many years hooked on one guy who wasn't good for me. He finally broke up with me and broke my heart."

"Oh. He broke up with you?"

"Yeah, he sure did. I think your first love is the hardest to get over. It took me quite a while to mend my heart. It turns out that the breakup was for the best, though. I learned he'd been cheating on me."

"I'm sorry. What a fool he was."

"I really didn't want to date after that."

"I can understand why. I'm glad you didn't marry him. It could have gone that direction, and it would have gotten really ugly. Kelly is rather naive when it comes to dating. She hasn't dated as much as her other girlfriends. You could say I was a bit protective of her."

"Oh, I can see the protective part. But you gave her a good upbringing, so now you'll have to trust her."

"I guess. Well, I'm beat, so I'll say goodnight, sweetheart."

"You did a nice thing today for Cole, Grayson. Have a good rest of your evening."

We finally said goodnight. I could actually feel his exhaustion through the phone. I, too, was tired and ready to retire. I'd really had a good day visiting with Kate.

The next morning when I awoke, I made the mistake of checking my phone before getting out of bed. I had to read the text twice before I could fully comprehend Cher's message and write her back.

[Cher]
They took Ericka to the hospital in Green Bay last night. George is with her, and I'm waiting to hear from him. I'll let you know. I'm so worried.

[Claire]
Thanks for letting me know. Prayers coming for our friend.

I couldn't believe how quickly Ericka had gone downhill. When she learned about her cancer, she seemed to give up. I think she felt it was a death sentence. I wasted no time in asking God to protect and heal her. Cher's text certainly took the wind out of my sail for the day. I went downstairs to feed Puff and start my coffee. Minutes later, Cher called.

Chapter 28

"What's the latest?" I asked quickly.

"Her breathing is a real issue, and they have her on a ventilator. George isn't going to work today. He said he'll just stay there with her. I begged to visit her, but George said that couldn't happen. It's so sad, Claire. I hope she pulls through. In other news, guess who I just heard from?"

"Who?"

"Laurie Rosenthal from Trinkets."

"Really? What did she want?"

"Well, tomorrow night she said she wanted to take us up on your offer to meet her at Bayside after work. I hope it was okay that I said yes. I figured we could also call Rachael since it's a Saturday night. I bet she'd love to see her old working buddies."

"I'm sure she would, and yes, I'm up for it. But are you sure you're in the mood to do this?"

"May as well. Might do me good. Laurie said to tell you that she appreciated that you sent someone to her store by the name of Kate, I believe it was, from Missouri. She evidently bought a lot of fun things for her garden."

"Yes, her name's Kate, and you'd love her. She and her husband sat with us at the fish boil, and then she and I had lunch together. They're visiting from Missouri if you can believe it. I knew Kate would like Trinkets."

"Wish I could have met her. So, about tomorrow ... Do you want to call Rachael, or should I?"

"I'll call her. What time were you thinking?"

"I guess around six o'clock after Laurie closes the shop. Since she lives upstairs, that shouldn't be a problem for her."

After we hung up, I thought of Ericka and how nice it would be to have her join us for this girls' night out. From what Cher said, though, those days are over. Girlfriend time is precious indeed. I didn't waste any time calling Rachael.

"Oh, Claire, I'm sorry I didn't answer sooner. I just came in from outside. What's up?"

"Well, it's a last-minute invite with a long story, but are you free tomorrow night?"

"Me? Just me?"

I had to chuckle. "Yes, just you."

"Yeah, I guess so. Harry hasn't mentioned any plans."

"How would you like to join some of us at Bayside, your old stomping grounds, for a girls' night out?"

She paused. "What brought this on?"

"Well, Cher and I met this woman Laurie, who owns Trinkets here on Main Street. We found out she's single and from Missouri. We thought we'd go to Bayside to get to know each other better and then thought of you since it's Saturday night and that was your work shift pre-Harry. I'm sure you could use a night out like that. Am I wrong?"

"Oh, of course, it sounds like fun, but I don't know if you've noticed that I'm not single anymore."

I chuckled. "And? Does this mean a girls' night out isn't permissible?"

"Yeah, I can just hear Harry. He'll think it's a trap to get me to come back to work at Bayside. You know how opposed he was to that."

"Raech, you'll just have to convince him. I'm sure everyone would love to see you."

"And I'd love to go. I'll see what Harry has to say, but it sure does sound like fun. I'll get back to you."

When I hung up, I was feeling anti-marriage again. How would I handle a simple invite like this if I were married? Asking permission to go out with girlfriends rubbed me the wrong way. Would I just announce I was going if we didn't have any plans as a couple? I'd like to eavesdrop on that conversation between Harry and Rachael.

I was lacking creative motivation once again as I thought of Ericka lying in the hospital. I hoped I'd find my muse again soon. My painting procrastination couldn't go on much longer. I started doing small domestic things to tidy up the cabin. The fireplace needed a good cleaning, and apparently, today was the day. I knew I'd be using it on a regular basis soon.

As I took a bucket of wood ash out to my firepit, Tom, who was working next door, came walking toward me.

"Hi there. Can I help with anything?"

"I'm good, but thanks. I can feel the cold coming on, and I needed to get this done."

"Yeah, some of the folks down the road have already started their fires. It looks like you still have plenty of wood. You know, Claire, when I see you, I still feel bad about your quilt show getting rained out. I'm going to help with the fall festival coming up in Sister Bay."

"Yeah? Doing what?"

"I have a friend who works for the city, and they need volunteers to help set up things in the road and in the booths. That event gets bigger and bigger each year."

"I'd love to go, but parking is such a problem."

"Yeah, parking can be tricky. It helps if you have a place to go. They'll feed the helpers, too, which is a bonus."

"That's so nice of you to volunteer, Tom."

"Say, I'll be starting on your leaves next week. It seems they come earlier each year."

"Thanks. It seems like we just had winter."

"The Farmers' Almanac says we're in for a rough one."

"I guess I'll muddle through as long as you can hang all my Christmas lights."

"You bet! Are you going to work at the tree farm again this year?"

"Yes, and this year they've added something for fall. I'm in charge of the gift shop now, so I'll be busy."

"Yes, you will. I'll see you next week then, Claire."

Tom was so good about helping me. He certainly made it easier for me to manage living here by myself.

After a shower and fluffing my pillow, I was ready to indulge in a good movie, so I turned on my favorite movie channel. *The Big Sleep* was just about to begin. Any movie with Laureen Bacall and Humphrey Bogart had to be good. Maybe I was just too tired to get into the story, but Humphrey was the detective, and the plot got complicated rather quickly. I couldn't engage and went right to sleep with the TV still on.

Chapter 29

The next morning, I felt alert and ready to start my day. It was Saturday, and I had a fun night to look forward to with the girls. It was going to be beautiful out, and Grayson calling as I was enjoying my morning coffee put a smile on my face.

"So, what's my sweetheart doing today?" Grayson sweetly asked.

"Ahh, what a sweet greeting! It sounds like you're in a good mood. No work today?"

"None. I thought the two of us might take a drive through Peninsula Park today. Might be a good time to get out Chili Pepper, who has been terribly neglected."

"Chili Pepper?"

He chuckled. "That's the name of my vintage corvette convertible that I keep in the garage most of the time. I know it's a corny name, but it *is* a bit chilly out, right?"

"Indeed it is. I don't remember your mentioning owning a convertible."

"Perhaps I didn't. It doesn't get to joyride as often as it should. Anyway, do you have plans for the day, or can I whisk you off for a while?"

"No plans till six o'clock this evening. We have a little girls' night out planned."

"That sounds fun, but I'm sure I'll have you back in plenty of time. How about I pick you up around eleven o'clock? Bring a jacket!"

"Very good. I'll see you then!"

I hung up realizing I'd learned something new and fun about Grayson. A spontaneous invitation was also a bit unlike him. Perhaps he was feeling more liberated with Kelly gone.

I'd never driven through the entire park before. I knew it was about 4,000 acres, and eight miles of it were on the Green Bay shoreline. The park dated back to the 1900s, and my own cabin had been built here before it was moved to its current location in the 1940s. I'd never asked Cher where in the park the cabin used to be. The last time I was there, it was to take a photo for Mr. Adams's painting. I'd gone to the very spot where he proposed to his wife. I bet there were a lot of memories in that park. Now I was going to build one with Grayson.

I rushed around preparing for a fun day. Layers would probably be the most practical for the park. I decided on jeans and a flannel shirt with a jean jacket. I also grabbed what I called my picnic quilt. Mom had given me a scrappy nine-patch quilt that we used many times as a family for outdoor events. Sometimes as a teenager I'd place it under our big tree when my friends would come to visit. It was always in the wash, but it held up well and stored a lot of memories. One time, I took it with me to the high school football game so I wouldn't have to sit on the cold, concrete bleacher seat. I'm fairly sure my boyfriend at the time,

Jimmy, gave me a kiss that night. Perhaps today this blanket would get me another kiss.

Chapter 30

When I happened to look out my front window, I saw Grayson drive up in his snazzy red convertible. The color red certainly flattered him. I flashed him a big grin when he came to the door.

"Hubba-hubba! So, this is Chili Pepper, huh?"

"That's my girl. What do you think of her?" he asked modestly.

"I'm impressed, but I'm dying to know why you named your car Chili Pepper, besides the fact that it's red."

"Well, the friend I bought it from had a little to do with that. He told me it was fun and hot to drive. He said, 'Ya know, it's hot and spicy, and like a chili pepper, you keep coming back for more.' I had to laugh, but when I got in the car to drive it for the first time, I decided the name was perfect and quite fun."

"Well, all righty. Let's see how this hot and spicy car of yours rolls!"

It was great seeing Grayson in such a good mood. I tried to act like I'd been in a convertible before, but I couldn't remember if I ever had. It was a little awkward for sure, like the whole world was watching us. The cool air blew my hair every which way even with the side windows up. I'd have been too cold without my jacket.

I loved seeing the scenery up close and personal in this topless car, but Grayson had to compete with the wind when he'd say something. He had to almost shout for me to hear him, but he was clearly enjoying his man toy.

Without notice, Grayson pulled into one of the viewing areas offering a gorgeous view of the bay. I followed him as he climbed out of the car.

"I have a little surprise for you, Claire. I bet you're hungry and a bit thirsty, right?"

"You're always so good at reading my mind," I blushed.

Grayson opened the small trunk and pulled out an old-fashioned picnic basket with a bottle of wine sticking out of it. I shook my head in disbelief. He'd thought of everything.

"There's a nice spot over here where we can sit. You may want to bring your quilt."

"I'll grab it. This is pretty secluded, Grayson. Have you been here before?"

"I can't tell a lie," he said with a grin.

"Do I want to know the story?"

"Marsha and I would drive through here occasionally. We'd see couples parked here and there. I could never try to persuade her to stop, though." He shook his head with disappointment. "I'm glad you approve."

As I spread out the blanket, I realized this was the first time I'd ever heard Grayson complain about Marsha.

He began opening the wine. Inside the basket were two glass wine glasses, ready for filling.

"By golly, this is still chilled. I chose a Chablis. I hope you'll like it."

"It's perfect. Thank you. So, what else do you have in your basket?"

Grayson carefully pulled out a platter of small chicken salad sandwiches, which looked like they were from a deli of sorts. Then he pulled out a small bag of grapes and a nice round hunk of Gouda cheese. I was impressed with his choices.

"What a nice spread, Grayson!"

"Well, you can thank the Fish Creek Market for that."

"I love their sandwiches. You're amazing, honey. This was a great idea."

As we ate, Grayson began describing exactly where we were and what we were seeing.

"Look at the colors over this way," I said, pointing to the west." I wish I had my paint and palette. Nature is the best artist."

"I wish you had your palette as well. I'd love to watch you work."

"Well, right now, the best I can do is take some photos while we're here."

I enjoyed every morsel of food he'd brought, and the wine paired perfectly. We kept smiling at each other as I rotated to get photos, including some cute selfies of my sweetheart and me.

Chapter 31

If I could stop the clock in my life, I wanted to do it right now. Grayson was completely relaxed, chatting about the water, the park, and the view. I think both of us realized we were creating a perfect memory together.

"It means a lot to have you here with me, Claire," Grayson said with sincerity as he caressed my hand.

"Something tells me you should take time more often to relax like this."

"I'm starting to give myself permission to do so."

"Why is that, do you think?"

"I've put Marsha on a pedestal since her death, and I'm just beginning to see how much I missed being married to her. Our marriage wasn't perfect by any means, but I think I wanted to convince myself that it was."

"None of us are perfect. We just do the best we can."

"My point. I felt the harder I worked, the happier she and Kelly would be. I had it all wrong. Even Kelly tries to convince me I work too hard. Wait till I tell her we had a picnic in the park." I grinned, but part of me felt sorry for him. "I think you and I should plan a trip together. Please think about it."

"I couldn't agree more, Grayson. I have nothing tying me down, and the more places I travel, the better my creativity gets."

I could tell I had said just the right thing, as he embraced me even closer.

"Did you know there's a graveyard close to us?"

"Well, I know there's one in the park. Do you know how to find it?"

He nodded. "You can see a bit of it from the road if you don't drive too fast. A sign says it was established in 1904. Actually, there are two cemeteries. I know one is Pioneer Cemetery, which some call Thorp-Claflin. You may be familiar with the Thorp family who founded Fish Creek. Many of their family members are buried there."

"Have you walked it?"

"I have, but it's been a long time. The tombstones are really old. On our way home, we'll stop by there. It's gorgeous in the fall with its many colorful trees."

"There's so much to appreciate in this park. I'm so glad you brought me here today, Grayson."

Our time together was passing quickly. I knew I could spend all day here with him, and it still wouldn't be long enough.

We packed up and slowly drove down the road where there was evidence of a cemetery. How pleasant it must be for the families of the deceased to be buried here in this sacred park.

The trees were so vivid and varied. I was gaining a new appreciation for fall in Door County. We got out to walk around the cemetery and noticed that besides the tombstones, there were outlines in the concrete of small buildings that were once on-site.

"Oh, Grayson, look at this stone. Increase Claflin arrived in 1834 and was the first white settler in Door County. He was born September 19, 1795 and died March 27, 1868. The shape of this stone is most unusual. It must mean something."

"There are many unusual shapes in this graveyard. Unfortunately, you can no longer read most of the headstones."

"Did you notice that this stone has tassels and a braided edging? I can't imagine how difficult it was to create it. I have a friend who once researched textiles in stones. She said she could actually date the time of the stone by the textiles created."

"How interesting."

"If stones could talk, right?"

After we took photos of some of the tombstones, we took our time getting back to Fish Creek.

"I'm so glad you thought of doing this together, Grayson. This park is so close to my cabin, and I rarely drive into it. My brother Michael and his friend Jon really enjoyed their day here when they visited me."

"Do you look for them to return?"

"I do. I'm hoping they'll come for Christmas and bring Mom."

When we returned to the cabin, Grayson looked concerned about something.

"Now, I don't want you to have too much fun with the girls tonight," he teased with a grin.

I laughed. "I promise to make our evening as grim as possible. Thank you for this wonderful day."

Without speaking a word, he took me in his arms to give me a long, tight hug and then a heartful kiss. I guess he wanted me to remember this moment when I was out with the girls.

It was five o'clock when I stepped foot in the cabin. A fun evening awaited me, and I needed to get ready.

Chapter 32

Looking through my closet, I pondered what to wear. Dress up, or dress down? I ended up choosing to be comfortable. A nice sweatshirt and my favorite pair of jeans would do just fine. I didn't need to impress the friends I was meeting, and I certainly wasn't looking to attract a date.

Laurie, Cher, and I decided to meet at Bayside. I still wasn't sure whether Rachael would show up. Harry probably discouraged her. Even Grayson had his doubts about Rachael coming tonight.

Cher and Laurie were already at one of the high-top tables when I arrived. So far, no sign of Rachael.

After a friendly greeting, Cher asked if Rachael was coming.

"She certainly wanted to, but we'll see," I replied as I ordered a Spotted Cow beer.

"Cher tells me that you're dating that handsome president of our chamber of commerce," Laurie teased. "He's a pretty good catch. I wondered if he was married."

"He's a widower, so there are issues at times," I noted.

"Widower issues or not, he adores this gal," Cher added with a grin. "Claire met him at the Blue Horse Cafe."

"Oh, really?" Laurie asked. "I may have to start going there more frequently!" We chuckled.

"Hey, look who just walked in!" Cher observed. "The bartenders spotted Rachael right away, so we may not see her for a while."

"Oh, I'm so glad." I responded. "She'll know a lot of these Saturday night regulars, too."

"Rachael used to bartend here on Saturday nights," Cher explained to Laurie.

"Rachael has a nice barn quilt business, and she and her late husband ran a Christmas tree farm," I added. "She's newly married again. I help out in their gift shop there on a seasonal basis."

"How fun that must be," Laurie smiled. I nodded.

"So, Laurie, when do you close your shop for the winter?" I asked.

"Late November usually, but if the weather is still nice in December, I drag it out a bit for Christmas sales," she answered. "Almost everyone else is closed by then. If a bad snowstorm comes along, that may change everything again."

"It's so nice that your family is coming for the holidays," I relished.

"It really is," she nodded. "I'm really excited about seeing my sisters. They stay in Green Bay at Loretta's, but they spend most of their time in Door County. Lily closes her store when she comes because it's slow in Augusta as well when the weather turns. And Lynn closes her gallery; she's married to a lawyer and doesn't have to depend on her business as an income. We've developed some traditions when they come, like having dinner at the White Gull Inn."

"Oh, I'd love to meet them if that's possible," I said. "My only sibling is a brother. He's great, but I'm envious you have sisters to share things with."

"I want to join in the fun, too!" Cher chimed in. "Be sure to tell them about Carl's gallery. I'm going to try to convince him to stay open till after Christmas."

"You should," I agreed.

"My niece Sarah sometimes joins my sisters as well," Laurie added.

"So, is Lily single?" I asked. "You may have told me."

"Yes. We all thought that she and Marc would get married since they've been dating now for several years, but it seems they like things just the way they are. He's such a great guy, and a big St. Louis Cardinals fan."

"Of course!" I cheered. "Everyone from Missouri is a big Cardinals fan."

"Well, Miss Rachael, we wondered if you'd ever join us," I kidded when she finally walked our way.

"Oh my goodness. It's so fun seeing everyone again!" Rachael reported happily. "It's like nothing has changed. It still feels like a wonderful family here even though I was just part-time. I told them the next round of drinks is on me, ladies." We happily accepted.

Cher took over introducing Laurie to Rachael. They both thought the other looked familiar but couldn't figure out why. The noise and chatter at our table became louder and louder.

"By the way, ladies," Rachael said, getting our attention. "Sylvester, one of the regulars, has a habit of buying rounds of drinks for any group of ladies if he thinks he has a shot at meeting them." We roared with laughter. "Once in a while, he actually gets lucky."

"Say, Rachael, how did Harry take to the idea of your coming here tonight?" I bravely asked.

"Well, the look on his face was rather comical," Rachael said with a chuckle. "I must have really shocked him. He paused and then said, 'Well honey, if you really want to go, I guess, go.' I think he thought I'd back down, but I didn't. I told him what great fun it would be to see everyone again and basically left the room before he could change his mind!"

Chapter 33

"He wants you to be happy. I'm glad he didn't overreact," I replied.

The bottles of Spotted Cow kept coming. It was eleven o'clock when I asked Rachael if she was okay driving home. If not, I told her my couch was open for her to spend the night.

"Oh, thanks Claire, but I'm good since I ate so much food," she explained. "Harry goes to bed pretty early, so he'll never know when I get in. He and Kent are going to the home game opener of the Packers tomorrow. It's probably why he didn't make a fuss about my going out tonight."

"I should have known there was a game this weekend. I've been seeing Packers gear everywhere for the past couple of days," I noted.

"You should get Harry one of our Packers throws at the gallery," Cher suggested.

"Oh, great idea," Rachael responded. "Save one for me, will you?"

"Sure!" Cher agreed.

"I got one for Grayson already, but he's not the serious fan that Harry and Kent are," I noted.

"Well, guys, this has been a blast, but I'd better be on my way," Rachael confessed.

"Thanks for putting this together, Cher," Laurie expressed. "I'm so glad to have met you all. When my family comes in, I'll contact you about a meetup."

"We'd love that," I nodded with a smile.

"You know, if they have the time, they may enjoy the tree farm," Rachael suggested.

"I'll tell them all about it," Laurie smiled.

We walked to the door together, and I stayed with Rachael till I saw her drive off. She said she'd text me when she arrived home. I couldn't help but be concerned about her. I didn't know how much she'd had to drink, but she sure seemed to have a good time.

I was glad to be home and couldn't wipe the smile from my face from the fun at Bayside and the nice date with Grayson. I didn't feel very tired, so I turned on TCM. I couldn't believe one of my favorite movies was playing. *Gone with the Wind* had so many wonderful messages about selfishness, war, and love. Seeing Clark Gable reminded me of Carl, who looked like a younger version. I stayed glued to the TV till I heard Clark Gable's favorite line, "Frankly, my dear, I don't give a damn."

When the movie ended, I realized I hadn't checked my phone for a text from Rachael. Two hours had passed, and still no message. She'd probably just gone to bed and forgotten to text me, but I sent her a message.

[Claire]
Did you make it home? I'm worried.

I waited for a response, but none came. I sure didn't want to wake up Harry and her by calling. I tried to file my worry away so I could sleep.

It was a restless night between thoughts of the movie and Rachael. Finally, around six in the morning, I decided to call since I knew Harry was an early riser. It went to voicemail. I left a message about just wanting to know if Rachael had made it home okay. I hung up and went downstairs with Puff. All my tossing and turning hadn't been good for her sleep either.

It was Sunday, and I decided to go to the church close by. I heard a strong wind and pulled the curtain back to see leaves flying everywhere, and fast. I checked the thermostat, and the temperature had dropped to near freezing. Tom would have his work cut out for him. My yard was also in disarray.

Thanksgiving crossed my mind. I knew I had to get back to Mom about my plans.

I was upstairs getting ready for church when my cell phone in the kitchen started ringing. I flew down my narrow stairs, nearly falling down.

"Harry, is everything okay?"

"No, not really. Rachael had an accident coming home last night."

"Oh, Harry!"

"She said she had to swerve off the road to avoid hitting a reckless driver, and it took her in a ditch."

"Oh no. What kind of shape is she in?"

"One leg has a minor fracture, so for a short while her leg will be in a cast from her knee down to her ankle. Her wrist is hurting, too, but all in all she was pretty lucky. Someone saw her swerve and called the ambulance right away, which was good. She'll be fine in time. She's sleeping right now from the pain medicine. I have to say, I had a bad feeling about her being out last night."

"Oh, Harry, this is awful. I tried to convince her to stay at my place, but she assured me she'd be fine. Please tell her to call if there's anything I can do."

"I will," Harry answered sadly.

Chapter 34

Why did I let her go home last night? I should have insisted, as there are too many crazies out that late. She'd need my help now more than ever.

I quickly texted Cher to tell her what happened.

Church would have to wait till next week, but a walk sounded good as long as I bundled up. I deadheaded a few of my flowers and then headed in the direction of Sunset Beach. I kicked away layers of leaves as I prayed for so many in need.

The beach wasn't crowded. I sat down on one of the stone benches, and my cell rang. I was surprised to see it was from Rachael.

"Hi, Claire. Just to set the record straight, the accident didn't have anything to do with the drinks I had last night," she defended.

"Probably not, but having you out on the road that late wasn't wise. How do you feel?"

"Well, I'm pretty doped up from the pain meds, but I should heal in no time from what they're telling me. My right wrist is affecting how I write and paint right now, so that's aggravating. Things are going to be getting busy at the farm, and here I am laid up with a cast and sore wrist."

"If I can help in any way, let me know."

"Well, you're an artist who has held a paintbrush before if I'm not mistaken," she teased.

"Oh, no, don't get any ideas about me painting any of those barn quilts for you, girl."

"Okay, but maybe you should come out tomorrow. I have some things to get ready to ship. My wrist is taped, so it's awkward."

"Not to worry, Rachael. I'll be out first thing in the morning."

As soon as I hung up, Cher called.

"I just got your text. Have you talked to Rachael yet?"

"I did, and I'm going out tomorrow to help her with some things at the farm. She hurt her wrist besides her leg, so she's on pain meds right now. I really regret she didn't spend the night."

"Me, too. Oh, I talked to Carl. He wants me to work every day now if I can since we're so busy. I'm going to squeeze in a visit to Ericka at the hospital no matter what George says." She started to cry.

"Oh, Cher, I know this is hard for you. I just wish Ericka wouldn't have given up so quickly."

"Well, who knows what we'd do in her situation, Claire Bear. When I told George I was coming regardless, he said he'd try to get me in. I think her other brother is there already or is on his way."

"This really does sound serious."

"Very."

"I'm sitting here on the bay. I have so many to pray for."

"Thanks for the prayers for Ericka. I'll try to call you from the gallery tomorrow."

"Good. I love you, Cher Bear."

I sat staring at the water rushing by like it was any other day. I couldn't fight the tears as I realized Ericka was never going to come out of this. How does God choose who lives and who doesn't?

I wanted to call Grayson and cry on his shoulder, but he had a golf tournament today. Perhaps we could talk tonight.

As I walked home, I passed Church of the Atonement. I wanted to go in to pray, but the door was locked. I continued my journey home, feeling sad. Puff would have to be my comfort this morning. I picked her up and gave her a big hug when I reached the cabin. Tomorrow I'd be off again, leaving her alone. I decided I'd better get something done instead of just moping around, so I changed my sheets and did a couple of loads of laundry.

My easel remained quiet, and my unquilted hangings stayed near my sofa waiting for me to pick them up. I took a deep breath and prayed in thanksgiving for all I had.

Chapter 35

Harry and Rachael were early risers, so I started the day before I normally would. I eagerly greeted my first cup of coffee and checked my phone as I sat at the kitchen table. The darkness out the window did nothing to encourage my morning commute.

I sent Rachael a text I was on my way.

When I finally pulled up to the tree farm, I saw light peeking out the windows. Kent greeted me at the door.

"Well, I wasn't expecting to see you today," I said with a friendly smile.

"I'm helping Dad with some things today. I'm glad you're here to keep an eye on Rachael so she doesn't overdo it."

"Wish me luck. It's hard to keep her still."

"Coffee? I just made a fresh pot. By the way, I sure enjoyed the fish boil the other night."

"We did, too. That was so nice of Brenda to arrange things."

"That's her. She's a real sweetheart."

"Do the girls like her?"

"They sure do. Everything we do now, they beg me to ask her to join us."

"Kent, I'm curious. Is this the first relationship you've had since your divorce? If that's too personal, I understand."

He nodded. "It is. It's a funny thing, but the girls have never been close to their mom. When they have to spend the weekend with her, it's quite an ordeal."

"What a shame."

"I'm not sure their mom enjoys having the girls either, especially with her recent relationship. Dad says I should file for full custody."

"Oh my."

"Well, good morning, Claire," Rachael announced as she hobbled in the back door. "It's good to see you this morning."

"I'm here for you," I reminded her with a smile. "How are you feeling?'

"The pain is better with these meds, but I'm having a terrible time sleeping. Poor Harry has slept in the guest room. Thanks for making coffee, Kent."

"No problem," he nodded and smiled. "Harry's probably waiting for me outside, so I'd better go. You ladies behave yourselves today."

"We'll be fine," Rachael said, blowing him a kiss. "Kent and Harry are going into Green Bay today to look at some new equipment."

"Rachael, feel free to boss me around as much as you want today. I'm ready for my orders," I said, pulling out a chair for her to sit. "By the way, you look really uncomfortable."

She spent the next half hour telling me all her concerns about what she needed to accomplish before the holidays. Then she explained what she needed to pack up to send, which she explained was the tedious part of the quilt barn business. Honestly, having this quiet, uninterrupted time with Rachael was nice. Normally she was on the move when she talked to me. Our conversation today drifted in many directions, including Ericka's health. I also shared with her that Kent had told me some personal information about his ex-wife.

"Oh, it's a mess, Claire. I wish he had full custody. I think she wishes it, too, but she won't admit it out of spite. He's convinced she uses drugs, but he hasn't been able to prove it."

"Drugs? Oh gosh. Those girls are so sweet and well-behaved."

"That has everything to do with Kent. He's such a good father to them. They love being around Brenda, but she's old enough to be their grandmother. I hate to say that out loud."

"I know. I worry that if the relationship fizzles, the girls will be more hurt than anyone."

Just then, Clint, the UPS driver, tapped on the door. When he came in and saw Rachael's leg, he demanded an explanation. As she began her story, I started unpacking some boxes.

"Clint, this is the manager of our gift shop now, Claire Stewart."

"So you're the one making my job so much harder these days," he joked. We all chuckled.

Chapter 36

My day ended up being quite fun. Rachael and I ordered a pizza, and I arranged some of the new merchandise in the shop.

By three thirty, I could tell she was really tired, so I suggested we call it a day. She still wasn't steady on her feet, so I walked with her to the house. Harry would return soon, so I encouraged her to lie down and rest for a while. She agreed to call me if she needed anything. As I walked back to my car, I knew how hard this must be for her.

On my drive home, I thought of Cher visiting Ericka today for perhaps the last time. What a tough day. I planned to call her this evening if I didn't hear from her.

Back at the cabin, I saw two squirrels enjoying the pumpkins I'd set out for display. I chuckled as I chased them away. Pumpkin had to be a fine treat for a squirrel. They ran past the fire pit, which gave me the idea to make an outdoor fire tonight. Tom had so much kindling from the trees saved up for me that I might as well burn it.

Rachael insisted that I bring home the leftover pizza. That and a glass of merlot would work just fine for my dinner. I took a second look at the fire pit and decided it was more trouble than I was up for right now, so I went to the porch to eat instead. I sat thinking about all Rachael and I had accomplished. It brought a smile, but only a brief one. Cher was calling, and I worried about what she'd say.

"Claire, I don't have good news," Cher said between tears. "Ericka left us today around three thirty." She paused. I felt stunned and yet not.

"Oh, no, no! So soon? How could this happen?"

"I'll explain later, but I did get to see her. I'm not sure she heard or comprehended all that I said to her. George held one of her hands, and I held the other. Unfortunately, her other brother didn't make it here in time."

I held back my emotions to try to hear and absorb everything Cher was telling me.

"Are you with George?," I asked.

"Yes. He has really prepared himself for this, which is more than I can say for myself. There was a lot more to her condition that I didn't know about till today. She was so young to die, Claire." Cher began to sob. "I keep feeling like I failed her somehow. I'm sorry for crying in your ear. I guess I'm still in shock."

"Of course, you are. You just had a very close friend pass away. Take your time to absorb it all. Are you still at the hospital?"

"Yes. I want to be here for George as long as it takes. I may not come home till tomorrow. I plan to call Carl when I hang up to tell him I can't work in the morning."

"He'll understand. Try to get some rest, and please tell George how deeply sorry I am to hear this."

"I will. I'll call you when I get home."

"I love you Cher Bear," I said to reassure her.

I hung up and tried to digest every word Cher had reported. Ericka was gone forever. I couldn't believe it. If there was more to her health than she'd shared with us, it explained why she felt destined to die. Too numb to cry, I decided to call Grayson.

"Hey, sweetheart. What's up?"

"I just heard some terrible news," I said in a shaky voice.

"What's wrong?"

"Ericka passed away this afternoon."

"Oh, Claire, I'm so sorry. You told me about her cancer, but I didn't realize it was this serious."

"I don't think many of us did. Cher and George were with her in the hospital. She was such a good friend. I hope she knew that." I took a deep breath to contain myself.

Grayson, in his pleasant, sympathetic nature, tried to console me. It was just what I needed. He shared that he'd lost a good friend once and had mixed feelings about it. He told me he wished he could reach out and hug me. He even offered to come over to make me feel better, but I told him not to. I thanked him and said I needed to hang up.

I took the rest of my wine upstairs and begged for this sad night to end. I began to cry for so many feeling loss tonight, but especially for Cher and Ericka's family. I could only imagine how shocked her coworkers would be to hear the news.

I lay back in bed as tears ran down my face. I thought of that very first day that I arrived here in Door County. Being a good friend to Cher, Ericka willingly accepted me. She brought George and his friend to help me unload. We even celebrated with a quick drink at Bayside that night as my welcome to Fish Creek.

It was hard to put into words what she meant to me. When Cher and I heard about Ericka's cancer, we tried our best to cheer her up. We brought her a Christmas tree and a new quilt from the Jacksonport Cottage where Amy works. What else could I have done? Did I say the things to her that I should have? When she tried to talk about dying, did I listen, or did I brush it aside because it was uncomfortable for me? Was I a faithful friend?

I turned out the lights and let my tears put me to sleep.

Chapter 37

In the kitchen the next morning, Puff and I were dragging. I didn't sleep well, so she didn't either. She looked at her dish as if wondering whether she should eat, and I did the same. I wanted to talk to Cher for more details in the worst way, but I had to wait my turn. George needed her now, and she needed him.

I was staring at the front page of the *Pulse* newspaper when Mom called. When I said hello, she knew from my voice that something was wrong. I suddenly blurted out the news of Ericka's death, and it took her by surprise. She paused before answering.

"I know how you must feel, honey. When a person who has been close to me passes, I feel like I've lost part of my body and soul. You just have to be thankful you had that person in your life and try to go on, as cruel and difficult as that can be. I never met Ericka personally, but I sure was grateful she was helpful to you when you arrived in Door County."

"I know. Those memories keep popping up in my mind."

"And they'll stay with you forever. She'd love that. It's a way to honor her even in death."

"You're right, Mom. I know you've lost some very dear friends yourself, including Cher's mom. I guess now I can better understand the depth of that loss for you. How are you feeling today?"

"Just fine, dear. Bill and I have cards today at the senior center. We both look forward to that."

"I'm happy you have something fun on the calendar today. Well, I should probably get busy with something."

"Of course, honey. And I'm really sorry about Ericka. Get some fresh air later, okay? It'll help you feel better. Oh, and what about Thanksgiving? Have you given any more thought to coming home?"

"No, but I will. I love you, Mom."

We said goodbye, and I felt gratitude for her wisdom. She'd felt this kind of loss many times over the years. She was a comfort in my sorrow.

I dressed and tried to think of all the things I needed to accomplish today. My mind then went back to Ericka and what I could get to memorialize her. She'd helped with so many causes in her life. Perhaps she'd shared her wishes with George. I'd ask Cher about that. Meanwhile, Brenda texted me.

[Brenda]
Free for lunch? My treat. Need to talk.

Instead of texting her a reply, I decided to call. She'd gotten to know Ericka through Cher as well.

"Thanks for the invite, Brenda. I was going to call you and tell you about the passing of Ericka yesterday."

She was shocked, of course. I explained to her what Cher had shared with me.

"I'm so, so, sorry, Claire."

"I feel so bad for Cher. The two of them were close."

"I can't even imagine what it must be like."

"I know. She's having a tough time. She stayed with Ericka's brother George last night. They need each other right now."

"I hear you've been helping Rachael. It's such a shame what happened, and right before the holidays. I can go out there after my morning shift is over."

"She'll appreciate that, Brenda. Are you okay? You mentioned needing to talk," I reminded.

"Yeah, I need some advice regarding Kent. Our relationship is growing, and I'm not sure that's a good idea. The girls are really attaching themselves to me. I think sometimes they pressure Kent into including me on things."

"I see your point. I can only tell you from experience that the feelings between you and Kent should drive the relationship, not the girls. I let Kelly influence my relationship with Grayson, and that was a big mistake."

"That's good advice. Lucy, the oldest, said to me recently, 'I wish you could be my mommy.' I didn't know what to say to that, so I just smiled."

"Oh, I can understand. I can't believe they don't have greater affection toward their mom."

"Well, you don't know the whole story like I do. It's really a shame."

"They're lucky to have their dad. Now, have you and Kent talked about the future? I don't necessarily mean marriage. And you don't have to answer me. I know it's personal."

"No, we really haven't. It's only become a more romantic relationship since Rachael and Harry's wedding. I just can't believe this is happening, though, Claire. Our age difference isn't supposed to matter, but it does, at least to me. Those girls could actually be my grandchildren. Do you realize that?"

"Do you think in the back of Kent's mind he's looking for a mother for his girls?"

"Well, that's a scary thought. I adore those girls, but I'm too old to start a family."

"Are you? Many grandmothers are raising their grandchildren these days. This would be no different."

"Claire Stewart, you're making this even scarier for me."

I laughed. "Just go with your heart, and concentrate on Kent, not the girls. Would you be happy just being friends with him?"

"I think I would, but as you know, nothing stays the same."

"Don't I know it. Ericka's passing is another reminder of how every moment counts on this earth."

"You're right. I knew talking to you would help. Please let me know when funeral arrangements will be for Ericka, and I'll be there."

"I will. I'll also take a rain check on the lunch invite."

"I understand. Maybe I'll see you out at the farm tomorrow."

Chapter 38

It was near dinner time when I finally heard from Cher again. She said she'd be stopping by around seven to fill me in on everything.

Carole called a little later. It had been a while since I'd heard from her.

"I have a bit of news for you."

"Well, I hope it's good."

"I'll let you decide that. Okay, here goes: Austen has a girlfriend."

"Well, I think that's great. Anyone I know?"

"Dr. Mecker's ex-wife, Bridgett. Remember her?"

"Actually, I do. We occasionally were around them at functions. She's strikingly different, I guess is the best way to describe her."

"Linda said she saw them at a restaurant in Cape Girardeau. Of course, Jill said the hospital is buzzing about the news. They're shocked she's not put off by his wheelchair."

"Watch your mouth, girlfriend. That person could have been me."

"I didn't mean it that way. Jill heard through the grapevine that Bridgett's divorce was pretty ugly."

"Well, maybe she got ditched by her hubby, like Dr. Page did."

Carole chuckled. "Well, I'm glad he's moved on so he'll leave you alone. He'll have someone to travel with now. Oh, and I wanted to tell you that your mom and Mr. Vogel were at the Kiwanis's pancake breakfast. They're so cute together."

"I love to hear they're looking out for each other."

"So, will I see you at Thanksgiving?"

"I just don't know yet. If I come, I'd like to bring Cher like I did the last time, but she and Carl are thick now, so I doubt she'll want to."

"You know, you could actually be brave and ask Grayson to come with you. Don't you think it's high time that he sees where you're from?"

"Oh, good luck with that. Kelly will be home from college then, so that's a definite no."

"Hey, guess what? My coffee book is at the printer! Isn't that exciting? I guess everyone will get one for Christmas."

"Carole, that's the best news I've heard for a while. I look forward to getting a copy."

"It's smaller than my cookie book."

"Do you have your next cookbook in mind yet?"

"I'm still chewing on it, as they say."

I laughed. "You'll think of something. Give Linda my love."

"I will."

When I hung up, I realized I needed to stop procrastinating about my Thanksgiving plans. The holiday really wasn't that far away. Maybe I'd talk it over with Cher. I wanted to get some brownies made since she was coming over with dinner. As I stirred the brownie mix more and more rigorously, I thought about Austen being coupled with Bridgett. She'd be perfect for him. He liked having a trophy date, and people would definitely notice her in a crowd. It would serve his ego.

While the brownies baked, I vacuumed the first floor. I was just putting the vacuum back into the closet when Cher arrived. She showed up fifteen minutes early, and when I saw the look on her face, I gave her a big hug.

Chapter 39

"Come in and relax, my friend. Tell me as much or as little as you want. If you just want to relax with some wine and skip talking altogether, we can."

"I'm ready for some wine," she said with a smile. "Ahh, you've been baking brownies from what I smell. I didn't end up bringing dinner, so your brownies will have to suffice."

"You know how I love merlot and chocolate, so not to worry."

I left her to just sit a bit while I cut the brownies. I had a feeling we might need more than one each.

"Claire, I think Ericka's loss has affected me worse than when my own mother died. Isn't that terrible? I hate to even admit that out loud." I looked straight into her eyes.

"The two losses are completely different. You had lots of time to digest your mom's death coming on. It's easier to accept an older parent's loss because you know it's going to happen at some point. But when someone our age has a serious health issue and dies so soon, it's a shock. We like to think it would never happen to us."

"Maybe that's why it's been so tough. I think you're right. Ericka never had a chance to hope for recovery."

"It's so incredibly sad. How's George handling it?"

"I'm afraid he's reacting like someone else I used to know and using alcohol to overcome his grief. I hope it's temporary."

"Agreed. Everyone handles grief differently. What about her other brother? How's he taking the loss?"

"I don't know, honestly."

"Ericka had so much to give to other causes, but she couldn't help herself."

"That's so true, Claire. I got to thinking about how much she cared about the environment. I think I've thought of what I want to do in her memory."

"Good. I've been trying to think of a way to honor her, too, so I want to hear your idea."

"I want to start a tree fund because she was such a tree hugger. I remember when a recent development took so many trees. She was having a fit over it, and no one seemed to listen."

"Cher, that's a wonderful idea. I'm sure the folks at the clinic would help. We can suggest it to them."

As our time passed, Cher told me several stories about Ericka before I'd moved to Door County. Some were funny, and she nervously laughed with tears in her eyes. I knew I was what Cher needed right now since I shared their friendship. It made me wonder who would remain after one of us passes.

Cher stayed till nearly midnight. I wanted her to spend the night, but she had a busy day planned for tomorrow. She said Carl's sister would fill in for her as long as she wanted. I wanted to tell her about hearing from Carole and all the latest gossip, but this wasn't the time. I couldn't help but admire the friendship Ericka and Cher had with each other. I realized how lucky I was to still have Cher.

I gave Cher a hug and sent her on her away with tears in my eyes as I watched her drive away. I hoped I'd provided some comfort to her tonight.

Puff and I went upstairs to bed. Thinking about Ericka was exhausting.

The next morning, I felt refreshed. My grief had taken me into the long, deep sleep I needed. After I drank some coffee, I knew I had to get to Rachael's.

When Grayson called around ten o'clock, he was anxious to know how I was doing and if I'd heard from Cher. I told him about our evening and that George hadn't planned any funeral arrangements at this time, other than that Ericka had requested cremation. I knew Grayson was calling from work, so I didn't go into any details with him. He felt badly about my sorrow, but I didn't want Ericka's death to be about me. Having his arms to hold and comfort me would feel nice, though.

Rachael sent me a text telling me to come after lunch. She said Brenda would also be coming out. I was glad I'd see both of them today. I'd already lost one friend. I needed to treasure the ones I had left.

I spent some time finishing up *Quilted Leaves* so I could get it to the gallery before winter came. After I fixed myself a grilled cheese, I proceeded to Rachael's.

On the way out there, the wind picked up, and sleet and rain followed, which I wasn't expecting. Surely, it wasn't time for snow yet. My memories of past Door County snowfalls and ice weren't comforting right now.

Chapter 40

I parked next to Brenda's car. It felt good to be somewhere that was becoming my second home.

"Hey, Claire!" Rachael greeted. "I bet you could use a cup of hot coffee after your messy drive."

"Oh my, yes!" I replied in relief.

"Did you find the roads slick?" Brenda asked, pouring me coffee.

"No, but I was tense on my way here."

After I got my coffee, I joined Brenda, who was pricing some merchandise.

"These two barn quilts need to be wrapped for mailing," Rachael noted. "Claire, do you mind doing that since you've done it before?"

"Sure. How's your hand doing?"

"It's painful, if you really want to know," she complained. "I'll be so glad to get all this bandaging off. I can't even cook for goodness sake."

"I'm sure Harry can pick up the slack," I teased.

"He has, of course, but he has plenty of other things to do," she said, shaking her head.

"There's never a good time for an injury," Brenda noted. "Claire, what's the latest with Ericka's funeral?"

"Other than hearing she's being cremated, I know nothing," I confessed. "I'm trying to console Cher. She's taking this hard."

"That poor girl," Rachael said as she watched us work. "Is there something that we can donate to on Ericka's behalf?"

"Yes. Cher is starting a tree fund to plant trees in her name," I shared. "Ericka was quite the environmentalist."

"What a wonderful idea," Brenda responded. "Let me know where to send a check."

"I will," I nodded. "She's going to talk to the clinic to see if they'd like to help."

"Oh, Claire, I wanted to tell you that I love these cute ornaments you ordered," Brenda complimented.

"I see you're making your own pile to take home with you, which is a good sign," I noted.

"Isn't she a gem?" Rachael chimed in. "We're so lucky to have her."

"Any of your friends would help you," I assured her. "Is your leg improving?"

"Somewhat. I'll be fine," Rachael said as she looked at it.

"You know, Thanksgiving is when you really need to promote the Christmas decor," I encouraged. "You need to have some sort of event like you did with the Tannenbaum party last year."

"I agree," Brenda said.

"We need something to attract new customers and make the farm a Christmas destination," Rachael added. "I'll think of something and put an ad out."

"We can help," I nodded with approval.

Rachael looked around and smiled at all Brenda and I had accomplished today. I'm sure it was a relief to her. At six, Harry showed up with hot pizzas and cold beer, which was our treat for the arduous work. Harry had a way of making any get-together a party.

I got home round nine o'clock, feeling completely exhausted. It was good to occupy my hands today helping Rachael. The barn was always a happy place, and for a while, it took my mind off of losing Ericka. I took off my coat, picked up Puff, and went upstairs for the rest of the evening. My hot shower helped warm me up before I crawled under my layers of quilts on the bed. I was hoping sleep would come quickly, but it didn't. I kept replaying some of the conversations we'd shared during the day.

I was worried that Rachael alone wouldn't come up with a way to expand her Christmas business. She was way too busy to devote energy to that. How could I help? The last thing I wanted was for all that merchandise to remain on the shelves after I'd ordered so much. We needed to have an event similar to the pumpkin party we'd had before Halloween. I wasn't sure Harry and Rachael realized what a wonderful place they have for hosting venues. Perhaps in my dreams, something would emerge.

I tossed and turned till I wore myself to sleep.

As I sat at the kitchen table the next morning, a simple idea dawned on me for Rachael's gift shop. It was early when I called her.

Chapter 41

"Well, aren't you an early bird," Rachael answered.

"I know, but I slept on an idea for you."

"Okay. Just let me get my coffee."

"I'll wait." She came back a minute later.

"Ready. Now I have a pen in hand."

"All right. How about this? You could announce you're having a barn warming, which is really fitting for what you want to do. You could say you're warming up for the holidays with everything people might need for Christmas. Then list the new additions like Christmas lights, ornaments, candles, poinsettias, and decorative garlands. Invite them to gather around the potbellied stove with hot chocolate or coffee. They could also enjoy the outdoors by making s'mores and roasting chestnuts on an open fire. Someone like Billy could help outdoors with the kids."

"Go on, I'm listening."

"You could have a drawing for a free Christmas tree. Who wouldn't want that? You could build on the barn warming throughout the season, but if they know a one-stop shop can give them all they need, it will become a destination. You had a good turnout at the pumpkin party, and I know those same folks will return. So, what do you think? Have I hooked you?"

"I absolutely love the idea, Claire. Thanks for dreaming this up. I like the warm, family feel of it, and Harry will, too."

"We'll have to do more decorating inside, and I want to check on the poinsettia delivery so it's timely, but with more lights everywhere, it will be gorgeous."

"I'll want to add hot cider to the refreshments as well, don't you think? I love that smell at Christmas."

"Yes, of course. Overall, I don't think it will be awfully expensive to set up. Getting it in the *Pulse* newspaper is key, of course."

"How can I ever thank you, Claire?"

"Well, your part is convincing Harry, and then we'll need a little help. Also, I may be going home at Thanksgiving, so we need to factor that in."

"Don't you worry."

I hung up feeling excited about my barn warming idea. An event like that would feel more homey than commercialized.

I needed some things from Fish Creek Market, so I dressed soon after the call with Rachael. There would never be a parking place this time of day, so I decided to walk.

The air was cold and brisk and typical for a fall morning. Along the sidewalks were beautiful mums, pumpkins, and hay bales, which signaled that events like Pumpkin Fest in Egg Harbor were happening.

I had my hands full when I left the market. I forgot for a moment that I'd left my car in the driveway and would have to carry everything back to the cabin. I just couldn't resist a deli sandwich besides all the other things on my list. I'd intended to stop by Carl's gallery even though Cher wouldn't be there, but I'd do that another day. I needed to finish up a quilt or two to sell before Christmas.

The walk home was pleasant. I'd just set my bags down on the porch to unlock the door when I got a text from Rachael.

[Rachael]
Harry loved your idea and wants to know how soon you can come to lay out a plan. He reminded me about an old sleigh in the attic that we can use in the display. He said it needs a good cleaning, but I could tell he was excited.

I went inside and put my things away. What would my life be like without Rachael and Harry in it? I sat down to answer her text.

[Claire]
Great! I like the idea of a sleigh. I'll have to let you know when I'll be out again. I'm still waiting to hear details from Cher.

[Rachael]
We understand. See you soon.

I was making progress on putting bindings on two wall quilts when I heard a car drive up. I quickly looked out the window and saw it was George and Cher. My heart fluttered as to what this visit was all about.

Chapter 42

"Come in, come in," I invited them. "I'm so glad to see you, George. I've thought of you every day since we lost Ericka." I gave him a hug, as he looked so grave. "Come sit down."

"We just came from picking up Ericka's ashes," Cher revealed sadly.

"I'm sure that was hard," I said. "I still can't believe it."

"Claire, I told Cher we needed to thank you for all you did for Ericka," George said calmly. "She thought so much of you." I felt my insides crumble with humility.

"You and Ericka were so good to me from the very first day I arrived here in Door County, so I'm the one who's grateful. Tell me about what happens next." They both looked at each other with such sadness.

"There isn't much to tell," George began as he shook his head. "She was perfectly clear about wanting to be cremated with no fuss, service, or fanfare."

"Oh, George," I said in disbelief.

"You know her biggest disappointment in life was when the clinic didn't want her to return," George shared. "I think she felt she owned and ran the place, making her irreplaceable. But their actions toward her at the end told her she was."

"Oh my goodness!" I said in shock. "I'm sure some of them thought the world of her."

"Well, they were in a tough spot," Cher explained. "They couldn't have a sick person working at a clinic that helps others. I frankly felt they were patient with her in hopes she'd realize on her own that she couldn't handle the work."

"Ericka could be very stubborn," George added.

"How's your brother doing?" I asked him.

"He's already gone," he said, shaking his head. "They weren't close. When he found out there would be no service, he left."

"I see," I nodded. "Well, we're here. What can we do?"

"Well, the tree idea went over big at the clinic. Ericka would be pleased about that. I think they were relieved to have that to respond to."

"I want to buy a tree on my own and plant it right here at the cabin where I met her," I decided.

"Oh, Claire, how sweet," Cher grinned with approval. "Let George and I help, too. We also spent time here with Ericka before you moved to Fish Creek."

"I know you did," I acknowledged. "I want an evergreen planted in a spot where I can see it from my porch every day."

"That nursery in Baileys Harbor always has a nice assortment," George noted. "They can help you. You do realize it will take quite a generous hole to plant an evergreen, don't you? Do you even own a shovel, Claire Stewart?"

I burst into laughter. "No, I don't," I admitted. "Good advice as always, George."

"We'll help you plant it," Cher offered.

"Sounds like a plan," George nodded.

"Gosh, where are my manners?" I said apologetically. "I haven't even offered you any refreshment."

"That's okay," Cher said, standing up to leave. "We just wanted to stop by to give you an update. We both have things to do, and I'd like to go back to work tomorrow."

"I might see you there," I noted. "I should have another quilt finished to bring in. George, I'm sorry to see you under these circumstances."

"Just don't ever forget about my sis," he said as he hugged me with emotion.

"Never," I said with tears.

I was glad they'd stopped by. As I watched them leave, memories surfaced of how George kept asking to date me in those first weeks I was here. He was always a pure gentleman, even when I turned him down.

I made myself a cup of hot tea and sat down to finish my quilt. Binding a quilt is mindless, and it was just what I needed. Puff waited patiently for me to finish so we could go up to bed. Sleep would come easy with all the tears I shed today.

Chapter 43

Halloween was always a big deal in my hometown, and it was increasing in popularity across the country. It wasn't as big here in Door County, I suppose because of not having many young children in the tourist mix. This time of year was all about the leaf peppers coming to town to check out the foliage.

As I watered my ever-loving flowers the next day, I got a call from Michael.

"Hey, brother!" I greeted him. "How are you?"

"I'm good. Say, have you gotten a recent call from Mom lately?"

"It's been a few days. Why? The last time I spoke to her we talked about the passing of my friend Ericka."

"Oh, I'm so sorry to hear that. You spoke of her often. I remember your saying she had cancer."

"She was younger than I am, Michael. It's heartbreaking. Anyway, what about Mom?"

"Well, she made a desperate plea for me to come home for Thanksgiving. She seemed fine, but something felt different about it. I wondered what you thought."

"When I talked to her, she and Bill were going to the senior center later that day. You know she doesn't like talking about her health. So, are you going home for the holiday?"

"I talked it over with Jon, and he's willing to come with me. We'd talked about going skiing, but the way Mom sounded, I didn't have the nerve to tell her that."

"I guess I should go, too. Cher has plans with Carl, so she won't be able to go with me."

"You know you could ask Grayson to come with you. Mom loves him."

"His daughter is coming home from college for the break. He's been missing her something awful, so I doubt he'll want to leave her."

"Well, you won't know unless you ask."

"I'll think about it. So, you're definitely going?"

"It's not quite definite, but probably. I'll see if we can get a few days in the mountains while we're there."

"Thanks for the heads-up. I'll let you know more later."

After his call, I knew I had to get off the fence and confirm one way or the other about going. I just wasn't sure about asking Grayson.

I put my wall quilt in a bag and set off to deliver it to Carl. It was pretty cold out, but the sun was shining. As I walked, I passed many shoppers with bags. Commerce seemed to be good.

Cher was at the counter alone when I walked in. It appeared she was getting something framed, so I didn't want to disrupt her. I began to look for Christmas gifts and ran across the Green Bay Packers throws. That reminded me that Cher was saving one back for me. After a few minutes, Cher spotted me and came over.

"Hey, Claire. Did you bring your quilt?"

"I did. Just give this invoice to Carl."

"He'll be back shortly from running errands. Your little quilts sell very well. Thanks so much. Oh, and here's that throw for Harry before I forget."

"Oh, hi, Claire," Carl said, coming in as I was swiping my credit card at the register. "How are you? I have a check for you on my desk, so don't go away."

"I do love it when he says that," I chuckled. "Cher, I just want to say again how much it meant that you and George stopped by to see me. It made me feel like part of the family."

"Well, you are part of the family," Cher said with sincerity. "Let's go soon to get that tree."

The check from Carl left me feeling grateful I still had a small income. I decided to stop at Pelletier's on my way home to get a coffee to go. When I walked in and saw their good-looking home-cooked breakfasts, though, I changed my mind and sat at the counter. I ordered a stack of pancakes, two eggs sunny-side up, and two pieces of bacon. That would take care of my food intake for the day.

Puff was ready to play when I got back home, so I indulged her until my phone rang.

"Oh, hi, Mom. How are you?"

"I'm just fine, dear. I have Bill on the speaker phone because we wanted to ask you to come home for Thanksgiving. We'd like you to celebrate with us." I paused, not sure what she was referring to.

"Oh? What are we celebrating?"

"Hello, Claire," Bill joined in. "Your mother and I decided to get married, and we want to have a little celebration when you come home for Thanksgiving." I wasn't sure I heard him correctly.

"Married? You got married?"

"I hope that wasn't too much of a shock," Mom said calmly. "You know Bill and I have been friends for years, and we think the world of each other. We both were lonely and enjoy being together, so we talked it over and decided to live the rest of our lives with each other. We didn't want to make a big deal out of the ceremony, so a retired pastor friend of Bill's married us. It was simple and sweet."

"Wow. I don't know what to say. Of course, I'm happy for the two of you. I'm just surprised."

"We understand, dear. We thought we'd have our families get together for dinner and toast the occasion. We wanted it to be a surprise when you got here, but you and Michael wouldn't commit to coming, so we had to tell you."

"Well, I'm certainly not going to miss this occasion," I said, starting to cry.

"Thank you, sweetie," Mom replied with emotion. "You know you're welcome to bring that handsome Grayson with you."

"I sure would like to meet him," Bill added.

Chapter 44

"He'd be happy to know that, Mom," I answered sweetly. "Have you told Michael your big news?"

"We're going to call him next," Bill noted.

"Okay. I'm glad you didn't wait to surprise us," I said with gratitude.

"We love you, Claire," Mom reminded me. "Let us know what your plans are."

"Love you, too," I said, hanging up.

I stared into space trying to digest what I'd just heard. My mom, at age eighty-five, had just had her second marriage, and I hadn't been married once. I couldn't help but think about my father who'd passed away. What would he think of this? I felt my only comfort was to talk to Michael immediately, but I had to wait till they told him. I punched in his number anyway, but the call went to voice mail. I figured he was learning what I just had. Without a doubt, Michael would call me immediately when he finished talking to them. What would Cher, Linda, and Carole think? I tried to talk to Cher next, but her call also went to voicemail. She must be busy at work.

I started pacing the floor trying to decide if my mom had made a big mistake. Linda was my next call.

"What's happening, Claire? It's good to hear from you."

"Well, my mom just called and gave me the shock of my life. She and Bill just got married!"

I could hear Linda chuckle. "Why are you in shock, for heaven's sake? Is it because they're not as young as they used to be? They're a well-matched couple who wants to spend the rest of their lives together. Tell me more about what you know."

"Well, Mom called to be sure Michael and I were coming home for Thanksgiving so we could celebrate their occasion. A retired pastor who's a friend of Bill's married them."

"Well, it sounds perfect for them. Look, I can imagine how you feel, but there's nothing but happiness here. You and Michael live far away from her, and Bill can give her attention every day. He also has big-time resources, by the way, if you know what I mean."

"My mom is financially secure, so I doubt if that matters at all to her."

"That's good. Anyway, I think the news is just wonderful. I'll call Carole if she doesn't already know." Linda chuckled.

"Okay. You gave me some things to think about."

"Well, I suppose this means we get to see you soon then? Let's at least meet for coffee."

"Sure. Mom thinks I should ask Grayson to come with me."

"Your mom always has been a wise woman. Don't you want him to see where you grew up?"

"I suppose, but Kelly is coming home from college. She takes priority."

"My guess is that he's not going to refuse your offer. Kelly isn't going anywhere, and your mom doesn't get married every day."

"I'll think about it. Thanks for listening, my friend."

Linda was always more serious than Carole. She even made better grades in school than Carole and me. What she said about Mom and Bill was spot-on. My cell began ringing. Of course, it was Michael.

"Yes, Michael," I answered.

"So, I guess we have a new daddy," he teased.

"Oh, Michael, how could you say that?"

"Hey, if Mom's happy, everyone should be. That's the way it works."

"I know, but I just can't wrap my head around it."

"She's marrying up, as they say," he joked. "Bill made twice the money Dad made, so give her credit. She's still an attractive lady for her age, and her mind is still sharp."

"But what would Dad think?"

"He'd probably say, 'More power to you!'" he chuckled. "Bill and Mom have a great history together, which is awesome. Jon and I will be there, but only for two days before we go to Colorado. Mom said she hoped you'd bring Grayson."

"Well, we'll see. Does this mean we have to give them a wedding present?"

"I'm sure our attendance will be sufficient. Goodness knows, they don't need a thing. Mom said their finances would remain separate, so nothing should affect her will."

"She certainly told you more than she shared with me."

"That's because I'm the smart one, remember?" he joked. "You get too emotional about things like this."

"Yeah, you're right."

"They're doing all the planning for the dinner, so all we have to do is show up. Try not to overthink this, Sis."

"Okay. I'll try."

"Love you! See you soon!" Michael ended cheerfully.

Chapter 45

Now I had to do some serious planning. If Grayson agreed to come, it could change everything. I couldn't delay his call much longer if I was going to ask him.

"Hi, Claire," he answered.

"Hey, Grayson. Is this an inconvenient time to talk? I need to ask you something."

"It's fine. Just let me get to another room."

I felt weak, second-guessing whether I should ask him.

"Now, what's going on?"

"Well, my mom just called to tell me she and Bill got married."

"Oh, really? That's a good thing, isn't it?"

"I guess. I'm still in shock. A friend of Bill's who's a retired pastor married them. "

"I'm sure they'll be happy together. What did you want to ask me?"

"I feel bad even asking you this, and if you say no, I completely understand. You won't hurt my feelings."

"I see. Well, go ahead and ask."

"Well, Bill and Mom want to do a small dinner at Thanksgiving to celebrate their marriage. They'd been trying to get Michael and me to agree to come home, and we kept procrastinating, so they had to tell us what was going on."

"That makes sense."

"Anyway, here's where you come in. They've invited you to join us for their celebration dinner. I know Kelly will be home from college then, so I hated to ask you. I tried to tell them that, but they said I should ask you anyway."

"I'd love to, Claire."

"What?"

"I said I'd love to. I'm honored to be included."

"But what about Kelly?"

"Kelly will be fine. She'll be here for a good amount of time, and frankly, she'd love to have the house to herself for part of it."

"Wow. I can't believe it. We'd drive, of course, so you'd be gone a few days. Is that still okay?"

"You plan it as you like. Besides, it'll be nice to spend Thanksgiving with you."

"Oh, Grayson. You're so sweet to do this for me. Are you sure?"

He chuckled. "Yes, darling, I'm sure."

"Okay, I'll let you get back to work, and we'll discuss the details later."

"Sounds good."

"I love you, Grayson Wills."

"I love you too, Claire Stewart."

I was on cloud nine after we hung up. Maybe I was even happier than my mom right now. I needed to try calling Cher again.

"Oh, Claire, I was just going to call you. I was with George, and we picked out a perfect tree for you. I thought we could plant it tomorrow if that suits you."

"Wonderful. That'll work. Do I need Tom to come over and dig a hole?"

"No, George said he could do it all."

"I'll pay for everything. Thanks so much. I have something really big to tell you."

"Yeah? Spill it."

"Mom and Bill got married."

"Holy cow! When?"

"Recently, and they want Michael and me to come home and celebrate on Thanksgiving."

"Well, I hope you're going."

"I am, and guess who else? Grayson. Kelly will be on break then, but he acted like it was no big deal for him to leave her at home for a few days. I almost fell over when he said yes."

"That's great, Claire Bear. That means Grayson is going to see where you grew up and where Dr. Austen Page lives."

"What are you insinuating?"

Cher giggled. "Well, it's all part of the deal, I guess. Anyway, George and I will see you around ten o'clock tomorrow."

"Okay. See you then."

Chapter 46

Everyone was approving of Mom's marriage, so I guess I needed to also. It was nice Mom wanted to include Grayson. Mom and Michael would be surprised to hear he accepted.

I hadn't eaten since morning, so I made a salad and poured a glass of wine. As soon as I finished eating, I planned to tell Mom about Grayson's yes.

"Well, Claire, I'm glad to hear from you so soon. Is everything all right?"

"I just had to tell you that Grayson accepted your invitation to come. I truly can't believe it."

"Well, that's wonderful! Michael told me he's bringing Jon, so I'm happy we'll all be together. Would you like me to make your hotel reservations? We certainly want to pay any expenses."

"Oh, please don't, Mom. That's not necessary. We'll stay at the new Holiday Inn Express that just opened on the interstate."

"I wish we had a big enough house to accommodate everyone."

"We'll manage. By the way, George and Cher are coming tomorrow morning to plant a tree in my yard in memory of Ericka."

"From what you've told me about Ericka, she'd be delighted. What a nice remembrance of her."

"Well, I'll let you go now. Oh, out of curiosity, Mom, did you take Bill's last name?" I paused, hoping she hadn't.

"I did. You know we're from the old school, Claire. I was proud to do so, and Bill was thrilled."

"Okay, Mrs. Vogel." Mom chuckled.

The next morning, I got up early and dressed so I could go outside and assess once again where I wanted Ericka's tree. I wanted people to see it from the road, yet not too close to my other trees.

It was chilly outside, so I didn't dally in my decision-making. I put some cinnamon buns in the oven for us to enjoy with coffee. The cabin smelled heavenly.

I watched the two of them get out of George's pickup truck, and there was my nice tree, just waiting for us to plant it. I greeted them before they had a chance to knock.

"Oh, George, this is perfect," I praised. "Here's the spot where I'd like it to be."

"That's a nice location," Cher said with approval.

"Now, would you like to come in for some coffee before you start digging, or wait till it's done?" I asked George.

"Let's get this done," George said as he removed his shovel from the truck. "This may take me a bit, so you might as well wait inside where it's warm."

"No, I want to witness the full process," I said, pulling the hood over my head.

"Contributions continue to come in, I'm told," Cher shared.

I nodded. "Ericka would be so pleased."

As the hole grew bigger and bigger, we remained silent as if we were performing a ritual. George finally found the right depth and poured in some water, and we all helped situate the tree and add more soil around it, patting it in to secure the tree. We took turns adding the last couple buckets of water. When we finished, George leaned on his shovel, and we stood back and admired the new addition to the yard. I felt I should say a few words.

"Thank you, George," I began. "Ericka, if you're listening, I want you to know I'll always remember you, but in this very spot, you'll live on. I'll never forget that you were my first real friend here in Door County. You made sure I had everything I needed." I choked up with tears. "You continued to be my friend up until the end. You even shared your best friend with me." I started wiping tears from my cheeks.

"Oh, Claire. That was special," Cher said as she began to tear up.

"Okay, ladies, I know my sister wasn't much for sentiment, but she loved you both," George confessed. "Now, she wouldn't want us to freeze out here, so let's go in and have a toast with warm coffee."

Inside, George started a fire for us while Claire and I got out the rolls and coffee. At any moment, I expected our beloved Ericka to join us, but she was there in spirit only.

Chapter 47

The next morning, I texted Grayson about whether I should make our reservations for Thanksgiving or whether he wanted to. He quickly responded by saying to go ahead since I was familiar with the area. He told me he'd be leaving the coffee shop soon and stopping by to see Ericka's tree.

I jumped into action to make myself presentable. Shortly thereafter, I happened to see Tom coming toward the cabin with his ladder to put up the Christmas lights. I smiled at the idea.

"Oh, it's never too early for lights!" I greeted. He laughed and said he agreed.

As Tom began unwinding the first strand of lights, Grayson drove up.

"Oh, yes," Grayson grinned as he exited his SUV. "This is the Christmas cabin in Fish Creek." We all nodded and chuckled.

"Do you remember Tom?' I asked Grayson.

"Absolutely!" Grayson responded. "He was one of the best quilt hangers during the quilt show. By the way, if you can spare some time, I need some lights hung at the office, Tom."

"Sorry, but I have more work now than I can handle," he said, shaking his head and pointing at all my strands. I giggled.

"Tom, you'll notice that I have a new tree over here," I announced. "We just planted it yesterday in memory of my friend Ericka. Even though it's small, would you mind putting lights on it also?"

"Of course," he nodded. "She's a beauty. Did you plant it yourself?"

"No," I responded. "My friend George did it. He's also Ericka's brother."

"Solid choice on the tree," Grayson said as he examined it. "It's a blue spruce, right, Tom?"

Tom nodded. "It is. Nice memorial."

"Grayson, come on in," I invited. "How about another cup of coffee?"

"I'll pass on the coffee. I can only stay a bit before I go into Sister Bay. Hey, what's this?" he asked, as he stared at Foster's painting of me and the sunset.

I was speechless at first.

"You bought one of Foster's paintings?" he asked in disbelief. "I don't remember seeing this the last time I was over."

"It's new. He gave it to me as a gift." There was a huge pause as Grayson continued eyeing it.

"I'd have to guess this is you staring into the sunset. Am I right?"

I paused. "It's supposed to be, yes."

Grayson turned to me and had a very strange look on his face. "You were actually standing there, and he painted you?"

I nodded and swallowed deeply. "I know, it's awkward, so don't go there. You know I went out with him a few times when you and I weren't together. He knew, of course, that I was still in love with you the whole time."

Grayson grinned. "I can't fault the guy for falling for you. I hope you've never regretted giving up that relationship with a famous artist."

I chuckled. "He never was my type even though I'd admired his work most of my life."

Grayson came closer and wrapped his arms around me. "Are you very sure?" he asked, as he put his lips on mine.

"Oh, I'm very sure," I whispered back with a smile.

"I like the painting very much," Grayson admitted. "Why hadn't I seen it sooner?"

"You have to ask?" I teased.

"Point taken. Okay, so what time are we leaving Wednesday?"

"If we leave by eight o'clock, we'll be there for dinner. By the way, Jon is coming with Michael. Mom's so happy we'll all be there."

"Good. I'm looking forward to meeting them. I told Kelly about our plans, and she's fine with them. She's invited to her aunt's for dinner, so it'll all work out. She and I will have plenty of time to do some fun things together when I return."

"I'd like to see her as well if that's okay."

"I'll tell her that. Well, sweetheart, enjoy all your lights, inside and out."

"I will. Thanks for stopping by."

With a wink and a kiss on the cheek, he went on his way. I took a deep breath, grateful the painting hadn't upset him.

Chapter 48

By the time Tom left, it was nearly dark, so I turned out some lights to get the whole effect of the work he had done outside. I paid special attention to the lights on Ericka's tree. It really looked adorable. I smiled even though my heart still ached from her loss.

I felt the need to have something warm, so I pulled out some frozen leftover soup for my dinner. I poured some wine and kept poking the fire that George had made this morning. I dreaded the frigid days and nights ahead, but I reminded myself I was in beautiful Door County.

As I ate my soup, I glanced over the latest *Pulse*. I read an article that thanked all the businesses for getting them through the busy tourist season. Quite a few of the shops used seasonal workers brought in from other areas. Temporary housing was always a problem, so many of the residents housed these folks. The article closed by announcing that the quiet season was just ahead, and locals could expect to see normal activity again. I hadn't been a local long enough to feel like either the tourist season or the quiet season was a bother or an inconvenience, but I knew some felt that way. The article also encouraged businesses not to close early so that locals could still enjoy themselves during the Christmas season. I had to agree with that one.

I lay there and checked my phone. I had an email from Marta canceling our quilt club meeting because our date would be too close to Thanksgiving. That was nice since I'd be going to Perryville. Marta also said that Lee had invited the club members and their spouses to a Christmas party at The Clearing. I knew Lee served on the board there. I'd have to remember to ask Grayson about joining me.

I went to sleep thinking of the large, beautiful Christmas tree they typically have at The Clearing. Sugar plums were dancing around it when I drifted off to sleep.

The next morning, I began packing for my trip home to meet my new stepfather. I could hardly say the word. I factored in nice clothing for the dinner, but I knew everything else would be casual.

I wanted to finish the painting of the shops on the hill. I'd already dragged it out too long. As soon as my signature dried, off to the gallery it would go. I'd hoped to take more inventory to Carl for the Christmas shopping crowd. I was close to finishing another *Quilted Snow* wall quilt, but this painting was my first priority today.

At noon, I made the dreaded call to Rachael to tell her I wouldn't be there for her Black Friday since I was going to Perryville. She took it in good spirits.

"Okay, Claire. We'll miss you."

"I'll miss you, too. I love the big meal you prepare with Harry's deep-fried turkey."

"Brenda can help out, and then the girls will join us for the meal. I may order some sides to-go. I still have barn quilt orders to finish."

"Did Kent bring in another big tree for us to decorate?"

"Oh, yes! You should see the place, Claire. Harry is pleased because some of the tree buyers want their tree before Thanksgiving. Every year, I seem to forget how beautiful the place becomes."

"I promise I'll be back out as soon as I return. Grayson is going with me for the first time."

"Whee!" she squealed. "I can't wait to hear all about it. Bringing him home to meet the family is a sure sign. I feel a wedding coming on."

"Stop it right there, Rachael. We've been there and done that. My mom was the one who invited him."

"Well, your mom is doing a better job in the marriage department than you are, my friend."

I laughed. "Oh, you're right about that. I'll know when it's right for me or if it's not."

Chapter 49

Later in the afternoon, Brenda called to see if I'd ride out to Door County Candle Company with her. Her friend Christiana had just purchased it and was having an open house. She suggested grabbing lunch somewhere, too, which sounded like an offer too good to pass up. I hadn't done much shopping other than the Packers throws at the gallery.

It was near freezing, so I dressed for the occasion in one of my warmest sweaters. I was pleased Brenda had thought of me. Shopping with friends was part of the Christmas experience.

She pulled up in her white, modest SUV.

"I'm so pleased you'll meet Christiana. She and her husband already own a company called Door County Delivered."

"Oh, sure. I sent my mom one of their boxes after she visited here."

"Well, the addition of the candle place is perfect for adding to their product. They have so many themes, but I guess you already knew that."

"I should order boxes for my friends Carole and Linda who help me with the quilt show."

"Oh, I remember meeting them."

"I'll see them briefly over Thanksgiving. Grayson is coming home with me, and he hasn't met them."

"Grayson is going with you?"

"I'm as surprised as you are."

"Your mom must be thrilled."

"She is. She'd like nothing more than to see the two of us together permanently."

We found a decent parking spot right in front of the candle shop.

"Oh, Brenda. You didn't tell me it was next to Door County Coffee and Tea!"

"Convenient, right? We can go there afterward if you'd like."

All we had to do was follow our noses to find the candle store. As soon as we opened our car doors, we could smell the wonderful scents coming from inside. I'd heard that they hand-pour the candles in small batches onsite. When we walked in, a pretty, young woman greeted us with a warm smile.

"Brenda! How nice of you to come!" I assumed this was Christiana.

"Meet my friend Claire," Brenda introduced. I shook her hand and told her I was happy to meet her.

"I'm so happy to meet you, too, Claire," she told me. "Please take a look around. I'm helping someone right now, but it's so nice you're here."

The scents were heavenly, and not too strong. It appeared there were stations of different scents, so we separated as we shopped. I spotted some folks dipping their own taper candles, which was fun to witness. A clerk explained that they could customize our scent choices into a unique candle. I was partial to the aroma of cedar trees since it reminded me of my childhood, but I also picked up candles smelling like fresh-baked brownies, cherries, lemongrass, orange clove, and red wine. The candles I collected would make perfect gifts. When I met up with Brenda, she thought Carole and Linda might like such a gift, too. I agreed.

As we were waiting to check out, I thought of our Christmas gift shop at the barn. I asked the clerk if she had any wholesale information I could take with me, and she handed me a brochure. After a hug goodbye to Christiana, Brenda and I were ready for our coffee fix.

Chapter 50

I loved visiting Door County Coffee and Tea. Before we sat down with our order, I stocked up on my favorite flavors. Cher had mentioned recently that they had a new flavor for the Christmas season called Candy Cane. I had to try some. When we settled in to savor our purchases, Brenda asked me about how it was going with Kelly.

"From what I understand, she hasn't objected to Grayson going with me to Missouri. That's huge."

"For sure. What are you giving her for Christmas?"

"Right now I'm not sure. Ideally, I'd like to paint something for her. What are you giving the girls?"

"I've been buying things all along for them. I do spoil them. I've already spent a fortune at a shop called Beach People. It's way too handy to stop there en route to work."

After I finished my cherry-cheese muffin, Brenda and I decided stopping for lunch may not be necessary. We were almost back to Fish Creek when Grayson called.

"Hey, Claire, would you mind if we left for Missouri a day earlier?"

"I think that would be fine. Why?"

"I have a distributor in Saint Charles, Missouri, and I'd like to set up a meeting with him."

"Sure. I love Saint Charles. It's a historic town along the Missouri River with dozens of cool shops."

"I figured it would be a place you could entertain yourself."

"Oh, yes. No problem there."

"Great. I'll give him a call back."

I hung up smiling. It was good Grayson would personally benefit from our trip.

Brenda dropped me off at home, and I told Puff I'd made some progress on my Christmas shopping. She barely looked up at me.

There was still time to deliver my last painting of the shops on the hill to Carl's gallery. I imagined that parking would be at a premium, so I decided to walk.

"Greetings, Carl," I greeted when I reached the gallery. "I have something for you that I hope you like." I began unwrapping the painting for him to take a look.

"I've liked everything you've sent here, Claire, but remember I'm not the consumer."

"This one was a challenge. I had a tough time achieving what I wanted."

"That happens sometimes with art, but it's all in the eyes of the beholder."

I held it up, and Carl gave it a long look.

"I see why you couldn't get as detailed as you have with the others, but I think people will appreciate this reminder of the quilt show. I like all the colors you've chosen."

"Really?"

"Yes. I have no doubt it'll sell, just like your other quilt show paintings."

"Thanks, Carl. Well, I'm off to my hometown in Missouri for Thanksgiving. I'm taking Grayson with me."

"That has to be a nail-biter, I suppose."

"Did Cher tell you my eighty-five-year-old mom just remarried?"

"I guess there's hope for all of us, huh?" We chuckled.

"Two old friends from the old school," I added.

"There's nothing wrong with that. Say, Cher mentioned that you planted a tree in honor of Ericka. I'd like to come by and see that some time."

"You bet! It's the small tree out front with some Christmas lights strung around it."

"Cher has taken Ericka's death very hard."

I nodded. "Yes, they were close, and I know she misses her. Well, I need to go, Carl. Have a nice Thanksgiving, and thanks for taking this off my hands."

I felt relieved that Carl liked my painting. Walking home put me in the mood for a warm fire.

Chapter 51

It was hard to believe it was Thanksgiving. I packed way more clothes than I needed, but our plans were varied, so I wanted to make sure I had options.

Grayson seemed excited when he picked me up. He'd contacted his distributor about meeting tomorrow morning, so in my mind I was already making plans to occupy myself.

"I made reservations at Country Inn & Suites, which is in the historic district along the Katy Trail. I hope you approve."

"That sounds great. Thanks for taking care of that."

"When we get to Perryville, we'll stay at the new Holiday Inn Express on the interstate."

"I'm not comfortable with your paying for these arrangements, Claire."

"You're my guest on this trip, Grayson, so just concentrate on entertaining your client." He grinned and shook his head.

"This is our first trip as a couple, you know," Grayson winked.

"I'm trying not to think about that," I responded. Grayson chuckled.

There was no doubt that seeing Grayson in my hometown would be surreal. We had a lot to catch up on in our conversation. As the afternoon wore on, I slept for a bit.

When we arrived in Saint Charles, it was dark. We wanted to stretch our legs from the car ride, so we walked to a nearby restaurant called Magpie's. Some were eating on the patio by the firepit, but I preferred inside. I'd heard about this restaurant from Linda and Carole. They recommended that I try the baked potato soup, and I wasn't disappointed. The warm soup and red wine were too filling to indulge in one of their many desserts.

I wasn't sure how our first night together in a hotel would go. We'd been intimate before our breakup, but since then, we were taking it slow. Grayson knew I was concerned about tonight, but I shouldn't have been, as he was a perfect gentleman. He invited me to rest my head on his chest for a few minutes as we first climbed into bed and then wished me goodnight as he kissed the top of my forehead. His actions only confirmed how much I loved him.

Grayson was up before me. He'd showered and was ready to meet with his client for a nine o'clock appointment. I took my time since I knew the shops wouldn't open on Main Street till ten.

The Christmas decorations in Saint Charles were appropriate for the historic area. The light posts lining the street were decorated with live greenery. Trees were strung with white lights that shined spectacularly in the darkness of evening but still remained on as I walked the street this morning looking for a shop called The Written Word. It was Carole's favorite, and she'd told me to ask for Julia, the owner.

After walking a few more blocks, I spotted the sign I was looking for. Inside the store were such pretty papers, stationary, pens, and gift wrap. I met Julia right away, and she asked where I was from. When I told her I currently lived in Door County, she said I should stop in the flower shop called Brown's Botanical and ask for Anne because she was going to Door County next week.

"She's been there once with a girlfriend and couldn't stop talking about it. This time her husband is joining her. I'm sure she'd love meeting you if you have the time."

"Sure, I can do that."

Before I left, I had an armful of greeting cards, note cards, and Christmas wrapping paper.

I found my way to the lovely flower shop where the freshness of the poinsettias welcomed me. There appeared to be several employees working there, but I approached the woman dressed in business attire.

"Hello, may I help you?" she asked politely.

"Would you by any chance be Anne, the owner?"

"I am," she smiled.

"Hi, I'm Claire. I just left The Written Word shop, and Julia told me I should introduce myself to you since I'm from Door County, Wisconsin."

"Oh, absolutely!" she responded. "You're lucky. I love Door County."

"Well, I'm originally from Perryville, where I'm going for Thanksgiving, but my boyfriend and I are starting our trip here in Saint Charles."

"Julia must have told you that my husband and I are going to Door County after Thanksgiving."

"Yes, and I wondered if I could be of any help," I offered. "I live in Fish Creek. Where will you stay when you're there."

"I stayed in Fish Creek on my first visit, but this time we're staying in Ephraim at the Water Street Inn. My husband Jack is a minister, and we want to attend the Moravian church in town."

"Oh, sure!" I responded.

"Tell her you purchased Christmas stockings for all of us at that Tannenbaum Christmas shop when you were there," Sally, her employee, noted.

"Oh, yes, they loved them," Anne bragged. "What a wonderful shop. I want to go back."

Chapter 52

"I agree it's a great store."

"We'll be hanging our stockings as soon as we take down our Thanksgiving decorations," Anne explained. "If you have a minute, can you chat in my office for a bit?"

"Sure. I have all day. It's been quite a while since I've been to Main Street."

"It's a magical place, I tell ya. Christmas Traditions is our biggest event, and they'll be decorating soon for that. Now, where in Door County did you say you lived again?"

"Fish Creek."

"Oh, I loved the White Gull Inn in Fish Creek."

"I live very close to it."

"How did a Perryville girl end up in Fish Creek?"

"Well, the cabin I live in now belonged to an old school friend. So, when she had to come back to Perryville to take care of her aging mother, I decided to move and take it over."

"That had to be a big decision."

"I was ready for a change, and Door County has a thriving artist community, as you may know. I like to paint and quilt."

"I purchased some nifty art on my last visit."

"You mentioned being married to a minister."

"It's actually a second marriage for me. Sam, my first husband, died from a sudden heart attack."

"Oh, I'm sorry. Did you have children together?"

"Yes. A son, Sammy. I'm afraid he'll have no memory of his father."

"Will you bring Sammy with you to Door County?"

"No, he'll stay with our longtime housekeeper, Ella. She's practically raised him, as I also run some greenhouses in addition to this flower shop. I only come into the shop a couple of days a week now, so I'm glad I was here to meet you today, Claire. My manager, Sally, runs the shop."

"Anne, I've really enjoyed talking with you today. I apologize for keeping you from your work."

"Oh, it's no problem. I don't suppose there's a way my husband Jack and I could meet up with you when we visit, is there?"

"I don't see why not. Here's my card. Perhaps my boyfriend Grayson and I could have dinner with you at the White Gull Inn."

"We'd love that, Claire. Thank you. Here's my card so we can communicate. I'm so glad Julia sent you here."

I said my goodbyes and then headed to nearby Grandma's Cookies. I'd never forgotten this place even though I hadn't been here in years. The sweet smell of the assorted fresh cookies made me swoon. I bought an assortment to take back to Grayson.

Once back at the hotel, I decided to take a nap. All that walking today wore me out.

Grayson returned to the room at six o'clock. He'd had a productive day with his client and was in a good mood. We'd be having dinner at an upscale restaurant called Napoli III that was located by the bridge in a section called the Streets of Saint Charles.

We were impressed the minute we walked in. The contemporary decor was warm and attractive. The host seated us in a half circle booth that encouraged intimate dining. Grayson commented that we should have more dinners like this, and I couldn't agree more. He suggested sharing calamari as an appetizer. I was a little skeptical since I'd never tried it before, but it was surprisingly delicious. I had the sea bass with asparagus risotto for my entrée, and my handsome date chose the salmon with a lemon caper sauce.

I had so much to share with Grayson about my visit on Main Street. He was interested in hearing about Anne and the flower shop, but my mention of Grandma's Cookies really got his attention.

When we got back to the hotel, I had to pinch myself to make sure I wasn't dreaming. This trip with Grayson was turning out even better than I could've imagined. It was good to be with him in such a different environment. I knew, of course, this was not what normal life would be like with him, but it was indeed a treat.

Chapter 53

We arrived at Mom's house around ten o'clock the next morning. Mom and Bill were in the kitchen cleaning up from breakfast. They looked especially happy and comfortable together, like they'd been married much longer than a week. I introduced the men, and they shook hands. Mom gave both of us warm hugs and told Grayson how happy she was he could come with me.

"Michael and Jon will join us for dinner tonight at the country club," Mom announced.

"They have good home cooking, and your mother won't have to bother," Bill noted.

"What time would you like us to arrive?" I asked, as Mom served us coffee.

"We're seniors, you know, so we planned an early night," Mom joked. "Cocktails are at five o'clock, and dinner's at six." We nodded and grinned.

"That sounds good to me," I responded with a smile. "I'll be ready for bed by eight o'clock." Everyone laughed, but I felt a little awkward afterward since Grayson and I weren't married.

We conversed about the history of our house and family. Grayson admired the photographs Mom had placed throughout the room and asked questions about several of them. Bill was interested in hearing more about Grayson's business. I gave Grayson a tour of the house and shared a few childhood stories.

We went back to the hotel around three to freshen up. I'd brought a simple black dress and a strand of pearls that Mom had given me when I turned fifty. I looked more like I was going to a funeral than a wedding. Grayson wore a lavender shirt and plum tie under his pin-striped, gray suit.

Grayson knew my nerves were all over the place. On the way to dinner, he squeezed my hand and tried to reassure me that everything would be fine.

The country club looked more refined than when I was there last. White starched tablecloths and triangle-fold cloth napkins covered the round tables. The centerpieces were tall vases of red, orange, and yellow roses surrounded by three white votive candles. The glow from the candles created a nice ambiance.

We were the last to arrive of my family. Jon and Michael had saved us a couple of seats next to them. They looked so handsome. It was their first time to meet Grayson, but shortly after the introductions, they were acting like brothers.

Bill's daughter Candice was the last to arrive. Mom had told me she'd been divorced for about fifteen years and wasn't seeing anyone. She stayed close to Bill, showing little interest in getting to know us.

The server brought out our dinner family-style. The roasted turkey was the highlight, but we also had mashed potatoes and gravy, green beans topped with slivered almonds, Brussels sprout salad, cornbread dressing, rolls, and a sweet potato souffle.

Before we were able to make the first toast, Bill stood up and got our attention with his deep, serious voice.

"What a joyous occasion this is for Mary and me," he said, beaming at her. "We thought long and hard about how to share this moment with all of you. We didn't want a fuss with our wedding ceremony since we'd both already had that with our dearly departed spouses. We're so grateful all of you were able to join us this evening for our special occasion and the spirit of the Thanksgiving season. I'd like to make a toast to my new bride and all of you for continued good health and happiness."

"Hear! Hear!" we all cheered.

"It's my turn," Michael said, standing up. "I'd like to toast the happy couple and welcome Bill into our family." We all cheered and clinked our glasses.

"If I may add on to Michael's toast, I'm honored to be included on this happy occasion," Jon interjected. "May you have many good years together."

Jon was such a dear. Next up was Candice.

"My dad has always been a wise and loving man," she began. "Dad seems to have found what was missing in his life now that he's with Mary. It's been beautiful to witness their relationship grow. Mary, I adore you and wish you both much happiness in the years to come." All eyes were now on me.

"I don't want to cry, but this has been such an emotional and wonderful experience. Seeing my mom happy is precious indeed. I think I can speak for all of us here when I say that we'll always be here for you if you need us. Best wishes for continued happiness." I walked over to Mom and gave her a big hug as tears rolled down my cheeks. I gave Bill a bear hug as a way of welcoming him to our family.

When I returned to my seat, Grayson was there to offer his own hug. Part of me felt very foolish, but this was an occasion like no other.

Chapter 54

Michael surprised us by bringing out a cart that held a small single-layer round white wedding cake topped with miniature red roses. It was a sweet touch. Watching Mom and Bill pose before they cut the cake was both awkward and adorable. I presented them with two dozen long-stemmed red roses. Everything went smoothly overall, and broke up at an early hour. I teased Mom about needing to get on their way for their honeymoon.

Once we said our goodbyes, Michael, Jon, Grayson, and I went to the lounge for a drink. We couldn't convince Candice to join us. The four of us shared some good laughs and memories that would have amused Mom. As we were about to leave, I got a text from Carole.

[Carole]
Will we see you tomorrow for coffee? How about ten o'clock?

I leaned toward Grayson to get approval, and he happily said yes.

[Claire]
Sure! See you at Villainous Grounds.

Before we left Michael and Jon, I pleaded my case for them to come to Door County for Christmas.

"I have to think of Mom somewhat," Michael responded. "I think Bill is going to have a knee replacement the first of the year, so they won't be going anywhere. Jon hasn't seen his mom for some time, so that's somewhere else we need to be."

"Of course," I nodded.

We said goodbye with big hugs. Who knew when we would see each other again?

The next morning, Grayson and I were still tired from the evening's activities, but I told Mom we would stop by to say goodbye after we had coffee with Carole and Linda. She sounded elated about how well the evening had gone.

We were ten minutes late to the coffee shop on the town square, where Carole and Linda were waiting eagerly.

Grayson made friends with them instantly. Carole and Linda already had their coffee, so when Grayson went to order ours, the girls gave me a thumbs-up.

"What a hunk," Linda said with her back turned to Grayson. I chuckled.

As we visited, Grayson had many questions for the girls. Of course, they made exaggerated remarks about me, to Grayson's amusement. He thanked them for helping me with the quilt show and encouraged them to come back to Door County sometime soon.

"So, will there be a show?" Carole asked with interest.

"My gut says something different will happen," I replied. "We learned a hard lesson about the liability involved. We have a nice donation from one of my quilt club members, and we'd like to dedicate what comes next to her."

"How nice," Linda added.

"Cher and Claire are quite the duo, as you know," Grayson noted. "Whatever they come up with will be grand."

"We were so sorry to hear about the passing of your friend Ericka," Carole sadly noted.

"Thanks," I acknowledged. "I now have a small evergreen planted in my front yard in memory of her."

Carole had always kept track of those who died from our class and reminded us that we all were getting to an age where anything could happen.

An hour later, we said our goodbyes and drove to Mom's house.

Mom and Bill had just made a fire in the fireplace. It was good to see it come alive again, as Mom was hesitant to have a fire in the years she was by herself. Bill was taking such loving care of Mom. The idea of them being married was starting to grow on me.

Chapter 55

As we said goodbye to Missouri, Grayson and I made small talk about all the events that had happened during our trip. He mentioned how much he enjoyed meeting more of my family and friends.

"In regard to Christmas, Kelly and I have always gone to Marsha's sister's house. This year, I hope you'll join us."

"We'll see. But you and Kelly should keep your traditions."

"I suppose your mom will be adjusting some of hers, just like many of us will." I didn't know quite what he meant by that.

"So, have you heard from Kelly while we've been away?"

"Yes. She sent a text that she had a fun time with her aunt and cousins. I told her I wouldn't be coming home till late tonight."

"I bet she'll be happy to see you."

He paused. "She's been changing quickly since she's been away at college. I guess I should have expected that. All the childlike things we used to do are now too silly even to mention."

"She'll always be your little girl, Grayson. Oh, I forgot to tell you that Lee and Dr. Chan invited our quilt group to a party. It's at The Clearing, where Lee is on the board. It's always gorgeous this time of year. When I find out more, you may be included in that invitation."

"How nice that they invited your group. You'll enjoy that."

"I guess we won't be attending a Bittner Christmas party this year if they go to Florida early. I think it was always Cotsy's idea to stay in town till Christmas."

"I'm trying to convince my staff that we should just do something modest and in-house this year instead of a grand party. Planning a grandiose event is a lot of work, and I'm not sure it's genuinely appreciated."

"It's always fun to shake things up and try something new."

We didn't arrive in town till eight o'clock due to the heavy construction we ran across in several areas. I knew Grayson was anxious to see Kelly, so I suggested he just drop me off instead of coming in. He gave me a hug and kiss and told me he really appreciated our first Thanksgiving together.

I picked up and cradled dear Puff once I set my bags down. I could tell she wasn't happy with me. I gave her one of the treats I reserve for special occasions. After she consumed it, she jumped out of my arms and curled up in her favorite chair.

I went upstairs to unpack and take a shower. I'd had fun in Missouri, but I was mentally and physically drained. I had to get some rest for a long day tomorrow at the barn.

When I climbed into bed, I quickly called Mom to let her know we'd gotten home safely. She wanted to talk longer, but I told her I was tired and would call her again soon. As soon as I fluffed my pillow, I was ready to put the wedding and my trip with Grayson out of my mind. Cher called and foiled my plans. I answered in a groggy voice.

"Oh, no. Did I wake you?"

"I just got into bed. The trip to Perryville wore me out."

"Oh, what was I thinking? I had you on my mind the whole weekend. Did everything go okay?"

"Yes, it was perfect. The newlyweds seem incredibly happy."

"I figured as much. Did they accept Grayson with open arms?"

"Very open. How did things go with you and Carl?"

Chapter 56

"Carl asked me to go with him to his sister's. His mom and many other family members were there also."

"Oh, so you met Mom?" I grinned.

"Yeah, it was strange. I got neither a warm nor a cold response. I don't think she could figure out our relationship. Neither can I."

I burst into laughter. "How did he introduce you?"

"He called me just a friend, which was fine by me."

"Well, I took a lot of reception photos I need to share with you sometime."

"Oh, I bet your mother looked beautiful."

"She really did. Bill looked pretty nifty himself for a big, old guy."

"I'm going to be working a lot at the gallery with the Christmas season and inventory. I'm trying to talk Carl into doing an open house, but so far, no luck."

"I'll be working a lot at the farm."

"You seem to enjoy that."

"I really do, especially close to Christmas. There's so much excitement, and this year we have a lot more products than last year."

"I wish Carl would let me do more of the buying. He rarely asks for my opinion."

"Well, at least he has good tastes in artists, like me!" We chuckled.

"I'd better let you sleep, Claire. I know you're exhausted. Thanks for talking to me for a few minutes."

As soon as Cher hung up, I fell fast asleep. I set the alarm quite early, which didn't sit well with Puff. She changed her tune, however, when she saw me go downstairs for breakfast. She wasn't going to miss that opportunity.

Ericka's small, lit tree stood out among the darkness of the morning and made me smile. I think it may have even grown a bit since we planted it. Oh, we would miss her this Christmas. After I fed Puff, I went upstairs to dress. I'd need warm clothes even with the wood stove in the barn. Every time the barn door opened, the chill air from outside wafted in.

The sunrise on the drive out to the Rachael and Harry's provided a nice backdrop. I had high hopes for a great winter day in Door County.

When I walked into the barn, the warmth of the stove was great, but my timing wasn't. Harry and Rachael were in a pretty heated discussion about some property that Harry wanted to buy. She often disapproved of how Harry spent his money. They stopped their bickering when they could sense my discomfort.

"Pardon us, Claire," Harry apologized. "How was your Thanksgiving?"

"Good. Grayson came with me for the first time to Mom's. Hey, the farm looks great. You two have been busy rearranging. I really like the way the gazebo lights up and has a tree in the center."

"That was Kent's idea. We did move some things around, but have no fear, we got the boss's approval on everything." Rachael grinned at his reference. "Well, I'll let you ladies get to work and catch up."

"Oh, Claire, I'm so sorry you had to see us argue," Rachael said once Harry was out of earshot.

"Hey, pay me no mind. I just work here."

Rachael chuckled. "I think you're more than that, my friend. Now, look at these Santas with the quilts. Are they not the cutest things?"

"I have to say they're cuter in person than they were in the catalog, and reasonably priced too."

"So, where do you want me to start today?"

"These two trees need water, and the floor needs attention. Please have some coffee first. Harry made his gumbo for lunch today. I hope it's not too spicy for ya."

"It sure smells good. Harry needs to cook for the customers. Folks would love his food."

"I know. He needs to do a lot of things. Hey, I want to know every detail of your trip, but I've got to get this barn quilt ready to ship."

Chapter 57

Once I got my cup of coffee, I began my list of tasks. Folks started to come in as I was watering the trees. The kids found some of our merchandise amusing, which I was happy to see. This year was truly a learning curve on what to buy for the gift shop.

Many customers complimented the outdoor lighting. And several asked whether the food they could smell was for sale and where they could get it. I was certain Harry was paying attention. It was interesting to watch Rachael's reaction to their comments. Many business owners were coming in to get Christmas greenery and other decorations, which made me think of Grayson. He hadn't mentioned coming out here this year.

I finally took a lunch break to enjoy Harry's gumbo. It did have that bite Rachael warned me about, but I was ready to go back for another bowl after my first.

When there was a quiet break, Rachael came toward me and wanted to share what she and Harry had been arguing about.

"Harry wants to buy twenty more acres that just went up for sale near us. The property would be perfect for growing more Christmas trees, and we could open that up to folks cutting their own. You know, Charlie always wanted to do that, but we could never afford to buy more property. Harry has money to burn, but I warned him that he could get in over his head."

"I understand what you're saying, Rachael. Plus, bigger isn't always better."

"It would be more work for me, and I can hardly keep up with my barn quilts as it is. I'm happy with the way things are right now, but Harry says he wants to look ahead to our future."

"Well, I hope he doesn't do all this without your blessing."

Kent interrupted us when he came in for some gumbo. We exchanged greetings, and he mentioned that Brenda may be coming out later. She must be working at the inn now.

"Claire, we sure enjoyed meeting Kate and Cole at the fish boil," Kent commented.

"It was fun. I went to lunch with Kate the next day, and Grayson and Cole hit it off on the greens."

"If you plan on seeing them again, Brenda and I might want to join you."

"I'll let you know. I think they may be back again closer to Christmas."

"Sounds good. Well, that gumbo hit the spot. I guess I'd better get back to work."

This was my third year helping at the farm, and a lot of folks recognized me from previous experiences here. Most didn't know my personal life, though, and occasionally a man would flirt with me, which never hurt my ego. I knew I was lucky to have found Grayson.

"Hey, Claire," Rachael called out from behind the back room. "Don't forget we're having our traditional Christmas Eve party again. You should invite Grayson to come out and join us."

"I appreciate that, but I truly haven't thought about my plans yet."

Rachael brought in a stack of the smaller barn quilts that displayed a simple twelve- or eighteen-inch quilt block. They were great sellers for Christmas gifts. She told me that many were purchasing them for interior homes and businesses instead of barns.

"Next year I'm not even going to offer the wall quilts to match the purchased barn quilts. People seem to like getting the discount instead."

"Good call. I don't know how you've managed so far. You know, if you could quilt two of this pattern in black and white, I think Cher would like it for her apartment. Her living room and dining room are that color scheme, and I never know what to give her. Would you have time to do that for me?"

"Sure. By the way, what are you giving Grayson this year?"

"So far, I just have a Packers throw, which I also bought for Harry by the way."

"Oh, he'll love that. Why didn't I think of that?"

"They sell them at Carl's gallery if you want to get one for Kent."

"Oh, absolutely! Kent and Harry are going to a game tomorrow. They're playing the Bears, so look out. Remember when I tried to fix you up with Harry?" We both burst into laughter.

"Yeah, well, we know how that turned out, don't we?"

Chapter 58

I came home with the Christmas spirit, despite working pretty hard at the farm. I meant to check with Kent about the delivery of my tree, but other things preoccupied him today.

Puff was ready for some snuggles and one-on-one time. I made a fire and poured a glass of wine before I heard someone knock at my door.

"Surprise!" Kelly called out when I opened the door. Grayson was at her side and gave me a wink.

"Kelly! How good to see you!" I responded. "Come on in."

"We should have called first," Grayson said apologetically. "We just left Husby's to have a pizza, and Kelly suggested that we surprise you. I was glad to see your car here. Have you been home long?"

"Just long enough to start the fire," I noted. "Let's sit. I want to hear all about school."

"Don't get her started or she'll never stop," Grayson warned.

"So far, I like my professors, but some really load up on the homework, which I struggle with sometimes. I'm being lobbied to join a sorority, but Dad doesn't want me to do it my first year."

"So, tell me. Are there a lot of cute guys?" I teased.

"I really don't want to hear this part," Grayson joked.

"Most of the good-looking ones are spoken for. I do have a good guy friend, Toby. We hang out a lot, but we're not connected." Grayson chuckled. I knew what she meant.

"Romantically you mean?" I asked with a smile.

"Let's change the subject," Grayson suggested. "How about offering me a glass of that wine?"

"Of course! How about some hot chocolate, Kelly?"

"Sure!" she responded eagerly.

Kelly played with Puff and told me Spot had been doing well in her dorm. She was happy her school had begun allowing pets in certain dorms a few years ago. She joked that her dad would have locked Spot up in her room at home till she came home again. Grayson was getting a kick out of her description.

As we sat by the fire, Kelly drove most of the conversation, which was fine by me.

"Dad said your mom is really nice," Kelly shared.

"She adores him as well. Did you have a nice Thanksgiving?"

"I did. There are three of us cousins in college now, so we had a fun time."

"How's your quilt holding up?"

"Good, but I need to wash it. I was going to ask you about that."

"Hey, just drop it off. I can do that for you."

"Really, Claire?"

"Absolutely. I can't promise miracles, but I really don't mind laundering it for you, Kelly."

"That's mighty nice of you, Claire," Grayson complimented. "Well, we'd better get going. Will I see you at the chamber meeting this week?"

"I'll see if I'm needed at the farm," I explained. "It's their busy season."

Grayson gave me a slight hug and a kiss on the cheek as we parted ways.

I tidied up the kitchen and went up to bed after I put out the fire. With Kelly still on my mind, I wondered what I could give her for Christmas. If I had a good picture of Spot, I could try to paint him.

As I pulled up my covers, my text went off. I figured it was Grayson or Cher. Instead, I was shocked to see it was from Foster.

[Foster]
I'm lying here thinking of you, Miss Stewart. I'm hoping to convince you to have a Christmas drink with me. I want to share some news.

Chapter 59

I took a deep breath. Should I respond or ignore him? I didn't want to be rude.

[Claire]
I suppose I could. You have me in suspense.

[Foster]
Good. I'll call you tomorrow.

I didn't want to respond again to encourage further conversation. This text was the last thing I needed as I tried to get to sleep. I wanted to tune everything out.

With little sleep, I woke up later than planned and texted Rachael I was running late. Over breakfast, I considered my text from Foster. What was his news? I looked out the window and couldn't believe my eyes. Snow! I still had plenty of leaves that hadn't been picked up. When I glanced at Ericka's tree, I could just imagine her standing there, loving the snow. It seemed so real in my mind that I almost waved to her. Of course, she wasn't there. I sat in Puff's chair shaking, and my eyes were tearing up. Ericka loved winter and teased me for being such a wuss when I moved to Door County.

I felt I had to talk to someone who would understand. Maybe Cher had experienced something similar. I decided to call her.

"Hey, Claire. You just caught me. I was about to leave for work. What's up?"

"I just had the most surreal experience, and I had to tell someone."

She listened intently while I described in great detail what I'd experienced looking outside. It took me a while, but she didn't interrupt. When I finished, I waited for her response.

"George is having some of the same experiences and doesn't know what to make of them. He, too, said she looked happy."

"Well, I'm glad it's not just me."

"Now I, on the other hand, might share this. Have you heard of a cardinal appearing after someone has passed? Some folks claim the same thing about a butterfly."

"Yes, I've heard of that."

"I know it's crazy, but ever since Ericka died, I see cardinals in the most interesting places and wonder if she's giving me a sign. I told George about it, and he absolutely thinks it's her."

"I don't know what to think."

"Well, I'm glad you don't think I'm crazy. Maybe you did see her this morning."

"Thanks for listening, Cher Bear. I feel better. I'd better head to work now. I'm already running late."

"Be careful out there, Claire Bear. The roads may be slick now that the temperature has dropped."

"Oh, I see a call coming in from Rachael. Bye, Cher."

"Good morning, Claire," Rachael began. "I'm glad I caught you. Please don't drive out today. The roads out here are terrible. Kent wanted me to tell you he'd get your tree to you this week, so make room for it."

"Thanks for letting me off the hook for driving in this weather. That's great about the tree. I'll use my free time today to get ready for it. If Mother Nature cooperates tomorrow, I'll come out then."

"Yeah, we'll see. Enjoy your day off."

I took a deep breath knowing Rachael has just given me the gift of time. Since I was dressed already, I began moving things around on the sunporch to make room for the tree. Hopefully, Puff would remember the routine from last year and let me do my business. I also put on my boots and went outside to the shed to retrieve my Christmas ornaments. I had to admit that it was rather fun being out in the snow. I found three big boxes to take inside.

As I ascended the couple of steps to the porch, I glanced at Ericka's tree once more. Just then a red cardinal perched himself right on one of the limbs, causing the snow to fall under its weight. I thought of what Cher had told me, and all I could do was smile. In Missouri we had a lot of cardinals, but I didn't recall seeing many here in Door County.

Chapter 60

I set the boxes on the porch and walked toward the tree. I was close enough to reach out to touch the bird, but it finally flew away. I couldn't believe it trusted me so much. If that wasn't a sign from Ericka, it was a sign from God, or what I've heard termed a God-wink. I had goosebumps all over. The cardinal was my second gift of the day. I walked away and picked up my boxes to return to the warmth inside.

I thought about calling Cher to tell her the cardinal had paid me a visit. I changed my mind, deciding the moment was meant for just me.

These Christmas boxes I brought in wouldn't unpack themselves, unfortunately. Puff watched me with caution, as she knew what was coming. I put one box in her chair, and she ran under the couch till I restored order.

The snow was now quite heavy, which somehow felt fitting here in Door County. It took a few years, but perhaps I was finally acclimating to Door County winters.

I built a fire and made a mental list of the best use of my time till Kent delivered my tree. I had a few small quilts to finish for the gallery as well as Michael's quilt for Christmas. I was pretty certain at this point I wouldn't see any of my family for Christmas. Mom and Bill would want to enjoy their first married Christmas at home and take it easy in preparation for his upcoming surgery, and Michael would likely be with Jon and his family.

I took another look at the bookcase quilt for Michael. There were many improvements I could make, but time was running out. I decided to go ahead and bind it.

My mind drifted to Grayson and Kelly. I really needed to get serious about their presents. I also had to fit in some shopping, but working for Rachael had left little time for that.

Tomorrow was the Christmas parade in Sturgeon Bay, and I suspected rain or shine wouldn't spoil it. There was so much to do this time of year, but I had to keep in mind I was a resident and not a tourist. Some things would just have to wait.

After I finished binding Michael's quilt, I made popcorn to munch on while I watched the Packers play. I knew Kent and Harry were likely having fun watching the game in the snow. The team played in whatever weather Mother Nature dealt them.

I wasn't a devoted fan and dozed off for a nap. The sound of my cell phone ringing woke me up.

"Claire, it's Foster."

"Oh, hello."

"I figured you might be snowed in. Is this a good time to talk for a few minutes?"

"Sure. Where are you?"

"In Green Bay now, but I'm headed to Florida in the morning for a week or so. I'll be back for that Christmas drink we talked about."

"Florida sounds like a nice break from this snowstorm."

"I have a boat rented in Miami where I have some friends. Are you taking time to paint at all?"

"Not much these days. Mostly I've been quilting. Finding inspiration to paint has been an issue for me lately. What inspires you?"

"I think of something that excites me and makes me happy, like you, Claire Stewart."

"Oh, Foster, you don't mean that."

"I'm serious. I feel I had the opportunity with you and messed it up."

"Foster, let's always be friends. You know how fond I am of you."

"Well, if you ever change your mind ... I won't forget about that drink."

"Have a great trip. Goodbye, Foster."

I lay back down on the couch wondering what would have been different if I'd encouraged Foster and let thoughts of Grayson go by the wayside. We were artists with great admiration for each other, yet we were so different.

I looked over at the TV and saw a report that the Packers had won again. They didn't need my help at all.

When I got up to change for bed, my text went off.

[Rachael]
Take another day off. Harry said more snow is coming tonight. I keep painting, and Harry keeps cooking.

[Claire]
I wish Harry was in my kitchen. Maybe I'll get some painting done tomorrow. Just let me know when you need me.

Chapter 61

I sometimes envied what Rachael and Harry had together. I just bet Harry would be adding a food component to the business soon.

Puff was already asleep when I settled into bed to watch a movie. TCM was showing vintage Christmas movies, and *Christmas in Connecticut* with Barbara Stanwyck was on now. In the movie, Barbara is a magazine food critic living in New York City but writes about her supposed life in the county with children and farm animals. Things get more complicated when a war hero enters the picture. The movie's a bit corny, but it's fun to watch.

When the credits rolled, I turned out the lights and peered out the window to see the snow accumulation. Ericka's tree was nearly covered now. I missed her dearly, but I was thankful she was my friend for a short while.

I rearranged my pillow and fell into sleep.

I did manage to get some shut-eye, but my dreams involved Foster and Barbara Stanwyck. The sunlight shone brightly in my room, which prompted me to get out of bed and start my snow day at home.

I heard a noise out front and looked outside. To my delight, Tom was clearing snow off my car. I wasn't planning on leaving the cabin today, but it was nice to know I wouldn't have to brush off the snow or scrape my windows later. He really spoiled me.

My priorities so far involved feeding Puff, getting my first cup of coffee, and building a fire. Once I finished those, I moved out to the screened porch to watch Tom for a few minutes. It was always chillier out there since that room only had a space heater, and I hadn't turned it on. I heard a text alert from my phone in the kitchen, so I returned inside.

[Grayson]
Are you snowed in and staying warm?

[Claire]
Yes. The fire is going, and my coffee is working its magic.

[Grayson]
I canceled the chamber meeting because of the weather.

[Claire]
Well, that's a nice gift. How's Kelly?

[Grayson]
She's going skiing today. I wouldn't let her drive, so she's getting a ride.

[Claire]
Mean dad. I'm watching Tom shovel my place.

[Grayson]
I'll try to stop by after work.

[Claire]
Great!

Maybe I should have asked him to dinner. He knew my dislike for cooking, but it would have been a nice offer. Right now, I just wanted coffee.

When Tom finished outside, I heard him knock at my door. I still had on my robe, so I pulled it tight before answering.

"I guess you heard I was here. I hope I didn't wake you, but I had to come early. Busy day ahead."

"No, I was happy to see you. You must be cold. Would you like a hot drink?"

"Thank you, Claire, but I'll take a rain check on that. You stay warm now." He waved as he walked away.

Chapter 62

Another free day. I went back to the porch to stare at my easel. I'd have to ask Grayson tonight about a photo of Spot. It was the best idea I could come up with for a painting Kelly would like.

Thinking of Grayson stopping by later made me more conscious of the disarray of the cabin. I had a lot of things to tidy up. I finished the porch and living room and had a brainstorm about how to decorate my mantel and staircase. I put on a coat and hat and stepped outside to trim some greenery. Soon my tree, wreath, and garland from the farm would arrive, but I could bring the outdoors in with my own touches now.

When I finished putting the greenery on my mantel, I pulled out the box of Door County ornaments I'd collected. They'd look nice on the mantel instead of mixed in with my other ornaments on the tree. Why hadn't I considered that before?

This collection of ornaments included a few of the cherry variety, a Green Bay Packers jersey, a Door County trolley, two lighthouses, an Al Johnson's goat, a Tannenbaum church, and the lovely one of the White Gull Inn that

Brenda had given me. My phone rang as I stood admiring my new display. It was Michael.

"Hey, Sis," he greeted me.

"What's up?'

"I have an idea to run by you. I've been wondering what to get Mom for Christmas, and Jon took a really nice photo of all of us with his tripod at Thanksgiving. It was right before we started making toasts. I like it very much, and I think Mom and Bill will as well. What if I have it blown up and framed and say it's from both of us? I'll send it in a text after we hang up."

"I love that idea, Michael. Just let me know what I owe you. I may send her some Door County coffee she liked while she was here. I'll say it's from the two of us as well."

"That works!"

"How's Jon?"

"Good. He's been playing around with photography a lot. I got him something for Christmas that he's been wanting for his camera. And what might my sister be asking Santa for this year?"

"How about something you've written? I feel I'm missing out on some of your great articles and all."

"Just anything?"

"Yes. Anything but your last grocery list."

He chuckled. "Okay, no listing of carrots and celery then. Oh, and don't totally rule out a Door County visit from us for Christmas. I know you sometimes decide to go places at the last second."

"Oh, I'd love to see you, Michael. Just let me know what you decide."

After we said our goodbyes, I realized Michael was no longer speaking just for himself. He was bringing Jon into our family, and I felt completely okay with that. My relationship with my brother had truly improved the past couple of years. Perhaps Jon had something to do with that. I'm so glad I decided to make Michael the tie quilt. He'd be shocked and hopefully pleased.

It was time for me to shower and change now that the cabin was looking respectable again. I heard my phone ringing when I stepped out of the shower. It was Grayson.

"Hey, sweetie. How would you like to have a nice dinner at Lure tonight in Sister Bay?"

"Oh, that sounds heavenly! I've been wanting to try that place since it opened."

"Great. I went ahead and made a reservation hoping you'd say yes. I'll be at your place in about half an hour to pick you up if that works for you."

I quickly changed my wardrobe plans. With the wintery mix outside, I decided to wear my black dress slacks with boots, paired with a black mohair sweater that was a gift from Austen. I wouldn't mention that to Grayson, of course.

Grayson arrived right on time wearing his red woolen scarf with his overcoat. That look was still a turn-on for me.

"Hey, was I supposed to bring you a Christmas tree?" he joked when he saw the empty area.

"No, but perhaps tomorrow Kent will deliver mine. Come look at my fireplace mantel and what I did with my Door County ornaments."

"It looks great, Claire. But you look even better." I grinned as he pulled me close and kissed me.

Chapter 63

Lure used to be a church but was now a charming white tablecloth restaurant located in a little slice of land on the main drag in Sister Bay. Their Christmas lights were a warm invite to passersby. I was impressed from the moment we walked in. Our host escorted us to a lovely, intimate booth.

"This was a great idea, Grayson. I don't get to these finer restaurants very often."

"The good folks who own this do an excellent job. You must try their clam chowder."

After we made our drink and dinner choices, Grayson told me he'd received an email from Cole Alexander.

"Oh, nice. What did he have to say?"

"It looks like he and Kate will be returning close to Christmas. He's smitten with a piece of property right outside of Sturgeon Bay on the lake side. It has a fairly large cabin with a garage located in the woods. He said if they liked it, he may purchase it while they're here."

"Wow. I wonder if Kate is on board?"

"Most likely. She certainly loves Door County."

"It's nice she has help to run the guest house when she's gone."

We enjoyed the chowder that Grayson suggested, as well as their halibut special of the day. When it was dessert time, Grayson ordered a piece of key lime pie, but I was too full even to take the bite he offered me.

"I really like this place," I said. "Thanks for suggesting it."

"Thanks for indulging me. Kelly doesn't enjoy fancy places. She's all about pizza when she's home. She goes back tomorrow, but at least she'll be home again soon for Christmas break."

"How are you managing?'

"Well, when she's home, she's more independent now. It's not like it was before, and I'm still getting used to that."

"You know, I was once a daughter like Kelly. My folks seemed thrilled when I came home, but I also knew they were glad when I left." He chuckled and nodded.

When we pulled up to the cabin, the lights Tom had strung for me welcomed us back.

"If my tree arrives tomorrow, I'll be perfectly lit up for the season."

"You're really a Christmas nut, aren't you?"

I grinned and nodded. "I always have been. I remember feeling pretty bothered when I learned that Santa Claus wasn't real."

We stayed in Grayson's SUV talking for about an hour. The lights from my porch and outdoor trees were just enough to provide a romantic backdrop.

The next morning, I still had a smile on my face from the previous night. I sat at my kitchen table to check my messages. There was an email from Marta reminding us of our next quilt meeting and telling us to bring a gift for an exchange. Anna was going to provide refreshments. I'd missed these friends since our group didn't meet last month.

I decided to call Rachael and ask when Kent would deliver my tree and when she needed me to work again.

"Good morning, Claire. You just caught me leaving for a doctor appointment. I'm getting an x-ray to check on how my leg is healing. Sometimes I wonder."

"Do you need me to come out? And do you know if Kent is going to deliver my tree today?"

"You stay put. I know Kent was loading up some trees, so you're probably on the list. Harry will be here by himself."

"Are you sure Harry's okay running things by himself?"

"Yes, this weather won't bring out many folks. By the way, I won't be at the quilt club meeting. I'm too far behind here at the farm."

"Oh, sorry to hear."

"The Christmas lights you ordered are almost gone. We'll need to order more next year."

"I'm glad customers are buying them. Well, good luck at the doctor, and be safe on the roads."

I was excited to learn my tree was likely on its way. I went upstairs to pull out the red-and-white quilt that I always put under the tree. It had become a favorite of Puff's.

I put on some Christmas music and wondered what I should bring for my quilt club gift. I could be generous and give them the *Quilted Snow* I'd just finished, but I'd planned for it to go to the gallery. The thought disappeared when I saw Kent pull in front with my tree. It was like seeing Santa come. I quickly put on my coat to go out and greet him.

Chapter 64

"Need some help?" I called out.

"Sure!" he said with a chuckle.

Kent was strong, but as I took hold of the top, I knew why he'd accepted my help. I'd chosen a bigger tree this year, and it felt a good deal heavier. Now I had to hope it wouldn't be too tall for my porch. As he placed it in its stand, I held my breath.

"Wow, this barely fits in here," he noted. "You may have to trim it a bit." I nodded.

As the branches relaxed, it was perfect. Kent made a few magical improvements and was ready to move on.

"The rest is up to you, Miss Claire. I noticed the new little tree on your lawn you have all lit up."

"Yes, that's for Ericka."

"Oh, of course. Brenda told me about that. I'm sure she's smiling down on it."

I nodded. "Thanks to Tom, I have my lights up. You probably remember meeting him at the quilt show."

"I do. You're lucky to have him."

I filled up Kent's cup with hot coffee, and he was on his way.

"Okay, Puff, we're on a mission here with this tree, so stay out from under my feet while I decorate," I instructed as if she could understand me. She gave me a meow and walked to the couch.

I hated stringing the lights on the tree, but the glow made it worth the drudgery. I had to use my step stool, but I finally arranged the strands to suit me. With my Door County ornaments placed elsewhere, I had more room for the other ornaments.

As I placed each ornament, I thought of Mom and what kind of tree she would have this year. Would she and Bill agree on how to decorate?

By late afternoon, I was finally ready to place the quilt under the tree. I stood back to admire and watched Puff prance about the outer edge of the quilt to check it out. Finally, her memory returned, and she found a place to get comfy.

I put a baked potato in the oven for my dinner and poured a glass of wine. I was pleased with the progress of my day. I'd just finished my light dinner when I saw a car pull up. It was Laurie Rosenthal.

"What a surprise, Laurie! Come on in!"

"I hope you don't mind the intrusion. Cher had explained to me recently where your place was. I just came from the White Gull Inn from dinner, and I had to stop when I figured out this must be your cabin. Your lights really add a nice glow to this whole area of Cottage Row. It's spectacular."

I grinned at her compliment. "Thanks. The more lights, the merrier! Would you like some wine or coffee?"

"Coffee would be great. It's so darned cold out. I was going to call you and tell you we have definite plans now for my sisters coming."

"Oh, you must be so excited about that! I can't wait to hear about it. About the coffee, would you like to try the last of my Christmas coffee from Door County Coffee and Tea? It's called Candy Cane, I think. It's so yummy for the season."

"That sounds wonderful, Claire. A salesperson I buy from frequently took me to lunch there. I couldn't pass up cherry bread pudding for dessert. What a treat!"

"I know what you mean. Okay, so tell me all about your plans."

Chapter 65

"Well, the group will be a little smaller this year. They're staying in Green Bay with my sister Loretta and her husband Bill. Lynn, the one from St. Louis, isn't going to have her husband with her this year. Their marriage is a bit on the rocks, and they'll likely divorce. Ellen, our half-sister from Paducah, Kentucky, isn't coming, but Lily, the sister from Augusta, is able to make it."

"Yes, Lily is the one I'm most eager to visit with. Poor Bill will be the only guy? What a sport. Now, did you tell me Ellen is the one who volunteers at the National Quilt Museum?"

"Yes, that's right."

"I've been wanting to check it out. From their mailing list, I know they just had a Shakespeare exhibit."

"The museum is really something. Bill won't be joining us girls, as you can imagine. I'm going to his and Loretta's house in Green Bay for dinner on Christmas. A couple of years ago, their daughter Sarah went into labor then, and we all ended up at the hospital and having a late dinner."

"Oh my. What an exciting Christmas!"

"It was wild and crazy for sure. So the twenty-third they'll come here, shop, have lunch, and then eat dinner at the White Gull Inn as in previous years."

"What a lovely tradition. Were you ever in a relationship when they visited?"

"Unfortunately, no. I have to say, you seem to have found a good one, Claire."

"Yes, Grayson's great. I do wish I had a bigger place to entertain all of you, but that would be a tight squeeze here."

"It's okay. My sisters like going to the same places every time they visit. Maybe you and Grayson can join us sometime."

"That would be lovely. It's nice meeting other folks from home."

"Claire, it's been wonderful visiting with you this morning. This peppermint coffee has certainly enriched my Christmas spirit. I'd better be on my way, but thanks so much."

As I walked her to the porch, she stopped to admire my beautiful tree Kent had delivered. She loved the way Puff wasn't the least disturbed and continued to nap on the quilt below.

"It's Puff's seasonal home, I'm afraid. Do you have a pet?"

"I had one named Sassy, but she ran away and never came back. I hope she found a loving home."

"I'm sorry you lost her. I worry where Puff is every time someone opens my door. When Cher moved back to Missouri for a while and I rented the cabin, she said the cat came as a package deal. And that's how I came to inherit a cat!" Laurie chuckled. "When Cher moved back, I tried to get them together again, but neither one of them would have it."

"Sounds like Puff was meant to be yours. Thanks again, Claire, for the visit. I'm ready to go to Bayside again anytime you're up for it."

"Sure. Keep me posted on everything."

As I tidied up and put out the fire, I thought about how lucky I was to have gotten to know Laurie better.

I crawled into bed, joining my sweet kitty, when I heard my text go off. It was from Foster, of all people.

[Foster]
Took this photo out on the water today. The blue water is the same color as your eyes. Thinking of you and wishing you were here.

How in the world should I respond to that? He was flirting again, and I was uncomfortable responding. He was probably having a couple of drinks, which encouraged his sense of romance. I decided to ignore his text and let him think I was already asleep. What would Grayson think if he knew about Foster's message?

Chapter 66

The next morning, I reluctantly wrapped up one of my *Quilted Snow* wall quilts to take to the club for our Christmas meeting. I hoped whoever ended up with it would be pleased to have it.

The snow was finally showing signs of melting, so I was ready to see my quilting friends again.

The library was all decked out for Christmas, as was our meeting room, which had a lovely Christmas tree of book ornaments.

"Merry Christmas!" Marta greeted me as I walked through the door. "Help yourself to some Christmas tea and sweet little treats that Anna brought."

Anna had beautifully arranged a large tray of German delicacies, with touches of holly and berries around the perimeter. I could see her cherry strudel, fruitcake, and heart-shaped Lebkuchen and gingerbread men. Her fruitcake looked more like my mom's Christmas stollen. I had to try one of each.

The chatter grew louder as our group size increased. Marta encouraged us to put our gifts on the round table covered with a red tablecloth. It appeared everyone but Rachael had shown up today.

"Welcome," Marta said. "It's so good to see everyone so merry today. Let's begin by thanking Anna for making all these delightful treats for us today. She said she's willing to share the recipes, so just let her know if you'd like one." Anna blushed. "I didn't prepare a program today because of our gift exchange. I know we'll have some Christmas show-and-tell, so that will be all we need for a little party. I suggest we start with the show-and-tell. I know Lee brought a piece I saw of Christmas carolers, so you're first, Lee."

"Thanks, Marta," Lee began. "I'm going to donate this wall quilt to my church to use at Christmastime, but I wanted all of you to see it first. I got this idea off of a card. I love the different nationalities of the four choir ladies." Lee had lots of time to make detailed quilts. She received many compliments today on her handiwork.

"Greta has a log cabin that's about to be a Christmas gift. Right, Greta?" Marta asked.

"Yes, I'm pleased that I'll be mailing this soon to my nephew in Oregon. I'd always promised him a quilt. He has no idea it's coming this Christmas, so I decided to make it red and green." Several cheers followed. Ginger stood up next.

"I'm making these patchwork stockings and table runners for my shop," Ginger told us. "I'm having trouble keeping them in stock because they make such nice gifts." Amy, Frances, and Marta expressed interest in buying one, which pleased Ginger.

"Well, I was hoping this would be done for Christmas," Olivia expressed as she held up quilt blocks to her chest.

"It's a Christmas sampler that has been fun to piece. As you know, I don't do appliqué. I hope it will go together quickly. This is just for me, and I like to use a black background."

"It's beautiful," Lee said. "Everything you do is so striking."

"I'm afraid my show-and-tell isn't done, so I'll bring it the next time," Marta apologized. "Thanks, everyone, for bringing your things. Before we exchange gifts, are there any announcements?"

Greta raised her hand. "The Holiday Harbor tree lighting is tomorrow in Baileys Harbor," she proudly said. "It's a wonderful tradition."

"Have you seen the additional Christmas lights in Fish Creek this year?' I asked. "They've really outdone themselves."

"And let's not forget the Christkindlmarkt in Sister Bay," Ava reminded. "The booths will have something for everyone this year."

"Has anyone seen the Festival of Trees at the Maritime Museum in Sturgeon Bay?" Amy asked. "I took my daughter for their kids' day with Santa, and it was delightful."

"Yes, my husband loves the ships and tugboats that they light up around the marina," Lee added.

"Well, there's no shortage of things to see and do this time of year," Marta noted with a smile. "Now for the exchange, I'm told all the gifts are numbered, so just pick a number out of the hat and retrieve your gift.

We started row by row, and I had the number three. I received a lovely Christmas pillow that Lee made, so I was really fortunate. It had *Have a Merry* hand-embroidered on it. She knew right away I loved it.

Chapter 67

After the excitement of everyone showing their gifts, Marta got our attention.

"Thank you, everyone, for all your wonderful gifts," Marta said with excitement. "I wish all of you a very Merry Christmas. We'll see you back next year."

Cher kept giving me a funny look, knowing what I'd just experienced.

"You should have kept it for the gallery," she teased. "I love my tote bag from Olivia. I may use it every day for work."

"I love it, too," I said, somewhat jealously. "I'm too stuffed to go to lunch, aren't you?"

"Yes, plus I need to get back to the gallery," Cher admitted.

It took a while to say goodbye to everyone. We helped get Frances to Ava's car and then went our separate ways.

When I returned home, I sent Grayson a text asking for a photo of Kelly's cat. It took just a bit for him to respond.

"I have one of Kelly and Spot together. I'll send it along and see if you can at least get Spot's face from it."

Seconds later, a darling photo appeared. I played a bit with cropping to enlarge Spot's face. I thought it might work. His black-and-white face was so striking.

It took me most of the afternoon to get the sketch just right. I finally took a break and put a load of laundry in the washer. A welcome call from Cher interrupted my domesticity.

"Am I interrupting something?" she asked.

"Oh, I'm trying to be creative this afternoon, but it's frustrating."

"Well, I have just the cure."

"What's that, Cher Bear?"

"George called and wants me to meet him at Bayside Tavern. He said I should ask you to join us. Are you up to going?"

"Am I ever! I don't have anything in mind for dinner, so this is perfect."

I perked up, knowing there was relief in sight. I finished up some cleaning before I showered for the big evening. Ericka would have loved this last-minute meetup.

When I walked in, the place was packed. The regulars had to make space for all the tourists. George spotted me and guided me to their back room, where they had a few tables open. He gave me a big hug and told me how glad he was to see me.

After we placed our orders, Cher described her busy day at the gallery. She hesitated to mention that Foster had stopped by.

"I couldn't believe he had another painting for us. Did you know he was in Florida recently?"

"Yes," I blushed. "He called me from a boat of some kind and described the sunset to me."

"Oh my word," Cher gasped. "You didn't tell me that. Well, his new painting is quite lovely. Of course, he mentioned that the two of you were going to hook up for a Christmas drink. Is that right?"

"Well, well," George teased. "This doesn't seem quite fair to the rest of us handsome gentlemen. I thought Grayson was the apple of your eye."

"You and I are having a drink right now, George," I teased back. "Foster's awfully nice, so I don't know what to do about his invitation."

"You'd better watch out," Cher warned with a wink. "I think he'd like nothing more than to steal you from Grayson."

"He and Grayson are friends, so I think he just likes to tease me," I explained. "He knows how much Grayson means to me."

"The heart is a fickle thing," George replied as he took another sip of his beer. "It can change you on a dime."

"Oh, really?" I asked him. "And when did you become so wise?"

Chapter 68

"Well, George was wise enough to stop pestering you to go out with him," Cher teased. I nodded with a smile.

"George, you're a sweetheart, and I want you to know I was very flattered by your persistence, but your timing was terrible," I defended. "I'd just run away from a long-term relationship in Missouri, and getting close to another man was the last thing I wanted then."

"I know, I know," he said, putting his arm around me. "You know I'll always be your friend. And if Grayson ever treats you unfairly, be sure to give me a call instead of Foster." We all burst into laughter.

"Deal!" I nodded.

We'd just finished our Bayside burgers when Ericka's name came up. It stimulated our emotions, knowing she should have been there having a drink with us.

"You know, I have some things of Ericka's I need to find homes for, and I know she'd have wanted you two to have them," George noted. "One thing is that quilt you gave her. It should really go back to one of you."

"Cher, you should take it," I quickly responded. "It was your idea to give it to her."

"You've got time to think about all this, George," Cher advised.

"I suppose, but her lease is coming up, and I need to address getting her things moved," George replied. "How's the tree doing, by the way?"

"It's doing great," I reported. "Tom put white lights on it for me, and I love it. You should come and check it out."

"I will," he nodded. "Cher told me about the visiting cardinals, and I have to finally admit they're appearing to me as well."

"Are they?" Cher asked in surprise. "I've questioned a few other incidents too, but I'm keeping them to myself for now."

"We each should cherish the communication we still have with her," I began. "Let's have a toast to our dear friend, Ericka!" We all lifted our drinks and cheered.

I'd loved this time with our little gang. We decided to call it a night and had a group hug before leaving the tavern.

George offered to walk me home so he could see Ericka's lit tree. He was impressed and thanked me for lighting it up for the season.

Puff was already upstairs and barely moved when I crawled under the covers. I lay awake for a while and then decided to check my phone for messages. That turned out to be a big mistake. I noticed a text from Carole.

[Carole]
I hope you're sitting down. Your Dr. Page is engaged and planning a Christmas wedding.

[Claire]
Well, I was actually lying down, and now I have to ask who the lucky lady is.

[Carole]
The doctor from Cape Girardeau you told me about. I'll try to find out more.

[Claire]
How did you hear the news?

[Carole]
Jill said it's all over the hospital.

[Claire]
Of course, it would be. How is his walking? Any improvement there?

[Carole]
No, I'm not aware of improvement. What do you make of the engagement?

[Claire]
I hope they'll be happy.

[Carole]
Aren't you Miss Hospitality!

I chuckled.

[Claire]
Have you seen my mom lately?

[Carole]
No, but I have Christmas cookies ready to take to her.

[Claire]
Thanks so much. Looking forward to getting your new book.

[Carole]
I hope it's out before Christmas.

[Claire]
Say hi to Linda for me. Miss you two!

[Carole]
Miss you, too.

I put my cell away and thought about my dear Austen finally getting married. I waited five years for his proposal, and it never happened.

Chapter 69

Running on little sleep, I got up early to head to the barn. I was sure my paperwork was piling up, and with the break in the weather, they'd be busy. I was about to go out the door when Grayson called.

"What's on your mind, Mr. Wills?" I asked in a flirty voice.

"Miss Stewart is always on my mind," he replied.

"I figured you might be on your way to Rachael's, but I wanted to tell you that I heard from Cole Alexander. Remember that I told you they were going to look at a piece of property in Sturgeon Bay?"

"Yes."

"Well, they've arranged to see it in person. I thought you might want to hook up with Kate while they're here. They're staying at the Stone Harbor Resort in Sturgeon Bay."

"Perfect. I'll see what I can do."

I hung up knowing we might have some Missouri friends soon right here in Door County.

I got to Rachael's around ten o'clock.

"Sorry, Rachael. I really intended to be here earlier. Grayson called just as I was leaving the house."

"Is everything okay?"

"Yeah. Remember the Alexanders who sat at our table for dinner at the fish boil? They might end up buying a place here. They're looking at a property in Sturgeon Bay."

"Good for them. We enjoyed meeting them at dinner that night. They seem like a nice couple. I'm afraid I need to help Harry with something now. Take your coat off and help yourself to some coffee."

"Do your thing. I'm sure I can find a lot to work on today."

"I know there's a box of lights to unpack. I left you a list."

"I'm on it."

I unpacked the box first thing, but then Kent's little girls burst in.

"Well, hello!" I greeted them cheerfully.

They ran up to hug me, giggling, before they headed to where Rachael kept a tray of Christmas cookies.

"Harry and Kent are very busy outside, so I thought you might be in here, too," Brenda noted. "Is there anything I can help with? Kent couldn't get a babysitter today, so here I am."

"Isn't it your day to work at the inn?"

She nodded. "Yeah, I just called for a replacement. Besides, this is so much more fun." I smiled.

Two customers came in then, so I took Brenda up on her offer to help. Everyone was in the Christmas spirit, and it was contagious. Buying or selling Christmas trees never got old.

After Brenda fed the girls, she decided to take off and find them a Santa somewhere.

By four o'clock, things had slowed down. Rachael wanted to know what my plans were for the evening.

"Well, I could wish for a knight in shining armor to bring me dinner, but I'm happy just being in front of my fire. I always appreciate having a good hot lunch when I'm here. Harry's chili was delicious as always. Customers were hoping for some, too."

"Well, there's plenty if you want to take some home."

"I'm stuffed right now, so I'll be on my way."

As I was about to turn onto Highway 42, Grayson called. I pulled over to see what he wanted.

"Hey, if you leave it up to me, I could pick us up a little dinner tonight."

I grinned. "I knew there was a Santa Claus! That sounds perfect."

Chapter 70

I was tired from my day at the farm with friends, but now I looked forward to seeing Grayson.

I gave Puff a hug when I got home and quickly ran upstairs to shower, wondering what kind of dinner I'd be having tonight.

I came downstairs and started a fire in the fireplace. Puff knew something out of the ordinary was up. She followed me around for a while and then finally gave in to a nap under the Christmas tree.

Grayson arrived at six fifteen and seemed to be in good humor. He warmed up by the fire after giving me a kiss. I noticed he had a bag of food from Barringer's, so I knew we were in for something delicious.

"How about I clear this coffee table and we eat in front of the fire?" Grayson suggested.

"Why, sure! What are we having besides wine, so I know what dishes to bring out?"

"You're about to have some amazing shrimp scampi with the best chopped salad in Door County," Grayson bragged.

"Oh, you must have remembered how much I loved that. I hope they threw in some of their warm bread."

Grayson poured us wine while I placed the dishes and silverware we needed. There was still room for a candle, so I found one and lit it. I turned out the lights to add to the ambiance. The reflection of the Christmas tree lights from the porch added to our romantic meal.

"You've got the touch, sweetheart," Grayson said with a wink.

"Well, if someone brought me this kind of dinner every night, I assure you I could take care of the rest."

"Hmm ... Well, I'll make a toast to the beginning of a great Christmas season."

"I'll toast to that! And the best part is that we're together."

We spoke little, truly savoring our food. I was counting my blessings as I sipped my wine, gazed into the fire, and sat next to this thoughtful man who made my heart patter.

I finally asked about Kelly and her plans. She was back at school for now, till Christmas. She had plans to go to Detroit with her roommate before she came back here for Christmas.

"So, do you think she's dating anyone at school?"

"I don't think so. She attends most gatherings in a group and doesn't mention any guys in particular. To be honest, I don't think she tells me everything. Speaking of guys, I ran into Foster yesterday at the office."

"Oh, really."

"He said he hoped I didn't mind that the two of you were going to have a Christmas drink together. It caught me off guard."

"He actually said that to you? And what did you say?"

"Well, I told him you were a single, grown woman who could have a drink with anyone she wanted."

"Wow. I can't believe you said that."

"What did you expect me to say, Claire?"

"Well, first of all, I was just trying to be polite to him."

"So was I. If you want to go, go."

I stood up in disbelief. "Just like that? You don't care whether I have a drink with Foster?"

"Look, Claire. Let's have a little history lesson here. A year ago, I wasn't husband material. You said you wanted to remain single and that you liked the way things were. I finally agreed to accept your refusal of marriage."

I took a deep breath in anger. "Well, remaining single is one thing, but giving another man your blessing is something else entirely," I said with an exaggerated tone.

"I think you're overreacting a bit, don't you?"

I felt. I picked up some of our dishes and brought them to the kitchen. Grayson followed shortly afterward.

"Maybe I'd better go before this gets more confusing," Grayson said, touching my shoulders.

I didn't know what to say. How do you tell someone you wanted them to be jealous? In my silence, Grayson grabbed his coat.

"You're leaving?" I finally asked, disappointed.

"I think I'd better."

"I truly loved the dinner. Thank you."

"I'm glad I did something right this evening," he said sadly.

Chapter 71

Out the door he went. How could this perfect evening go so wrong?

As I cleared the coffee table and put out the fire, I felt a mixture of anger and sadness.

As I went up to bed, I kept questioning what had gone wrong. Why was I so hurt when he was nice to Foster? Was he so sure of me that he thought it wouldn't matter if I had a drink with another man? Since spring, we'd seemed aligned in our thinking, confessing how much we meant to each other.

Guilt began taking over my mind as I lay in bed. Perhaps I should have made my feelings clear to Foster that I wasn't comfortable meeting up with him. I certainly would never do anything to hurt Grayson. As I tossed and turned, I wondered whether Grayson was also having a sleepless night.

I finally got up to think about tomorrow's agenda. I tried to think of anything that would divert my mind.

My morning plan was to go to the Pig. Then after lunch I'd help out at the barn. My mind kept returning to Grayson. Why hadn't he called? Should I call him?

Time was ticking away, and I wasn't getting anything done. I'd finally grabbed my coat to head out to the store when Mom called.

"How's married life, Mom?" I teased. She laughed, and I could just imagine her blushing.

"We're fine if that's what you're asking. We both have the sniffles, though. Jon and Michael stopped by for a short while yesterday, which was nice."

"I'm sure you enjoyed their visit. Did they say exactly what their plans for Christmas were?"

"They did talk about their ski trip, but I don't think they're heading your way. Bill's daughter Candice called a couple days ago and wants us to consider coming to see her for Christmas, but we decided we're not going anywhere. We did sign up to help serve those in need on Christmas day. Bill said he's helped for many years, and I think it'll be fun."

"Didn't you and Dad do that a long time ago?"

"We sure did. Now, how's everything with you?"

"I'll be going to the Christmas tree farm soon. This is their busy season."

"That's nice of you to help, dear. Claire, what would you like for Christmas? You know you'll get a check if you don't give me some ideas."

"Mom, I don't need a thing. Really."

"Well, if you think of anything ... How's that sweet gentleman in your life?"

"Grayson's fine. I'm going to be painting a picture of Kelly's cat for her if I can get a sketch done. I think she'll like that."

"I don't know how you do what you do, honey. Well, I'll let you get on your way. I sure miss you."

"I miss you, too, Mom. I love you."

I hung up with another pang of sadness. I wanted to cry on Mom's shoulders about Grayson, but I didn't want to give her anything to worry about.

I took off for Sister Bay trying to concentrate on what I needed for the Pig. The traffic became a nightmare once I hit Ephraim. I forgot today was their Santa parade. I was sure to run into detours. It was cute to see all the kids lining up on the street's edge hoping to get a glance of the old guy.

The detours finally guided me to another road that would take me to the Pig. I'd try to focus on what I needed and not let all their holiday offerings tempt me. The crowd was huge, and it took me much longer than I anticipated, so I called Rachael to warn her I'd be late. She understood and told me Harry had made gumbo for everyone's lunch. Now I just needed to get my refrigerated items home before heading that way.

As I passed Noble Park, I noticed a sign advertising tonight's tree lighting. The last time I attended was when I'd just moved here. Brenda was nice enough to invite me.

By twelve thirty, I was finally on my way to the barn. I was starving for Harry's good gumbo.

Chapter 72

When I arrived, the farm was bustling. I said hello to Kent, who was putting a tree on top of someone's SUV.

"You'd better get in there," Kent told me. "We've been slammed."

Sure enough, there was a line to check out. I threw off my coat and started helping a lady with a crying child in her arms.

"I wanted to look around more at all your new things, but this little guy wasn't having it."

"Well, he's adorable," I complimented. "Let me have him for a bit, and you can take a look around."

"That's an offer I can't refuse," she said, putting him in my arms. Rachael gave me an odd look.

Her son stopped crying right away and wondered who this new person was that was now in charge. I even got him to smile when I walked him over to his mom. I noticed our poinsettias had finally arrived. She had two plants in her hand as well as a tree topper.

"I'll trade you now," she said as we exchanged what we were holding. "I've been looking for a new tree topper, and I'm so glad I found this. Thanks so much."

"Maybe he'd like one of those Christmas cookies," I suggested.

"I didn't think they were for the customers. Do you have children? He really took to you right away."

"No kids for me."

"Well, you'd make a great mom."

No one had ever told me that before.

I noticed that she'd not only purchased a small tree, but a lot of greenery as well. How she did all this with that child amazed me. I wished her a merry Christmas as she left.

"Nice of you to help her," Kent said, coming toward me. "I thought he'd never stop crying. Hey, by the way, Brenda talked me into taking the girls to the Noble tree lighting."

"That's great. You'll enjoy it. They'll have hot refreshments, and Santa will likely be there as well. Main Street has added more lights this year, so it will be beautiful."

"Okay, good to hear. I guess it's why the girls like Brenda so much."

"They sure do. Oh, did Rachael tell you the Alexanders are coming back to Door County to purchase a property in Sturgeon Bay?"

"Well, I'll be darned. You mean they'll be moving here?"

"I don't believe so. They have a guest house in Borna, so I think it's just to have a place to get away."

"I see. I hear Harry calling, so I'd better see what he wants," he said, leaving me to go back inside.

I rushed in to help Rachael's busy line. It was one thirty before I finally got some of that gumbo.

As soon as I finished eating, I rearranged the poinsettias. I told Rachael I was glad she'd included white ones.

I loved having distractions to get my mind off of Grayson. I thought I'd have a chance to talk to Rachael about what happened last night, but we were too busy with the flow of customers. And by five o'clock, I was ready for some quiet time to myself. I put my coat on to leave for the day, and Rachael put two poinsettias in my hand to take home. She always felt she couldn't repay me enough.

I was happy to arrive back at the cabin and see it lit up. The place would look even cheerier with the addition of the poinsettias. I put one on the fireplace mantel and the second on my kitchen table. Thoughts of Grayson returned in my solitude.

I poured a glass of wine and sat down at my kitchen table. I couldn't let this drag on. It was nearly Christmas, and neither of us needed this aggravation. I took another sip of wine and said a little prayer before calling Grayson.

Chapter 73

"Grayson," he answered matter-of-factly, like he didn't know who was calling.

"Grayson, it's Claire."

"Oh, hello, Claire."

"I feel so bad the way we left things between us. I think we truly misunderstood each other. I wanted to tell you I had no intention of having a drink with Foster, knowing his intentions. I am 100% committed to you and ..." He interrupted me.

"Stop. It's okay, Claire. I know that, and I love you."

"You do? I love you, too," I said, starting to cry. "I'd never do anything to hurt you."

"I know you wouldn't, sweetheart. Do you feel better now?"

I audibly sighed. "Yes, I really do. I really do." He chuckled.

When we hung up, I felt the weight had been lifted from my shoulders. Mom had always said never to go to bed mad at anyone because you never knew whether you'd have another chance to make amends. She was right. That night I had the best night's sleep ever.

The next morning, my text went off early, waking me up. It was Rachael telling me she could really use my help. So much for trying to paint Kelly's cat today.

Tomorrow the Alexanders would be arriving, and I hadn't heard from Kate about wanting to get together. Rachael had to come first with my time.

I got up and hustled with showering, dressing, and eating breakfast. Puff couldn't believe I was off again. It's funny that I could almost read her mind. She wanted her breakfast, and since I left the tree lights on all the time, she was more than happy to nestle under the warm lights when she was full.

The weather was dark and dreary at this hour. I hated driving to the farm before the sun rose. I passed two accidents on the way there, making me nervous. I should have brought hot coffee with me to keep me more alert. When I finally reached the road that would take me to the farm, there was almost no traffic. I could finally calm down. A car going the opposite direction had a tree tied on top, which told me Harry was already doing business.

I hurried into the barn and cheerfully said hello to Rachael. I could tell something was wrong.

"Are you okay?" I quickly asked.

"Kent's had an accident. He says he's probably fine, but they're keeping him at the hospital for now. I think it did quite a number to his truck. Harry will be alone today. He'll have to pick the girls up from school unless Brenda can do it."

"Oh, Rachael, I'm so sorry to hear of the accident. There's so much fog out there that I'm not surprised. I was scared while driving here and saw a couple of accidents. If Brenda comes today, I can go out and help Harry. I'm so glad the girls weren't with Kent. I'm here now, so do what you have to do, okay?"

"I will. There's chicken and dumplings in the Crock-Pot for later, and the usual pot of coffee."

"You spoil me," I said, putting my coat away.

I checked the trees and got them watered before tidying up the place. Finally, Brenda arrived, looking distracted.

"How's Kent?"

"He's sore, but there's no concussion, thank goodness."

"That poor guy."

"He's not sure what really happened other than that the two vehicles just didn't see one another."

"Things could have been much worse. I heard you were going to the tree lighting. How was it?"

"Great fun, despite Kent not being too excited about it. I'm going to see if I can have the girls spend the night with me tonight. I think Kent might appreciate that."

"I'm sure it won't be a problem."

Folks started coming in, so we had to stop our chatter. Rachael came in to get coffee and warm up. I could tell she was anxious when she asked if I could come in tomorrow to work. I considered the Alexanders briefly but told Rachael that I'd be happy to help.

"Is it tomorrow that the Alexanders are coming?" I nodded. "Are you sure you won't have plans with them?"

"I'll be here, Rachael. Don't you worry. Now get back to work." She grinned with affection.

I was busy in thought, but a bell rang every time a customer came in. Looking up to see who it was, I couldn't believe my eyes. Foster. What was he doing here?

Chapter 74

"Good heavens!" I said in shock.

"Surprised? I just bought a beautiful Christmas tree for my place at the Blacksmith Inn. You can't have Christmas without a tree, right?"

"How did you know about this place?"

"I knew you were working at a Christmas tree farm, and Cher supplied me with the rest."

"Well, this is it," I said as I waved my arms around. "How about one of these barn quilts to go along with that tree you just purchased?"

He chuckled. "They are quite fun. Is the artist here?"

"She's outside helping her husband Harry."

"Oh, then I just met her. She helped me pick out my tree."

"Did you tell her who you were?"

"No, but she didn't ask. She just told me to take the ticket inside to pay."

"That's where I come in," I noted. Brenda was watching us intently.

When I took his ticket, I decided to be brave and bring up Grayson.

"I heard you ran into Grayson recently," I hinted.

"I did. I also met his lovely assistant Jeanne for the first time. She seems to be quite protective of him."

"That she is," I nodded.

"So, Miss Stewart, when can we have that drink?" I paused, as a customer came in the door.

"Brenda, would you mind helping this young man?" I requested as she came rushing over.

I walked to the other end of the counter, and Foster followed.

"I know you've been very kind and generous to me, Foster, but I just wouldn't feel comfortable having a drink with you, knowing you'd like our relationship to be more than friends."

"My dear Claire, I wouldn't want you to feel uncomfortable. I was honest and told Grayson about it, and he didn't seem to have a problem with us getting together."

"Well, I don't feel that way, and I'd ask that you please respect my feelings."

"I absolutely will. Enough said. Now come outside and take a look at my tree." I smiled and nodded.

I rushed out in the cold to see what Rachael had helped him pick out. Of course, it was one of the best trees on the lot. I was shivering, so I kissed him on the cheek and wished him a merry Christmas. Then I ran inside to get warm.

"Well, well, well," Brenda teased. "I don't think I have to ask who that handsome man was."

I shook my head in disbelief. "I can't believe he came all the way out here."

"He's just pursuing you in a clever way. I think you handled it pretty well."

"It's tricky. I admire him so much, and I don't want to offend him."

The busy day continued, but at five o'clock Harry brought the girls into the barn. They ran into Brenda's arms, and she led them to the Christmas cookie tray. Rachael also joined us inside. She looked absolutely drained. Brenda told the girls it was time to leave, so we said goodbye. Rachael asked me to stay a bit and share a glass of wine with her and Harry. That sounded pretty good, as I had nowhere else to be.

"I think we broke a record with sales today," she noted as she sat down.

"I'm sure we did, but I'd like to do a few things differently next year," Harry said as he warmed his hands over the stove.

"Like what?" I asked innocently.

"We need to expand the white house and move trees further behind the barn," he began. "Did Rachael tell you I want to put a cafe where the white house is?"

"She didn't, but that doesn't surprise me, and you may have a great idea there," I added. "Folks want a hot drink or a snack. Driving out here is a destination, so it would be easy to get customers to stay for a sandwich, a bowl of soup, or a hot drink. Look how well the added merchandise has gone over."

"I bet you hear a lot of those remarks," Harry agreed. "Now, my wife thinks I move too fast on my ideas. I want to add more property while it's for sale so we can grow our own trees." Rachael just shook her head in disbelief.

Chapter 75

"I think I've convinced Kent to come work for us full time when we get things going here," Harry revealed. He's encouraging me to think ahead because you know I'm not a spring chicken anymore." We chuckled. "Rachael needs to stay focused on her barn quilts, which she loves to do. She doesn't need to be coming outside to help me load trees."

"I completely understand," I nodded.

"I'm looking to start in January, so we still may need your help now and then," Harry noted.

"Well, in the meantime, merry Christmas and happy New Year," I said, raising my wine glass. "I know you're both thinking of Charlie, and he'd want this business to grow."

Rachael started to tear up. "I know, you're right," Rachael confessed with a shaky voice. "Kent said when the time was right, he'd ask Brenda to quit her job at the inn and work in the cafe. He said she'd told him one time it would be fun to have her own cafe."

"Well, that sounds like a nice little arrangement for a married couple," I teased. We all chuckled.

"Brenda is aware of that happening, so I'm surprised she hasn't said anything to you."

"Well, I'd rather hear it from both of you," I noted. "I can't guarantee how much help I'll be because I want to get back to serious painting. I'll do what I can, though."

"That's all we're asking," Rachael added. "We're good with any amount of your time. You've been more than generous with us."

"Well, I wish you all the best and think you're going in the right direction," I claimed.

Harry and Rachael wanted to take me out to dinner somewhere, but I bargained for a night in front of a fire. They truly did appreciate having me as a sounding board.

"Well, I don't think I can handle any more surprises here, so I'm heading home to that fire and another glass of wine."

I hugged my dear friends goodbye and went on my way. I had to digest all the news on my drive home.

Back home, I checked my phone for any messages. There was a text from Kate Alexander.

[Kate]
I'm so glad Grayson could join us at the property. Hope to see you soon to celebrate.

[Claire]
Congratulations! I look forward to having you here.

I built my fire and decided to have a cup of that Christmas Candy Cane coffee I'd purchased with Brenda. I'd eaten a late lunch of delicious chicken and dumplings, so dinner wasn't necessary. I relaxed with my feet up and made a to-do list for tomorrow. I needed to mail my out-of-town packages.

After falling asleep with the news on TV and my fire already out, I went upstairs at a late hour.

I woke up the next morning with a sore back, so I took a long, hot shower. It did seem to help. I checked my phone over breakfast.

I was pleased to hear from Anne, the floral shop owner I'd met on the trip with Grayson. She said her husband, who was a pastor, would be attending a conference in Green Bay and she'd have a lot of free time to spend in Door County. We were in a popular tourist area, so she'd have plenty to do. I really liked Anne. She mentioned at our lunch that she had a son named Sammy, but it didn't sound like he was coming. I gave her my phone number so we could arrange a time to get together.

It appeared I could be getting lots of company, so I decided I'd better start cleaning the place after my trip to the post office. I had a package for Mom, Carole, Linda, and Jon and Michael. Mailing their packages made me a little sad because it meant I wouldn't be seeing them for Christmas.

Chapter 76

After standing in line for so long at the post office, I decided I deserved my favorite latte at the Blue Horse. It was late enough that I wouldn't be running into Grayson. The Blue Horse was busy, as usual. As luck would have it, Jeanne, Grayson's secretary, approached me in line.

"Well, hello, Claire. How good to see you. You just missed Grayson."

"Oh, I just assumed he'd be gone by now."

"Well, we just had a little Christmas celebration, I guess you'd say. I'm sure he told you the office party would be in-house this year."

"Yes, he mentioned it," I nodded.

"I think it will be much more fun this way. Of course, I'm in charge, so I'd best get back to work."

"I'm sure it'll be great. I hope you have a merry Christmas, Jeanne."

"You too, Claire," she said, as she left.

I got my drink and bagel and decided to stay here for a bit since I'd spotted a seat on the porch. The view of the bay was pretty no matter what time of year it was.

I sat there realizing that once again, this woman from Grayson's office had gotten a rise out of me. I was disappointed Grayson hadn't asked me to the work party this year. I needed to get home and forget about Jeanne.

The first thing I did back at home was write a few Christmas cards. I wondered about Austen and whether he was a married man now. It was around two o'clock when I heard from Kate.

"Hey, Claire. We're here. I decided to stay with the guys. The weather isn't looking too good, so I don't want to be driving around. I guess I'll see you at dinner if all goes well."

"Oh, okay. Where are we having dinner?"

"Right here in the lodge. They have a nice restaurant, so Grayson will pick you up sometime before seven o'clock."

"That sounds wonderful. Tell Grayson I'll be ready."

"I will. He's been so helpful. We'll fill you in on everything tonight."

I was somewhat relieved that no one needed me till dinner time. I'd have a chance to do more around here. I'd catch up with Kate and Cole soon enough.

Mom called when I hung up with Kate. She'd just found out about a friend of hers at church who had died. They already had another funeral to go to on Monday. Her voice was so sad.

"Oh, Mom, I know how difficult this must be."

"Bill holds in all his emotions, but I just had to talk to someone. I hope you're not in the middle of something."

"I'm never too busy for you, Mom. You know that. You can call me anytime. Women need their friends."

"I know. I miss Hilda so much, especially with the holidays coming."

"Cher's been missing her, too. And now she also has to deal with the loss of Ericka."

"My heart goes out to her. Maybe I should call her."

"That would be nice, Mom. I know she'd love to hear from you. Oh, I mailed your package today, so I hope it gets there by Christmas."

"Bill put yours in the mail yesterday. I sure hate knowing you won't be here."

"I know, but this year you're starting a new tradition with Bill."

"Oh, yes, don't I know." She chuckled. "He's determined to have a real tree."

"Well, your house will smell great. Mom, do you remember when I told you about Kate and Cole Alexander who own Josephine's Guest House? Well, they're in town from Borna, and it appears they've purchased some property. I'll see them tonight at dinner with Grayson."

"How nice it'll be to have friends there from Missouri."

"I'll keep you posted. Now, try to cheer up and enjoy that new Christmas tree that's on the way. Maybe you could even string some popcorn like we used to do when we were kids. Tell Bill to send me a photo of your tree once it's decorated."

"Okay, honey. I sure do love you."

"I love you, too, Mom."

Grayson had sent me a text while I was talking to Mom.

[Grayson]
I'll be there around six thirty, sweetheart.

I smiled.

Chapter 77

I changed into a red, cable knit sweater with black wool slacks, which made me feel really festive. I looked out the upstairs window and saw snow starting to fall. Driving was now going to be a challenge for us. I was glad Grayson was picking me up.

It was six forty, and Grayson wasn't here yet. He was never late, so I began pacing the floor, worried something had happened. He finally arrived five minutes later.

"Hey, sweetheart," he said, coming in the door with snowflakes on his overcoat shoulders.

"Oh, Grayson," I said, giving him an extra tight squeeze. "I'm so glad to see you,"

"Nice welcome, sweetheart. I'm happy to see you, as always. Why don't we just stay here in front of the fire?"

I grinned at his suggestion. "Part of me says yes. So, how are the roads? And did everything go okay today?"

"The roads aren't great, but yes, the real estate transaction is a done deal. It's an amazing place sitting high on the lake with a decent house and garage. Kate's already planned the decor, so you'd better hope the rest goes okay." I chuckled.

"She said maybe they could rent it out for the months they're not here."

"Good idea."

"Well, we're running late. It's a good thing Kate and Cole can stay in their room till we get there. With tonight's weather forecast, I wanted to cancel, but the Alexanders wanted to celebrate in the worst way."

"Let me find my warmest coat."

Grayson's SUV was covered in snow in just the brief time he was in the house. He brushed the windows with his scraper, and off we went. Seeing the Christmas lights glowing in the falling snow made the trip to the lodge a beautiful one. The traffic was slow and cautious. Our drive was quiet so Grayson could concentrate on the roads.

We finally arrived at the restaurant, and Grayson sent Cole a text that we were here. We went ahead and got a table, and they joined us a few minutes later. One side of the restaurant was glass overlooking the lake. Our viewpoint from the table allowed us to see the lights on the marina behind us and the bridges.

"I guess Grayson told you we said yes pretty quickly to the property," shared Cole.

I nodded. "He sure did, and I couldn't be happier for you."

"Oh, Claire, I don't want to go home. I want to move in right now," Kate gushed.

"I can imagine," I giggled. "You know you could be like me and never look back."

"Now that we have our drinks, I'd like to make a toast to welcome Kate and Cole to Door County," Grayson said, holding up his glass.

"Hear, hear," we all said together.

Kate quickly got on her phone to show me pictures of every detail. She talked so fast about her plans that it was hard to follow her.

"Kate's done a fantastic job on her guest house and our new home behind it, so I know she'll love getting her hands on this place," Cole bragged.

"I haven't shared with you, Claire, that I look after my Aunt Amanda. She also lives behind our guest house. She moved to Borna from Florida, married shortly after, and then her husband passed away. I don't like to be away from her too long. She's such a dear."

"I totally understand," I responded. "She's lucky to have you."

"I can't wait till we tell Kate's son in New York that we're buying a place here," Cole revealed.

"Are they coming for Christmas?" I asked.

"Yes, he and his wife come every year," Kate explained. "So far, no grandchildren."

We enjoyed a delicious dinner with this couple we'd be seeing a lot more of in the coming years. Cole and Grayson got sidetracked with the real estate details, and Kate and I had our own conversation, which happened the last time we'd had dinner together. Grayson was getting nervous as he checked the weather on his phone. We decided to part ways before the roads got even worse.

Grayson went to get our car while I waited for him in the lobby. It wasn't long before he returned on foot.

"I'm afraid we aren't going anywhere. I hear Highway 42 is closed down with several accidents. I suggest we spend the night here and go home in the morning."

"Are you sure?"

"We have no one waiting for us, and it's the smart thing to do. You stay here, and I'll see about booking a room."

Chapter 78

The restaurant was closing, and Grayson still hadn't returned. I went to the lobby desk and found Grayson standing at the counter with other folks looking very frustrated.

"Honey, I'm sorry I didn't get back to you, but this place is booked. They're trying to find us a room elsewhere, but nothing close by seems to be available. It's going to be a while before this storm lets up."

"Grayson, this is awful. What do we do?"

"For now, grab us one of those comfy couches over there and wait for me," he said sweetly with a kiss on my forehead.

I found a large, leather couch near the lobby door and fireplace. I staked out our place as I watched Grayson continue to converse at the lobby counter. Finally, he walked toward me.

"I'm afraid we're stuck right here till morning, my dear," he said in frustration. "The lady at the desk assured me all of us staying here would get blankets. It's the best they can do."

"Well, then we need to make the best of it," I conceded. "Have a seat. This couch is comfortable, and look how close we are to the fireplace and complimentary coffee."

He smiled. "You're right, honey. They said if we needed anything, they'd do what they could to accommodate us."

"What time is it anyway?"

"It's almost midnight. The bar is closed now, so we'll just stay put. You can lie right here in my arms by the warmth of the fire." This might not be so bad after all.

We took off our coats and used them to cover with. A nice employee came by and offered us an additional blanket or pillows. We declined, but an elderly couple across the couch from us took him up on the offer.

Grayson put his feet up on the coffee table in front of us and began to relax. I snuggled up into his shoulder, which made a perfect pillow for the time being.

"A guy sure can't complain too much," he chuckled. "Here I am spending the night with my best girl in front of a warm fire."

"You're something, Grayson Wills," I bragged, kissing him on the cheek. "I wonder when we'll be able to leave?"

"Right now, I don't care. When I think about the mess we could have gotten ourselves into by leaving, I'm thankful for being here on the couch with you. It's a good thing we had a nice big dinner."

"Look at that sweet couple, Grayson," I said, pointing to the elderly couple who were already fast asleep.

"You and I will be them someday," he whispered. "They have each other, no matter what happens next." We both smiled.

The lobby became increasingly quiet as everyone settled in for the night. Not every seat was occupied, but those settled here felt comfortable enough to sleep. How lucky I was to be with the man I loved under these circumstances. I wanted to fall asleep, but I was too busy smelling Grayson's cologne and enjoying the softness of his neck. Every man I'd ever known could fall asleep the minute he stopped talking, and Grayson was no different. I could feel and hear every breath he took. I didn't want to disturb him, so I just recalled the moments of the day and how, right upstairs, Cole and Kate were fast asleep in their room.

Hours later, I heard someone poke the fire. By that point I was lying on the couch using Grayson's lap as my pillow. The lodge was quiet and dark, so I fell back to sleep.

The next interruption was much louder, and both of us jumped.

"Did I snore?" Grayson asked with a grin.

"I have no idea," I said as Grayson got up and put his suitcoat back on.

Dawn had come, so Grayson walked over to the counter to find out what was happening with the roads. The little couple across from us were gone. We'd made it through the night safe and warm. I went to the restroom to freshen up.

Chapter 79

When Grayson returned, he said the roads were open and asked if I wanted to get a bite to eat before heading back.

"Sure. I'm ready for some coffee."

After we sat down, Grayson called Cole to tell him we'd spent the night in the hotel. He left out the part about us sleeping on the couch in the lobby using our coats as blankets. He hung up, and the two of us moved on to other topics, including the in-house Christmas party at his work.

"Yes, I heard it firsthand from your assistant, Jeanne, when I saw her at the coffee shop. I think she's delighted not to have to share the evening with me."

His phone rang, and he said it was a call from Alice, his older family friend from the Moravian church. When I'd met her a while back, she seemed quite protective of Grayson. He stepped out to the lobby to take her call, and I ordered food for both of us: two coffees, biscuits and gravy for him, and a ham and cheese omelet for me. When he returned, he filled me in.

"Alice says they've canceled the early service at church, which was disappointing to her. No, I didn't tell her I'd just spent the night with Claire Stewart." We both chuckled.

"How's her health these days?"

"Not good, and she doesn't have any business being out in this freezing weather. I sure wish she'd agree to an assisted living facility, but she refuses. She pays for people to do what she needs, like take her to church. That house is too massive for her, but it's where she says she wants to die."

"Well, it's her life, and she's fortunate to be able to afford what she wants. It's sweet the way you continue to help her."

"I never really shared the whole story with you, but my family owes her in a big way. I promised I'd be there for her since my parents are gone."

"Of course. You're doing a good job keeping your promise."

We finished our huge breakfast and were ready to tackle the journey home.

Getting into Grayson's cold car was a jolt from our cozy experience in the hotel. We drove slowly, but at least we were moving.

Tom had already cleared my driveway for me, so pulling in and parking wasn't an issue.

"Well, Miss Stewart, it appears your marathon date with me has come to an end. We made the best of an unpleasant situation, and I think it went pretty well. I must say, though, my sore back will be happy to be in a comfortable bed tonight." I kissed him and told him I hoped his back felt better tomorrow.

"I'm headed home to take a hot shower, so that should cure my back. If I hear from Kate, I'll let you know." After a big hug, off he went.

My cabin seemed especially cool. I called out for Puff with no response. Where could she be? I checked the food bowl I left her, and at least she'd eaten. Her water bowl looked mostly untouched. I threw off my coat and went upstairs calling her name. There she was all snuggled up on my pillow. It touched my heart, and I felt guilty for being away. I picked her up to cuddle, but she wasn't receptive. I tried to explain my absence, but she wasn't having it. Hopefully, she'd forgive me given a little time.

After a hot shower, I built a fire and decided to make some soup from things I had left in the fridge. I piled everything in my Crock-Pot so I could smell it cooking all day. At noon, I heard from Cher. She was supposed to be taking inventory today at the gallery.

"Hey, Cher. Is the gallery closed while you do inventory?"

"Yes, unless someone knocks on the door to pick something up. But I'm taking a break to check on you because you've been MIA for a while." I chuckled as I began telling her what happened last night at Stone Harbor. She was amused by it and couldn't wait to tell Carl.

"Anna's having an open house this coming weekend, and so is Amy's quilt shop. Are you interested in going?"

"I suppose so, if the roads are good."

"I'll drive. We need to support them. Did you see in Anna's email that there would be a surprise?"

"No, I guess I missed it. Maybe she's going to expand."

"That's what I'm thinking. I'll pick you up at ten o'clock. We'll go to Anna's first and then Amy's."

"Great!"

Chapter 80

Later that night I heard from Grayson.

"I'm about to get a good night's sleep, but I feel there's someone special missing," he said.

"That's sweet. I miss you, too."

"I grabbed a pizza on the way home, made a quick call to Kelly, and then decided I needed a good night's sleep."

"Is everything okay with her?"

"Yes, she seems way too busy if you ask me, and I worry about her grades. I've got the worrying part of fatherhood down."

"I'm sure it's hard not to worry, but she'll figure everything out. I've been working on the sketch for her painting. You didn't tell her, did you?"

"No. Mum's the word."

We hung up, and I got to thinking about the *L* word. It seemed hard for Grayson to say he loved me, but when he did, it felt really special. His actions told me how he felt. People use the word *love* so casually today that its significance has been lost.

I went up to bed, and Puff left her warm quilt under the tree to follow me. It didn't take long to fall asleep after last night's unusual arrangement.

The next morning, I checked out the latest *Pulse*. The Christmas activities seemed to expand every year as more and more tourists stayed in the area. I had my shopping done, and I didn't need to bake cookies since I was going to Anna's Bake Shop later. Maybe Carole would send me some of hers like she has in the past.

As much as I dreaded going out in the snow, I needed to go to the post office. The snow had stopped, but roads could still be messy. If I was heading out anyway, I might as well make a stop for coffee.

I bundled up, and the cold wind hit my face. I looked one direction and noticed Ericka's tree standing tall against the challenges of the season. I could learn a thing or two from that evergreen. When I looked the other direction, the Bittners' house was snow covered and inactive. It gave me a lonely feeling.

It took me quite a while to scrape the deep snow and ice from my windshield. No warmer temps were in the forecast for the next week, so I figured I might as well tackle my car now. The inside of my Subaru was warming up with each minute I spent clearing off the outside.

I took my time driving to the post office to avoid sliding. Fortunately, someone had plowed and salted the lot, and other cars occupied only two of the spaces. I was pleased to find a few Christmas cards in my box.

One card caught my attention immediately. It was from Austen. I kept reading it over and over.

I want to wish you a merry Christmas. If you haven't heard, I'm about to get married. We're building a home in Cape Girardeau to accommodate my circumstances, so this will be my new address. I'll never forget your love for Christmas, and I'll never forget you.

Love, Austen

Why on earth did he think I needed to know his new address? Actually, why did he have to say anything at all about anything? Yes, I'm certain Christmas did remind him of my fondness for the holiday, but sending me this note seemed odd. Did his bride-to-be know he was sending this?

Another card was from Michael and Jon. That seemed odd as well because Michael didn't typically send me a Christmas card.

The last card I opened was from Foster. His card was a lovely winter scene of the Blacksmith Inn. He didn't include a note but had signed it *Love, Foster.* I chuckled to myself that I had three Christmas cards signed with *love.* I put them in my purse with a couple of bills and drove to the Blue Horse for coffee.

With the harsh weather, there wasn't a line this morning, which was a rarity. I looked at the painting I'd done of the Blue Horse after one of our quilt shows. An employee had purchased it at the gallery, and it always made me smile to see it hanging here. Oh, why did that last show have to go so wrong?

Chapter 81

"You just missed the guy with the red scarf," the girl behind the counter joked. I looked at her strangely. "That's your friend, right? I can't think of his name right now."

"You must be referring to Grayson Wills."

"Yeah, that's it. I should remember his name by now. He's here almost every day."

"This is actually where I met him." She nodded and smiled.

Today I left with hot chocolate instead of coffee. It sounded like a good complement to my cinnamon bagel. It was sweet of the girl to think of Grayson and me together. I should have asked her if he was with anyone this morning. On second thought, I didn't want to know if he was.

Instead of going home, I turned right to drive to the shops on the hill. I wanted to see their Christmas decorations close up. Every business did its own thing, and shop owners really outdid themselves decorating. Many of their customers were tourists who had gone back home; the decorations were for the locals who remained.

When I returned to my cabin, I placed my new Christmas cards on the mantel with the greenery, as I always did. I finally got busy with Kelly's painting. Puff hadn't moved from under the tree, but she was watching me. I had made just a little progress when Ava called.

"Claire, how are you?"

"I'm good. What's up?"

"I was wondering if you were planning to be at Anna's open house tomorrow."

"As a matter of fact, Cher and I plan to come together. How's Frances?"

"She's moving quite slowly and doesn't care to get out very much. I told her she needed to go tomorrow, but she can be stubborn. She's had some success with her predictions lately, so she has me doing all sorts of nonsense."

I chuckled. "Is she still going to the cemetery?"

"Only when I agree to take her. You know what horrid winter we've been having. The last time I took her she told her husband she'd be with him very soon."

"How sad. Maybe when she sees all of us, it will cheer her up."

"I hope so."

I hung up feeling guilty that I hadn't gone to see Frances very often. At least we saw her at quilt club once in a while.

By the end of my day, I'd made some progress on Kelly's painting and finished up my veggie soup. Now I was ready to relax and turn on a movie. I was pleased to see one of the old *Christmas Carol* movies was on. Even though I knew the ending well, it wasn't Christmas unless I saw the ghosts of past, present, and future spook Mr. Cratchit.

The story's message was that if you were cruel and selfish, there was a price to pay. I often wondered whether the movie ever changed someone's life after watching it. I watched till the very end and turned out the lights.

I lay there thinking of Frances. I wondered if she had a prediction that she was going to die soon. She had a surprisingly good track record with her predictions. When I first moved here, I told her I was looking for a place to sell my work. She said go to the guy who looks like Clark Gable. I chuckled, but as it turns out, Carl was that guy.

I hoped I wouldn't dream of all the ghosts from the movie, but they did manage to creep into my dreams in a strange way. I woke up and took a drink of water and then reached out to Puff to comfort me. All was well at the Stewart cabin.

Chapter 82

Cher picked me up at nine thirty, and we headed to Baileys Harbor, where Anna's Bake Shop was located. Cher was chatty. She always had more stuff to talk to me about because of her job with the public.

"Laurie Rosenthal has been stopping by the shop more these days. She keeps wondering why we don't go to the chamber meetings like we used to, especially with Grayson as president."

"I guess I should feel bad about it, but the timing never quite works out for me. Did Laurie say when the sisters were getting together?"

"Yes. Next week. She really wants us to meet them."

"I'm looking forward to it also. I think they want to stay on Main Street somewhere."

"That would be convenient for all the shopping they want to do. So, did Kate and Cole buy that property you told me about?"

"Yes. They're quite excited about it. I think Grayson is a little jealous of the spot they found."

"I'm sure you'll be invited to come over."

"I hope so."

The parking lot at the bakery was full when we arrived. When we walked in, I immediately saw Frances and Ava at a table. Anna spotted our group once Cher and I sat at a table for four nearby.

"I'm so tickled you all are here," Anna gushed.

"Well, we're eager to hear what the surprise is," I said.

"Oh, it's not much. We wanted an excuse to thank our customers since it's the holidays and all. Marta is in the kitchen, but she'll be out shortly to see you."

Anna engaged in conversation with Frances and told us to stay put, as there would be coffee and sweet treats coming out soon. The place was getting louder, which made it harder to actually visit. I kept my eye on Frances. She seemed uncomfortable.

All of Anna's baked goods were amazing as always, but my favorites were her apple strudel and cheesecake. Anna reminded me of Carole since both of them showed their love through baking. I needed to remember to take some goodies home with me. I served Frances a piece of cheesecake, and she seemed happy to connect with me.

"Oh, Claire, I've thought of you so often. I sensed someone other than Grayson was pursuing you and wondered how everything was working out."

"Well, that's true," I chuckled. "I did go astray for a bit, but Grayson and I have confirmed our relationship. Are you doing okay?"

"I'm just biding my time, as Ava may have told you," she said in a weak voice.

"Did she tell you we have a puppy at our house now?" Ava interrupted. "Her name is Polly, and we love her, don't we Frances?" Frances had no reaction.

"I worry when Ava goes out at night to walk her," Frances added with concern. "Our neighborhood isn't as safe as it used to be."

"We even took her with us to the cemetery, didn't we?" Ava bragged.

Just then Anna stood on a bench to get everyone's attention.

"Welcome to all!" she began loudly. "I want to thank you for coming out today to celebrate Christmas with us." Everyone cheered. "I also brought you here today to meet someone special in my life. His name is Pearson Schmidt, and he's from Germany also." More cheers erupted. "Pearson and I are happy to share that we're getting married on New Year's Day!" Now the crowd really got loud. We all looked at each other in surprise. Who knew?

Pearson had been standing next to Anna for their big announcement. He was a handsome man and did indeed look German. He seemed rather shy and was blushing from the attention. Marta beamed with pride as if it were her own daughter getting married. Minutes later, Anna rejoined us, and we were able to hug her and offer our congratulations.

"So, tell us about this big wedding!" I requested.

"It's just going to be a small gathering with family. We're too busy to plan much this time of year. Pearson will move in with me upstairs for now, but he loves construction, and he'd like to build us a house somewhere close by."

"That sounds perfect," I replied. "We're all so happy for you."

Many were eager to congratulate her, so she moved on, and we decided to head out. I picked out some pastries to take home with me and put in the freezer. I was glad to be leaving all the commotion.

Chapter 83

The Jacksonport Cottage quilt shop, owned by our friend Amy, was our next destination. Most of our chatter on the way there was about Pearson and Anna. What a surprise that was.

"Sometimes I feel like I'm the only single woman in the world," Cher said sadly.

"Besides me, you mean," I added with a grin.

Amy seemed happy to see us when we walked into her shop.

"Oh, I bet you came from Anna's open house," Amy surmised.

"We did, and we brought you a piece of cheesecake," I said, presenting it to her. "It was a great turnout."

"Thanks for thinking of me," Amy said. "Were the Quilters of the Door present?"

"Besides Marta, Ava and Frances were there," I recalled. "They have a new puppy named Polly to add to their lives. Ava seems more enthusiastic about it than Frances does."

"What was Anna's big surprise?" Amy asked.

"Well, you're not going to believe this, but Anna is getting married on New Year's Day to a man from Germany!"

I shared. "She was so happy to announce and introduce him. His name is Pearson, and he seems like a nice, quiet guy. Now we need to have a shower or something for her."

"That's such great news," Amy said, grinning.

"Well," Cher said, looking around the store. "What if we all chipped in and gave Anna a nice quilt? I happen to know someone who has a quilt shop." Amy beamed. "What pattern would you suggest, Amy? I don't know Anna's color preferences.

"What a great idea, Cher," I nodded.

"Now, you know I'd offer a wholesale price if you did such a thing," Amy added.

"Let's just do it," Cher announced. "Anna said they hoped to build a home in the future, so they'd be starting from scratch."

"You could always buy a gift certificate so she could pick out her own quilt," Amy suggested.

"That's probably the best way to handle it," I agreed.

While Amy helped a few customers, Cher and I looked around and decided on an amount that would get Anna something in the average price range. I was glad to get all that settled before we left the shop.

We were in a good mood and ready for a late lunch. Chives restaurant, one of my favorites in Door County, was nearby, so we decided to stop.

There were so many favorites on their menu. I decided on their French onion soup and a Caesar salad. Cher had their special of the day, which was chicken pot pie. We enjoyed our food tremendously as we jumped around topics of conversation.

"Now, Cher, you haven't given me an update on you and Carl in quite some time. How are things going now that you've met some of his family?"

She grinned. "Nothing has really changed. I know he cares about me, but he's never said the *L* word. I'm not sure he ever will."

"Are you in love with him?"

She looked at me for a while before answering, like she had to think about it. "I don't know. I find myself holding back because I don't want to risk someone hurting me. Neither one of us has really revealed how we feel."

"Well, this ambivalence could go on for years, Cher Bear, if someone doesn't make the first move."

"I think for now we're both happy with the status quo. We have to be careful not to show any affection in the shop, so I guess that adds to the confusion. You were a bit like that with Grayson for a while. Remember?"

"Well, not like that exactly. By the way, I don't think I told you I got a Christmas card from Austen."

"Oh really? Isn't the doctor supposed to be getting married soon?"

"Yup. He wanted to make sure I had his new address in Cape Girardeau, like I may need it."

"Oh, brother. What an ego that man has."

"I think he still considers me unfinished business. As always, he has to have the last word."

"Carole and Linda asked again if we were going to have another quilt show. I guess we need to decide that soon."

"I don't know about a quilt show, but we have money to do something somewhere. We owe it to Frances since she donated $1,000. We could do something in her honor."

"It has to be in Fish Creek, don't you think?"

"Yes, definitely Fish Creek. I guess we're partial to what it has to offer. I'm sure we'll think of something."

Chapter 84

The next day I decided to do something I hoped I wouldn't regret. I kept thinking about what kind of quilt event Cher and I could have other than an outdoor show. Foster was creative and had lots of contacts, so I sent him a text inquiring whether he had any ideas. I just hoped he wouldn't read into anything with my text.

I looked at my easel and was determined to finish Kelly's painting today. Rachael would need me at the farm again soon, so I had to make the best of my time. Thinking back on the early days of Kelly acquiring Spot, Grayson's initial resistance, and Puff meeting Spot helped me find my groove. I spent the next few hours bringing her cat to life on my easel. I was planning to have the picture framed at the gallery. I really hoped Kelly would like it.

My stomach started to growl, so I began preparing some chili. The phone rang, and I didn't recognize the number.

"Claire Stewart?"

"Yes."

"This is Anne Fletcher from Brown's Botanical."

"Well, of course. I'm so glad to hear from you again."

"When we talked at my shop, I told you that my husband and I planned to get back to Door County, but so much has changed that I felt I needed to give you a call."

"Is everything okay?"

She snickered. "It will be. We just learned that I'm pregnant. So pregnant that I feel ill almost every day."

"Oh my, but that's wonderful news for you."

"The timing isn't good. I thought I just had the flu till I went to the doctor. With the holidays, my shop is really busy, and I've not been much help. My Sammy is five years old now. This pregnancy has really caught the reverend and me off guard."

"Perhaps it's your Christmas miracle," I teased.

"We feel that way a little bit. It's Jack's first child, so he's over the moon with excitement and very protective of me. Fortunately, Sally, my manager, has gone way beyond the call of duty these days. Leaving now just isn't possible, so we've postponed our trip to Door County."

"Anne, I'm so happy for you. Have you told Sammy?"

"We have. Jack didn't want to wait. Ella, our housekeeper, is also excited about the news. She helped me so much when Sammy was born."

"I have a feeling you'll get back to Door County someday."

"We will for sure. I've told Jack all about it. He says when we go, we'll go as a family. I don't think I mentioned to you before that I'm a writer. I'm nearly finished authoring a book about the Taylor house, which has a long history, as you know. I do wish you could see our historic home, Claire. We've put so much care and love into the place."

"Well, I look forward to reading your book one day and, who knows, perhaps even visiting sometime."

"I took some time after we met at the shop to look up your website, and I must say, I'm so impressed with your art and your quilting. Some of my relatives were quilters, but I never had time to learn much. I do have a fondness for antique quilts. I'd love to show you an old quilt we found under my bench in the potting shed. The love letters pieced on the back revealed some surprisingly helpful family information."

"Wow! No wonder you're writing a book. Please stay in touch. I want to know more."

"Please visit us when you get back to Missouri. It feels like we've been friends for a long time even though we've just met."

"It feels that way to me, too. Thanks for calling to share your good news, Anne. I wish you and Jack all the luck."

"Thank you. I wish you and that significant other in your life a very merry Christmas."

"The same to you, Anne."

Chapter 85

As I stirred the pot of chili, I thought about my visit to Saint Charles with Grayson and what a wonderful conversation I'd had with Anne. If we hadn't shared a Door County connection, we'd have never met. Now she was beginning to feel like a real friend. I could only imagine how surprised she must have been to learn she was pregnant. What a shame her first husband died before knowing she was expecting. God surprises us with joy and sorrow at the most unexpected moments sometimes.

I took my bowl of chili to the porch. The steam from my bowl warmed and comforted me as I gazed out onto the winter scene before me.

It occurred to me that perhaps I should make Anne a baby quilt. She mentioned how much she loved quilts, and a baby quilt would be a fun change for me. I could hide it under her potting bench.

I was curious about the book she was writing on the Taylor house. If I wrote something, maybe it would be the account of my own relatively new experience of moving to Door County. I could write about how the locals and the tourists depend on each other. Or I could write about folks like Ericka, who fought to keep Door County's environment safe and beautiful.

I loved reading the historical articles by Patty Williamson in the *Pulse*. So many communities have a historian like Patty who's responsible for taking notes and telling stories in their small town. I often wondered about my very own log cabin. All Cher had told me was that in the 1940s, it was reassembled here from its original location in Peninsula State Park. I didn't know much else, such as who'd built it and who'd lived here through the years. Perhaps Patty could help me research it one day.

All the paint had dried on Kelly's painting, so I decided to take it to the gallery before they closed. The sun was shining, so I decided to walk. I wrapped the painting carefully and put on my coat and hat.

I passed a few Christmas carolers singing "Oh, Little Town of Bethlehem" on the front steps of the community church. That song was one of my favorites as a child. Fish Creek was a lovely place to call home.

Cher was at the counter when I arrived at the gallery. When I explained the urgency of having Kelly's painting framed in time for Christmas, she didn't make any promises.

"Well, does it fit any frames that you already have?" I asked.

"I'll check and see. This is quite good, Claire. The cat's eyes look quite real. I'm sure that's not easy to do."

"Thanks," I blushed.

She went to the back room to look for frames, and Carl appeared at the counter. "There will be no charge, Miss Stewart," he said. "Consider it a Christmas gift from me."

"Oh, Carl. That's so sweet of you, but it's really not necessary."

Whispering, he said, "I insist. Now, if you can give me a clue as to what to give your friend Cher, let me know." I nodded and smiled.

I said my goodbyes. Snowflakes were beginning to fall as I left the gallery. Christmas was definitely on the cusp.

Chapter 86

When I returned home, I thought more about making a baby quilt. I'd have to make a trip to the quilt shop to gather materials. I decided to call Olivia.

"Well, how are you, Claire?" Olivia asked.

"I'm well, but I need some help," I answered. "I finished the tie quilt I was telling you about. I can't wait for my brother to see it. The next quilt I want to make is a baby quilt. I have a friend who's having a baby, and I'd really like to make something for her. My fabric stash isn't conducive to that."

"Making a tie quilt is on my bucket list. I'm sure your brother will love his. I'll do what I can to help with the baby quilt. We just got in a fabric group from Moda that's blues and yellows. If you don't know the baby's gender, that fabric might be a good one. The log cabin pattern might work for it. It's so easy, and everyone loves it."

"Oh, and I love Moda fabrics! Great idea!"

"There's a yellow checkered pattern that I think would be darling for the back. If you like, I can pull everything you need for it and bring it to our quilt club meeting in January.

What about batting? Do you want me to grab some of that also?"

"Wonderful, Olivia, and yes, please include the batting. I wasn't sure what people were using these days for baby quilts."

"Consider it done. Now I have a surprise for you."

"Really? What?"

"As of yesterday, I'm the new manager of Barn Door Quilts!"

"That's awesome! Congratulations! I can't say I'm surprised, though."

"Well, I'm still in shock. I think the current owner is considering adding a second shop somewhere, but that hasn't been announced yet."

"You'll do great! And if I don't see you before, have a very merry Christmas. I'll look forward to seeing the baby fabric at our next meeting."

I hung up feeling so happy for Olivia. Everyone loved her, but she often felt self-conscious as a Black woman living in Sturgeon Bay. She'd probably share her news about the shop at show-and-tell next month.

I was smiling when I climbed into bed that night. I decided to text Cher about the phone call I'd had with Olivia. Cher didn't respond, so perhaps she was already asleep.

I still felt wired, so I turned on TCM and saw the beginning of one of my favorites, *An Affair to Remember*. I knew the movie word for word. The ending always made me feel terribly sad, so I only watched it for about forty-five minutes. Turning it off, I thought of Grayson. I was glad we had more going for us than an affair. My text went off. I thought it might be Cher returning my message, but it was Austen instead.

[Austen]
Hey. Just learned about your mother's wedding. Good for her. How do you feel about it? Did you get my card with my new address?

I shook my head in disbelief. Austen was using my mom's wedding to start a conversation. He may have unfinished business with me, but I was finished with him. His poor wife was in for a real treat. I was satisfied in knowing that they truly deserved each other. I turned over my pillow and decided to start my prayers. Austen's text didn't deserve an answer.

Chapter 87

Kate texted me the next day to say that she and Cole had to return home, but they'd return on the twenty-third to close on the property. She wanted to schedule a time for us to have a Christmas drink together. I told her I looked forward to that.

I wanted to ask Cher about Lee's Christmas party, so I sent her a text.

[Claire]
Good morning! Are you and Carl going to Lee's Christmas party at The Clearing? I'd mentioned it to Grayson that night we were snowed in at the lodge, but I haven't talked to him about it since then. Maybe just the quilting friends should go together.

[Cher]
I asked Carl, and he hasn't committed. Maybe you should talk to Grayson about it again.

[Claire]
I'll call him now.

"Hello, Claire," Grayson answered.

"I'm sorry to bother you at work, but I kept forgetting to follow up with you about the Christmas party at The Clearing that Lee from quilt club invited us to. It's tomorrow night. She's trying to get a head count."

I gave him more details, and he checked his calendar. He told me he could go, but he had to move some things around first.

"Formal attire, I presume?" he asked.

"Yes, likely so."

"I'll see you around eight o'clock tomorrow then, gorgeous." I smiled.

I wanted to finish my Christmas shopping today. I had in mind to go to the Christkindlmarkt in Sister Bay. I'd never been there before, but Cher and Brenda had raved about it. The Historical Society hosted it for three weekends, and this was the last day for it. The weather report told me it was thirty degrees outside, so I bundled up in layers before heading out the door.

Finding a parking spot was challenging because of the crowds, so I had a bit of a walk. There was still snow on the ground from last week, so I had to be careful not to fall.

The homey feel of the market reminded me of the Tannenbaum Christmas party that Rachael and Harry had thrown at the farm as a way of remembering Charlie. I bought a cup of hot chocolate to carry around with me to help my hands stay warm.

There were so many vendors selling handcrafted items made in Door County. With the chilliness of the day, the Swedish-style sweaters, hats, and gloves were popular. I picked out a heavy sweater for myself in red and blue trim that had *Merry Christmas* across the chest. I bought a clever tree made from real branches as a gift for Tom and a painting of a sailboat I could give to Grayson for his birthday. I also found a nice grouping of hand-carved wooden ornaments for myself and to give as gifts. I chose a tin of popcorn for George as a thank-you for his help with the tree. I was getting hungry, so I located a seat under the tent to enjoy a hot grilled sausage sandwich on a pretzel bun. It was fun watching the children running around trying to follow Santa. If I weren't so cold, I'd have stayed at the market a couple more hours, but my numb toes told me it was time to head out.

I had a real handful going back to the car, but I managed. My shopping today certainly put me in the Christmas spirit. Now I could say I'd attended my first Christkindlmarkt.

On the way home, I stopped by the post office to retrieve my mail. When I saw a large, padded envelope from Carole, I knew it must be her new book. Before I tore it open, I also noticed a Christmas card from Alice, Grayson's friend from the Moravian church. Two years ago, I attended their Christmas service.

I quickly flipped through Carole's book on coffee. She'd even included a section on the history of coffee in different cultures. I decided that my evening plans would be to read each page in front of the fire tonight. Before I got out of the car in my driveway, I decided to give her a call.

"I got the book!" I said with excitement.

"Merry Christmas! I received your package, too. Next time I'm there, I want to shop at that candle place."

"Sure thing. It's a fun store. Your book looks great. I love the cover and plan on reading it tonight. I'll be ordering some for others."

"I took one to your mom with some cookies, and she seemed thrilled."

"Oh, thank you. Was Bill there?"

"Yes, he was helping her in the kitchen with something. The place smelled wonderful. She has a real tree in the living room now. It's pretty."

"Oh, you're making me homesick. I'm sure glad she has Bill there to celebrate Christmas with."

"They seem happy."

Chapter 88

I took a hot shower to warm myself from the Christkindlmarkt and built a fire. It felt good to thaw out from the day's chill. I couldn't read a book about coffee without some to sip myself, so I made a cup of decaf before settling in on the couch. I spent the evening going through Carole's book page by page. I enjoyed reading about unusual ways to transform your humdrum morning coffee into something much more flavorful. Puff stayed right by my side, happy I was home.

I poked the logs to rejuvenate the fire and heard my cell phone ring. It was Cher, and she sounded awful.

"Cher, honey, what's wrong?"

"Carl said he wasn't interested in going to Lee's party with me. He gave me no reason and said he hoped I understood."

"Oh, I'm sorry. That doesn't seem like him."

"I know him well enough to know this isn't a good sign. He knows how much I was looking forward to going to something this formal. I'd even mentioned that going would be good for his business at the gallery. What do you think might be going on?"

"I really have no idea, but try not to make a big deal out of this. Maybe something about it made him feel uncomfortable, or there was something else he was already committed to doing. Unfortunately, he might not share with you why he said no if it involves something personal."

"Well, none of these comments are making me feel any better. Carl had to know from my reaction I was disappointed. I've been with him in public before, so I don't think that's the reason."

"Yeah, it's a shame he wasn't clearer with you. You do realize you can go without him, right?"

"I know, but the event will be mostly couples, and being there alone will make me feel even worse."

"Suit yourself. You're also welcome to go with Grayson and me."

"Absolutely not, Claire. I'm not going to be your date crasher. I was really looking forward to seeing The Clearing at Christmastime. It's so beautiful."

"Please don't let this get to you, Cher Bear. I'm sure Carl didn't mean anything by telling you no."

I finally hung up and went to bed shortly afterward.

The next morning, I thought of Cher again. I hoped she'd gotten some sleep. Carl's response did seem odd, but I remembered Austen often having other motives for his actions. I always assumed it had to do with one of his patients. I didn't know Carl very well, so I wasn't much help to Cher in figuring out his motives.

Tonight would be my big social event of the Christmas season. I had a red dress appropriate for Christmas that I'd worn once with Austen, but Grayson had never seen me in it. The sleeveless gown had an empire waist, and tulle covered the floor-length full skirt. My strand of pearls would pair well with it.

Around noon, Carl called to tell me the wonderful news that Kelly's painting was ready for me to pick up.

"Great! I can't wait to see it, Carl."

"I like the way it turned out. You might think of painting people's pets as another niche for you. You did an excellent job with this cat's eyes."

"Thanks for the compliment, but I did this for someone special and don't anticipate painting any more cats." He chuckled. "Hey, I heard you won't be joining us at the party this evening at The Clearing."

He paused. "Was Cher really upset?"

"She was disappointed, but she's a big girl."

"It's a bit complicated," he told me.

"I understand. I'll be in soon to pick up the painting."

I hung up wondering just how complicated his reason was.

Chapter 89

I tried on the red dress, and the bodice was a bit snugger than when I'd worn it last, but it still fit well enough. I chose to wear my hair pinned up so that my dangly pearl earrings and pearl necklace would stand out more. Perhaps people's eyes would be on my jewelry and not my dress.

Grayson showed up looking dapper, of course. He surprised me by wearing a red bow tie for the occasion, which I'd never seen him wear before. He grinned with pride when I noticed.

"Well, it's Christmas!" he explained.

"I see we both got the memo to wear red tonight," I teased. "You look so handsome."

"Flattery will get you everywhere. And you, sweetheart, look stunning. How did I get so lucky?"

On the long drive, Grayson told me that Kelly would be home in a couple of days.

"So, when can we have our own Christmas?" I asked awkwardly.

"Christmas Eve we go to Marsha's every year, and you're most welcome to go with us," Grayson offered.

"Oh, Grayson, I don't know if I should do that." He looked at me strangely.

"Are you free on Christmas Day? Or evening?"

"Either one."

"I think the twenty-third is when Kate and Cole will return, and we need to see them."

"It may work out that the Rosenthal sisters will be there that day as well."

"That sounds like a party to me. If you need a big place, my home is available."

"That's so generous of you, Grayson. I should hear from Laurie any day now."

In the center of The Clearing's large event room was the statuesque Christmas tree that stretched all the way to the skylight ceiling. The tree was classically decorated with white lights, burgundy ribbon weaving through the branches, and gold ornaments. Lee and Dr. Chan welcomed everyone as they came through the door. I peered through the crowd looking for other club members, but so far, I didn't recognize anyone.

Grayson left me to get us a drink, and Ginger and her husband Allen walked over. I had to do a double take, as the last I'd heard, they'd gotten divorced. Ginger was chuckling at my reaction, and both of them were grinning.

"You're seeing correctly, Claire," Ginger noted. "We're back together again."

"You did surprise me, but I'm so happy for you both," I said as I hugged each of them.

"Our children are happy, too," Ginger added. "Isn't this party grand? Did you see Ava with her new beau?"

"Ooh, no, I didn't," I replied as I looked around.

"He's a policeman," Ginger informed me.

Grayson returned and handed me a cocktail. Amy and Anna had come to the party together and joined us a few minutes later. I didn't realize Grayson hadn't met any of them until he introduced himself. They had a lot of questions about his job, which he graciously answered.

We left the group and mingled about the room. The buffet tables extended twenty-four feet. Gold tablecloths covered the tables, and intricate snowflake ice sculptures flocked each end. The entire room looked elegant. They'd spared no expense.

Grayson recognized a few folks. We soon realized many of those in attendance were doctors and their spouses.

We found a table to sit at and were able to enjoy the delicious food. Everything around us was beautiful, but we locked eyes on each other. We were thinking about leaving when Ava and her escort came up to us.

"Claire and Grayson, I'd like you to meet Kevin Masters, a friend of mine," she introduced.

"It's nice to meet you," we both replied.

"Claire, where are Carl and Cher tonight? I thought they were coming."

"They had a change of plans," I replied. "Did Frances make it tonight?"

"This event would have been too much for her," Ava noted. "But she's getting excited about Christmas, so if you have time to stop by, please do." I nodded.

We said our goodbyes and thanked Lee and her husband for inviting us. It had been a wonderful evening.

Chapter 90

When we got in the car to leave, Grayson caught me off guard.

"How about we go back to my place tonight?" He'd never suggested that before, and I wasn't sure what to say.

"Is that what you really want?" I asked sheepishly.

"Well, you haven't seen my decorations, Miss Stewart. And it's nice and quiet there."

"In that case, I'd love to."

Grayson's lovely home on a small lake wasn't easy to find, but it stood out among the others with its many festive Christmas lights. I didn't recall him having outdoor lights before.

"Wow! Did you do all this?" I marveled.

He grinned. "I'm afraid not, but I have a client now who does this kind of work. He had all these lights up before Kelly left, and she loved it, of course."

"It's gorgeous!"

"Wait till you see the tree."

He was right. The pre-lit tree was large and stunning in his well-decorated living room.

"Now, how about a nightcap, Claire? I just bought a new bottle of amaretto, and I'm anxious to try it. On the rocks?"

"Yes, with lots of ice. Oh, Grayson, you even have the lake lit up with lights. Your sunroom always pulls me there. I think it reminds me of my little porch. It's a piece of the outside, inside the house."

"Come sit by me," he suggested sweetly. "We haven't had a chance to catch up much lately."

"Well, I can give you an update on the farm," I noted. "Harry is going to add a food venue to the place. You know how he loves to cook."

"That's not surprising. It will be an immense success, I'm sure."

Grayson turned to put some music on. It was a nice, unexpected touch. He took my hand as if he wanted to dance.

"Can we slow dance to 'White Christmas?'"

I chuckled and accepted his arms. "Now if 'Jingle Bells' comes on, we may want to sit that one out."

I loved when Grayson held me like this. I could feel his heartbeat against mine, and he smelled wonderful. His cologne was subtle compared to Foster's and Austen's choices.

We swayed to the music without saying a word as he began to caress my back. The next tune was "I'll Be Home for Christmas," which reminded me of my home in Perryville. Every now and then Grayson would kiss me tenderly.

"I want you to spend the night here, Claire," he whispered. Once again, I was without the right words.

I paused and pulled back from him even though I didn't want to.

"I don't think I can, Grayson."

"Why?"

"I feel the presence of someone else in this house. Out of respect for Kelly and your wife of many years, I just don't feel comfortable."

He paused and took my hand, and we both went to sit on the couch.

"Sweetheart, the last thing I want is for you to be uncomfortable. You're important to me, and I respect your feelings. But I love you, Claire, and I just want to feel close to you."

Chapter 91

I pulled his other hand into mine. "Oh, Grayson, I love you too, but I have too much respect for Marsha to be more than a guest here." Grayson paused and looked to the floor.

"I guess I was just getting caught up in the moment."

"Of course, as was I. I'm flattered at the thought, but I think you should probably take me home where I belong." He smiled and nodded.

In silence, the two of us walked out of his home hand in hand and drove back to my cabin.

When we arrived in my driveway, I sensed Grayson wanted to talk. He opened up about his feelings toward and memories of Marsha. They hadn't had the perfect marriage I'd imagined. He and I both had built her up into something she wasn't. I began to feel closer to Grayson as he talked about her tragic accident and how broken he felt in the years after she died. Memories of the past took over the rest of the evening. It's not how I'd imagined our evening would end, but it's what needed to happen. It was hard for Grayson to open up, but he trusted me enough to share what he hadn't told anyone else.

When I walked up the stairs to go to bed that night, I felt a sense of pride. It would be a night I'd always remember. Things with Grayson felt different somehow. Better. More honest. Would tonight change our relationship in any way?

The next morning I woke to my cell ringing.

"Wake up, my friend," Rachael's voice commanded. "If you're lying in that bed alone, I want you to tell me about the magnificent party Harry and I missed out on."

I chuckled as I gave a big yawn. "Good morning to you, too! Yes, I'm alone, and the evening was lovely, as you'd expect. The big news is that Ginger and her husband are back together. They looked so happy."

"Oh, that's wonderful!"

"Ava was there with a date, and Amy and Anna came together. That was it as far as club members unless I missed someone. Folks were coming and going."

"What was Ava's date like?"

"Handsome and built like a bodybuilder. I understand he's a police officer."

"Interesting. Hey, the real reason I'm waking you up is to see when you can come and help out. We especially need you on Christmas Eve if you're available."

"I can come out tomorrow and get things ready for the sale. Do you have a lot of trees left?"

"Very few, which Harry is pleased about. He's got his mind on the cafe now, so he's meeting with folks."

"There's no time like the present. You'll be set for next year's season. Have you seen Brenda lately?"

"Oh my, yes. She had the girls with her yesterday, and they took over my kitchen to make Christmas cookies for their dad."

"How cute is that! Their relationship is sounding more and more serious."

"Honestly, I've never seen Kent happier. Don't forget, we always have a party on Christmas Eve if you can stay."

"I may. Grayson has his traditional plans with Kelly, and even though he invited me, I don't feel comfortable going."

"Consider his invitation a compliment. Maybe you should reconsider."

"I'll think about it. See you tomorrow."

The next morning, the sun shining on my face woke me up early. I needed to stop and get my mail on the way to Rachael's. As I poured my coffee, I happened to notice Puff wasn't eating her usual breakfast.

"What's the matter, my Puffy Pooh? Are you getting tired of the same ol' breakfast? How about if we try something new I bought for you?" She ran to her spot under the tree.

I replaced her food with a new brand and left her for the time being to dress for the day.

When I returned downstairs, she still hadn't touched her food. I picked her up, gave her a hug, and headed out the door.

I arrived at the post office and was happy to see a package from Mom. Surprisingly, there was also a letter from Michael. I stayed in the car to open Mom's present instead of putting it under the tree. As always, Mom wrapped her Christmas gift in white tissue paper and a red ribbon. She said her mom used to do the same thing. That tradition always made me smile. I was surprised to see a professional photo of her and Bill. Part of me smiled, and the other part felt disappointment. The frame was lovely, but I wasn't quite sure where I'd display it. There was just a small handwritten note that said *Merry Christmas.* I took a deep breath and went on to open Michael's letter.

Chapter 92

It read:

Dear Sis,

I regret that this Christmas keeps us apart once again. You requested I write something for you as a Christmas gift. As I think about your request, I can only write what is in my heart.

I owe you so much gratitude for continuing to keep our family's ties alive, even when my selfish career and personal life kept getting in the way.

We shared many good memories of our childhood, but one memory always comes to mind when I think of you.

Remember one year for Christmas when we each got a pair of roller skates? We were excited beyond belief and couldn't wait to get out to the sidewalk to try them out. I'm sure you'll remember what happened rather quickly. One of my skates fell into the sewer at the corner of our street as I was trying to adjust it. I'll never forget how my heart sank, and my tears were immediate. I knew I'd lost my new skate forever.

But you came rushing over to me and said I could have one of your skates. I couldn't believe your willingness to do that. Like the idiot brother I am, I took your skate and can't remember ever thanking you. You cheered me on when I put on your skate and flew down the sidewalk. I'm a little late, but I want to thank you ever so much.

Neither of us will be with Mom this Christmas, but luckily, Bill loves her and is taking good care of her. I think her present to us was to reassure us that she would be okay.

So, Sis, I wish you and Grayson a very merry Christmas. He seems to think the world of you, as he should. If he's as smart as I think he is, he'll not let you get away.

Jon and I are heading to Canada where Jon's mother is living. We'll be able to do some skiing while we're there.

Please know I'll always be here for you even after Mom is gone.

I'll love you always,
Michael

My head dropped into my hands and tears rolled down my face. How lucky was I to have this loving, sensitive brother? So many times over the years I'd written him off as someone who wanted me out of his life. There were so many awkward conversations and months of silence. What made him change?

I put his letter back in its envelope and decided to get a cup of coffee at the Blue Horse. I immediately saw Grayson's SUV and decided to turn around. I was feeling emotional, and I couldn't take a chance that he'd be there with Jeanne or someone else. My cell was ringing, so I stayed where I was.

"Claire, it's me, Laurie!"

"Oh, hello!"

"I'm sorry I didn't call you sooner, but my family is in Green Bay now. They're all planning to be here on the twenty-third. Christmas Eve and Christmas Day will be at my sister Loretta's house."

"I'm so happy for you!"

"Well, about the twenty-third ... How about meeting up with all of us for dinner at the White Gull Inn? They'll be shopping all day, and that's where they always want to eat. They're excited to meet you."

"I suppose that'll work. We're also supposed to meet up with Kate and Cole from Borna. They're closing on a piece of property in Sturgeon Bay."

"Is that the couple who has a guest house you were telling me about?"

"Yes, that's them."

"Well, I'm sure my family would love to meet others from Missouri. I already have reservations, so I can just change the number with no problem."

"Oh, Laurie, that would be too much to ask. I don't know when they'll be free, so I'd have to get back to you."

"Not to worry. I'm so excited my sisters are here. I was hoping my niece Sarah would be joining them, but she couldn't take time off of work. I should probably get going because I have a lot to prepare for. I'm so glad we have some things planned."

"Thanks for checking with me. I'll get back with you to firm things up."

Feeling better and a bit more chipper, I decided I was hungry. The Fish Creek Market always had a delicious lunch special you could order out. I headed that way with my stomach growling.

Today's special was shrimp scampi and a roll, which sounded delightful. I ordered that and picked up a new kind of cat food and a toy for Puff and one for Spot. I was hoping that new food and a toy would perk up Puff.

Chapter 93

As soon as I got home, I checked on Puff to see how she was doing. Her food bowl in the kitchen was still full. I watched her take a sip of water and walk away.

"Oh, but wait, my sweet girl. Mama bought you some new food to try today." When she left the room, I put the new cat food in a clean bowl and called her name, to no avail. I went to the porch and picked her up. I wanted her to at least smell the new food, so I brought her back to the kitchen with high hopes.

She looked up at me when I placed her in front of the bowl.

"Try some, Puffy. You must eat." With that, she meowed and walked around the bowl. As she got closer, it was hard for her to resist the smell of fish. Once she took the first bite, she continued till her bowl was clean.

"Merry Christmas, Puffy," I said, dancing around the kitchen. When Puff was happy, Mama was happy.

I needed to decide where to put the picture of Bill and Mom. My mantel currently held my old photo of Mom and Dad. I supposed I should replace it with this new photo and put the old one in my bedroom. Now I just had to figure out where to keep Michael's letter since I knew I'd want to read it over and over again.

By two o'clock, I was ready for a short nap, but a call from Grayson interrupted my plan.

"How's my favorite girl?"

I smiled. "Couldn't be better. How is my favorite guy?"

"He's peachy." I chuckled. "I just heard from Cole, and their closing is still the afternoon of the twenty-third. They'd like us to celebrate with them that night if you're free."

"Maybe we could celebrate with them at the White Gull Inn where there would be another party going on."

I explained all the details from Laurie's call and how fun it would be to have all the folks from Missouri in one party. I went on and on excitedly. Finally, he got a word in.

"Everyone loves the White Gull Inn. Let's do it!"

"You'll let the Alexanders know then?"

"I'll tell them we'll have the champagne cooling for them."

When I hung up, I couldn't wait to call Laurie. The phone rang seven times, but she finally answered.

"Sorry about that. I had a customer."

"No problem at all. I'm just calling to tell you that the gathering at the White Gull Inn will work out perfectly. I can't wait for you to meet everyone."

"That's great! It will be quite a party."

Laurie hung up just as Mom was calling.

Chapter 94

"Am I interrupting your painting or anything?" she asked meekly.

"No, I've been sloughing off today, and tomorrow I'll be back at the Christmas tree farm. Are you calling to find out whether your photo arrived?"

"I suppose I am. But I also wanted to thank you and Michael for the beautiful photo from Thanksgiving and for the Door County coffee. The picture looks so nice hanging in the living room. It's a lovely reminder of our time together that evening."

"I'm glad you got our gifts. And I love the picture of you and Bill, Mom."

"Really? I was worried about it."

"It arrived this morning, and I couldn't wait to put it on my mantel. I also got a wonderful letter from Michael that made me cry. I asked him to write something for me, and he sent me the sweetest letter thanking me for being a good sister and telling me he'd always be there for me."

"Well, now I'm going to cry. I have to say, he's maturing and really starting to value his family more. Your news is the best Christmas present I could have asked for."

"How so?"

"There's no better gift than having your children love and respect one another." I smiled. "I'm also enjoying some of Carole's Christmas cookies, as well as her new book. She's really something, and so incredibly good to me."

"She's wonderful. I hope she keeps writing. By the way, the couple from Borna is coming to close on a wonderful piece of property on the lake."

"Will they move there and sell the guest house?"

"No, nothing like that. It's just a sound investment they'll be able to enjoy whenever they have free time."

"Good for them."

"Now, what exactly do you and Bill have planned for Christmas since Michael and I won't be there?"

"Church, as always. Bill said his daughter will drop by Christmas Day, so we'll enjoy seeing her. What about you and Grayson?"

"We just went to a lovely Christmas party together with some of my quilt club buddies. Grayson invited me to go with him and Kelly on Christmas Eve to his late wife's family gathering, but I'm going to pass. We'll be together on Christmas Day, I suspect."

"How nice. I was curious about all the ice shoves I keep hearing about on the news. I'd never heard of those until you moved to Fish Creek. You've had quite a winter there."

"The ice shoves are quite huge this year, especially down by Sunset Beach near my house."

"You should send me pictures. Oh, I just noticed the time. I need to get this chicken in the oven. I'm so pleased you like the photo, and thank you again for your thoughtful gifts."

Her priority was getting Bill's chicken in the oven. She couldn't be happier having someone to take care of.

I looked at my easel all covered up and felt like putting a sign on it that said, "See you after Christmas." My focus needed to be on the Christmas tree farm right now.

Why hadn't I heard from Cher about last night's party? She could have just come alone. I decided to call her.

"Are you at work?" I asked quickly.

"Yes. I'll be leaving shortly to go home and stew some more about Carl."

"Why don't you stop by for a cocktail instead?"

"Okay. That's the best offer I've had in a while. I'll see you in about half an hour."

She sounded so down. I knew she was bummed out about Carl not wanting to go to the party. I decided we needed a snack with our cocktail and conversation, so I put a pan of stuffed mushrooms and cocktail sausages in the oven. I checked on Puff, and she seemed back to her normal self. I guess she just needed a change like all of us do from time to time.

I greeted Cher with a hug before she even stepped inside.

"Thank you," she said as she walked in. "I needed that. What smells so good in here?"

"Just a little treat to go with your favorite wine."

"You're so kind, Claire Bear. So is Puff under the tree for the whole season?"

"Yeah, pretty much," I answered as we both took a seat on the couch.

"I'm so tired of winter. I can hardly take this cold anymore."

"Cher Bear, you've been in a sour-puss mood. Spill it."

"What do you mean?"

"Is it because Carl didn't go with you last night?"

"Maybe. You know, Claire, I'm not sure we'll see each other much when the gallery cuts its Christmas hours."

"Oh, I don't know about that. He cares a great deal for you. By the way, the group asked about you several times last night."

"It was fabulous, wasn't it?" Cher asked with envy.

"Indeed, it was. I won't lie. I couldn't help but wonder about having a quilt show there. It's such a nice building, and we wouldn't have to worry about rain."

"You would be thinking of that," she teased. "Weren't you going to ask Foster for a suggestion?"

"I did, and I've gotten no response, which kind of surprises me. I think he's starting to realize I'm serious about just being his friend and nothing more. Hey, did Laurie tell you that her sisters will be here soon?"

"She did, but I can't go. George is having all of their Hanson family over for dinner, and he wants me to be there. He said to invite Carl, but I may not. I don't want him to turn me down again."

Chapter 95

"Darn. I wish you could go. Kate and Cole are closing on their place and are going to join us that evening."

"Some people have it all, don't they?" Cher said with envy.

I continued to bring up things to try to lighten her spirits. She was moved when I read Michael's letter to her. When I showed her the photo of Bill and my mom, she didn't respond.

"Should I give you your Christmas present now to improve your mood?" I asked to tease her.

"I don't even have yours wrapped yet, so we'd better wait."

"When should we exchange?"

"Whenever," she said, shaking her head. "I guess I'm just not in the mood this year."

"Maybe this wine is making you whiny," I joked. "Is it Ericka's absence?"

She broke into tears and covered her face. "Oh, Claire Bear. You're such a dear to think of her. This is my first Christmas without her, and it's hard. I'm so glad we planted that tree, but looking at it is a constant reminder of her being gone. You know we're not getting any younger. I feel like my life is just passing me by sometimes." She blew her nose as she held back tears.

"Cher Bear, you know I'll always be here for you. We've been through everything together, and there's no getting rid of me now. You're healthy and you have a job you love, not to mention the handsome guy that comes with it. You need a lesson in gratitude, my friend."

She looked up at me. "Oh, Claire, I'm sorry," she said as she reached for another hug.

"I'll tell ya what. How about the two of us share Christmas Eve together, just like we used to do?" I could tell the words sounded comforting to her. She nodded and smiled, like a little child.

Cher left feeling a tad better. I was hoping some of my words would resonate with her. I hated to see her hurting.

It was getting late, so I cleaned up the kitchen, put out the fire, and went up to bed.

The early hour came sooner than I wanted it to. I peeked outside my bedroom window. It looked like it could snow again.

When I came down for breakfast, Puff was eagerly waiting for me to fill her bowl, which was a pleasant change from yesterday. It didn't take long for her to finish, and back under the tree she went.

I left for the farm in the early-morning darkness. Still half asleep, I arrived in the parking lot with plenty of other folks. If they were ready for the day, so was I.

Harry had just finished making the coffee when I walked in.

"Good morning, Claire. It's always good to see ya."

"How's the cafe coming along?"

"Things are moving as we speak. Enlarging the white house seems to be a much better plan than building a new structure, but I'm beginning to wonder if it's any cheaper."

"Well, it'll be worth it in the end."

"It's hard to make any progress on the cafe while we're finishing out the tree season. Hey, when you're hungry, grab some pulled pork from the Crock-Pot. I think you'll like it. It's a shame we didn't get to the Chan Christmas party the other night. I heard it was a dandy."

"It was. You two need to have some fun. It's Christmas, you know."

Harry burst into laughter. "I have fun every day here with that loving spouse of mine. Hey, speaking of Rachael, did she ever tell you about the book *The Christmas Tree Ship*?" I shook my head. "If you love Christmas trees, like I do, you need to read it. Once a year, in the early 1900s, a three-masted schooner festooned with lights would float down the Chicago River to supply Chicagoans with their Christmas trees. Some crew members on the ship didn't make it because of stormy, winter weather. I finally got Rachael to read the book to learn a little more history of the Christmas trees on the Great Lakes."

"Harry, we need to find that book to sell in the gift shop!"

"Good thinking, Miss Stewart. That's why we pay you the big bucks to work here." He roared with laughter and went out the door.

"Good morning, Claire," Rachael said as she came inside. Are you ready to work?"

"I got my coffee, so let's begin. Harry just told me about the book *The Christmas Tree Ship*." Rachael smiled and nodded. "I said we should sell it in the gift shop."

"Sure. Make a note for next year. Today I want you to check the inventory in case you want to put anything on sale before Christmas. Keep track of what things we can save in the warehouse for next year."

"I can do that."

"Brenda is coming in this afternoon after her morning shift. Everything is ready for the UPS guy on this side table. Today will be the last big rush before Christmas, so we'll be busy."

As the activity of the morning slowed down, Rachael wanted all the details about the Chan party. I caught her up and had just finished my wonderful BBQ sandwich when Brenda joined us. She looked beat.

"Brenda, you look so tired," I told her. "Are you sure you don't need to get home? Rachael and I have been doing fine."

"I'm just exhausted. We're busy at the restaurant with the holidays, and Kent has me doing child duty when I'm free."

"That's a lot," I agreed.

"Yesterday we took the girls to the PC Junction for lunch. Have you ever been there?"

"No, I haven't, but I heard kids love it."

"We sat at the counter, ordered our food, and it's brought to you on a railroad car. The train whistles are enough to drive you crazy, but all the kids are screaming with delight when it goes by. I've never seen anything like it. We enjoyed our hamburgers. Afterward we let the girls play in the area outside."

"I'm exhausted just hearing about it. You're a good sport to share that experience with them."

Chapter 96

The rest of the day wasn't quite as busy as expected, so I had a little more time to visit with Brenda before she left. I filled her in on meeting up with the Rosenthals. She actually remembered them coming to the White Gull Inn each year to have dinner.

"Your Christmas will really be different this year with Kent and the girls in your life. Have you purchased their gifts yet??"

She nodded. "Thanks to Kent. I'd be lost on what to get the girls otherwise. They're getting a puppy from Santa, and they'll be over the moon about that."

"Oh, how fun! How did the cookie baking go?"

"Is that what that was? It was a big mess; that's what it was. Never use sprinkles or glitter. I'm still finding evidence from that baking spree!"

"Are the girls ever with their mom?"

"Almost never. They throw such a fit if they have to go, and frankly we know she'd rather not have them. I just can't believe it. It breaks my heart."

By five o'clock, Brenda and I joined Rachael with glasses of wine. Rachael didn't think she'd need me tomorrow, which was fine by me.

The next morning, I thought more about spending Christmas Eve with Cher. I didn't need to be a fifth wheel with Grayson and Kelly. I hoped Grayson would understand. I opened up the *Pulse* at the kitchen table, and my cell rang. It was Michael.

"Hey, Sis. Are you up?"

"Yes, I'm just taking it easy. I worked at the farm yesterday, but things are winding down now."

"I just had to call and thank you for the gorgeous tie quilt you sent. I can't believe you really made that. I must have given you a real guilt trip when I gave you Dad's ties."

I chuckled. "In fact, you did. But once I came up with the bookshelf idea, I got excited about making it. I'm so glad you like it."

"I really do, as does Jon. I have it hung in my office. You know, I actually remember our dad wearing some of those."

"So do I. Who would have thought those ties would someday end up in a quilt? I must say, Michael, your letter was simply lovely. You have no idea how much it meant to me. I have it in my bedside table drawer to remind me about you once in a while." I could tell Michael wasn't sure how to respond.

"Well, mission accomplished then. I guess I'm better at writing my feelings than saying them out loud. It sounds like we're both happy about our gifts this year. That certainly wasn't always the case when we were kids." I chuckled, remembering some of the horrendous presents we'd gotten each other.

We continued sharing our plans for the holidays. He admitted that he really didn't know what to do with Mom and Bill's photo. I could relate.

We hung up, and I had a smile on my face. I was really beginning to like this brother of mine. I poured another cup of coffee and looked once more out the window. I saw Tom get out of his truck, so I went to the door in my robe to wave him my direction so I could give him his Christmas gift. I hoped he would like the hand-carved tree I purchased for him.

Chapter 97

"How ya doin', Miss Claire?" Tom asked. "Ya ready for Christmas?"

"Come on in from the cold. I have a little something for you. It's not much, but I thought of you when I was at the Christkindlmarkt."

"It's a neat place, isn't it? I helped them with the tents one snowy day. I won't do that again!" We both laughed.

Tom's eyes got big as he opened his gift.

"Oh my, Miss Claire. You didn't have to get me anything, but I really love this. I've always liked this guy's work. I wish I was a little more creative so I could make things like this. Thank you so much."

"I'm glad you like it, Tom. I don't suppose you've heard from the Bittners?"

He shook his head. "Usually I don't hear from them until they're ready to come home. They're happy when they don't hear from me because it means everything's fine at the house."

I chuckled. "Since they're not here, can't you let some of their snow pile up?"

"No ma'am," he said firmly. "They want me to do what I always do for security reasons mostly. It looks like they're home when their snow's cleared off."

"I understand."

It was easy to please Tom, and I was so lucky to have all this help through the year. I wished him a merry Christmas before he left.

Feeling more confident about my plans for Christmas Eve, I sat down by the tree and called Grayson.

"Hey, good looking! What's on your mind?" he answered cheerfully.

It took me a while, but I explained to him how down Cher had been since Ericka's death and that I wanted to spend the day with her to cheer her up. He didn't seem to mind much when I declined his family invitation. He probably expected it. He said Kelly returned home yesterday and had a present for me. I told him I was looking forward to giving her the painting of Spot.

"How about you and I exchange gifts after the dinner party at the White Gull Inn? Then Christmas night, you can come over, and you and Kelly can exchange."

"That sounds perfect."

"I'm taking Alice to an early dinner tonight, and Kelly promised she'd go with me. Alice loves her."

"That's nice of Kelly to join you. So, are you attending the closing with the Alexanders?"

"No, but I'm looking forward to celebrating with them afterward."

I was happy with how my holiday plans were shaping up. I couldn't wait to firm things up with Cher for Christmas Eve.

When I called her and told her I couldn't wait to spend the day with her tomorrow, she seemed to really perk up. She offered to make her mom's bread pudding recipe, which was tradition on Christmas Eve.

When we hung up, I made my grocery list and headed to the Pig. Driving through Sister Bay this time of year was always a treat. I loved all their decorations.

The Pig was packed, but it was all the excitement of things to come. I found a perfect turkey breast to fix for the two of us. I also bought my favorite cranberry relish from the deli. The rest of the sides would be easy enough to make on my own.

I ran into George as I was ready to get in line.

"I didn't know you liked to cook, George," I teased.

"When I'm in the mood, there's no stopping me. I'm going to fix a duck for Christmas dinner, which I haven't had in ages."

"Wow, I'm impressed. Cher and I are having turkey on Christmas Eve. Did she tell you she's coming over?"

"I'm so glad you made plans with her. We've both been down without Ericka. You're like family to her. Say, do you need help taking anything to your car?"

"No thanks, but if I don't see you, have a merry Christmas."

"You too, Claire Bear," he said lovingly.

On the way home, I felt the urge to stop in at the Hide Side Corner Store, where I always found delightful clothing. It would be nice to have a new outfit to wear to the White Gull Inn dinner. It didn't take me long to spot a three-piece burgundy knit outfit that was simple and stunning. It was on the expensive side, but I loved the color and fit. Merry Christmas to me! There's nothing like a new outfit to get you in a good mood.

Chapter 98

I had cleaning to do and preparation for my Christmas Eve dinner. Cher and Grayson's gifts were under the tree, but I wish I had more to give Grayson. What do you buy a guy who has everything?

Making Mom's recipe for dressing made me feel a little homesick. Hopefully, I'd remember everything because she never wrote it all down. I wanted to do as much as I could ahead of time to prep for our dinner. Tomorrow was going to be busy with the Missouri crowd.

As I was searching for my bottle of dried sage, a UPS driver stopping in front of my cabin interrupted me. He brought a large package to my door, which I could hardly wait to open. Then I noticed it was from Foster. Oh no. It was a sweet painting of quilts blowing in the wind on a clothesline. It was titled *Quilting Free*, which I thought was an odd name for it. Foster had signed it, which I hadn't expected. Quilts weren't normally something he painted. Attached was a note that said,

Someday you'll be as free as these quilts.
It was a quick paint, but I hope you like it.

Merry Christmas!
Foster

I didn't like the message he was sending me. I took the painting upstairs immediately so Grayson wouldn't see it, and I tore up the note. I didn't want to even think about it.

At five o'clock that evening, I got a call from Laurie to see if we were still on for our dinner at the White Gull Inn tomorrow. She said if they were a little late, it would be from their busy day of shopping.

"I'm excited to see everyone. Please don't stress yourself out over introductions. We'll be fine on our own."

"I'm excited to see Kate again, if she remembers me," Laurie noted.

We hung up, and I could only imagine how excited Laurie must be to see her sisters. I envied her. Cher and Rachael were the closest I had to sisters.

The last chore for the day was getting live greenery and berries from the yard to put on the kitchen table to make it look festive. I had a card table–sized Christmas tablecloth adorned with my grandmother's china that paired perfectly with my gold-rimmed crystal glasses. You would have thought the king and queen were coming to dine tonight. But Cher was worth it, and I could only hope this would cheer her up.

I went up to bed that evening full of excitement. Christmas was actually here, right in my own little cabin. I fell asleep and didn't wake up till eight o'clock the next morning.

As I nursed the delicious coffee I'd made using one of Carole's new recipes, I thought about what a big day this was going to be for so many people. Kate and Cole must be excited beyond belief about their new place, and Laurie and her sisters were going to have so much fun reconnecting. The sun was shining, but my phone said it was only fifteen degrees in Door County. I could imagine the Rosenthal girls flying in and out of stores to do their Christmas shopping, not even minding the cold. It was chilly in the cabin, so I decided to start a fire.

I sat in front of the fire with my English muffins and coffee. Right now, everything was so peaceful, and I was thanking God for this special day. I hadn't checked my phone yet. I'd missed a text from Grayson.

[Grayson]
Kelly's home. She tells me she now has a boyfriend at school. You should see her short haircut. I can't believe after all these years she'd do that. I'm not too happy about it. I'll see you at six o'clock, right?"

I had to chuckle.

[Claire]
Yes, six o'clock. Your daughter is growing up. Be happy!

I could only imagine the adjustments Grayson was going to have to make with Kelly in the next three and a half years. Kelly had told me she wanted to pursue a career as a vet, but we'll see. It's hard to figure out what you want to do with the rest of your life when you're eighteen.

Chapter 99

Linda had sent me an email wishing me a merry Christmas. She said she was still working on my Christmas gift, but she'd send it soon. She told me how much she loved the Door County candles. Oh, how I missed her and Carole. I really treasured these lifetime friends. We'd been in each other's lives for decades, sharing all of life's ups and downs. They were also so good to Mom in my absence.

By late afternoon, it was time to put on my new outfit and prepare for a fun evening. Knowing Grayson was coming here afterward to exchange gifts was making me nervous. I wondered what he'd give me this year. Why hadn't I tried to paint him something?

I decided this outfit called for silver jewelry instead of my usual pearls. I found some silver dangly earrings that would complement my hair's updo. My black heels would do nicely, but I sure hoped I remembered how to walk in them. I couldn't remember when I last wore three-inch heels.

I descended the stairs with care to keep from falling. I put some Christmas music on low and turned down the lights to create the warm feeling of Christmas. The lights from my tree, mantel, and staircase were all I needed.

Prince Charming then appeared at the door to pick up his Cinderella. I pulled him inside with open arms and followed his eyes up and down as they checked out my appearance.

"You look amazing, my dear," he said sincerely.

"And you look as handsome as ever," I replied, giving him a kiss on the cheek.

"I heard from Cole that all went well at the closing."

"Great! I'm so happy for them."

Laurie was waiting at the entrance to the White Gull Inn to greet everyone when we arrived. I was happy to see the healthy fire in the lobby fireplace to take off the chill. Folks whom I presumed to be her family filled the room.

"Claire and Grayson, welcome," Laurie said with excitement. "The gang's all here. Are you ready to meet them?"

"Absolutely!" I gushed.

"We'll start with Loretta and Bill," Laurie began. "As I believe I mentioned to you before, Loretta is a nurse, and Bill is a professor at the University of Wisconsin in Green Bay." The handsome couple were more than happy to meet us, it appeared.

"Impressive school," Grayson noted. "I wish my daughter would have chosen to go there." Bill chuckled.

"It's so nice to meet you, Claire," Loretta responded. "Laurie has been talking about you, and I'm glad to finally meet you, too. Our family just found out some exciting news. We're going to be grandparents again!"

"Congratulations!" Grayson and I said at the same time.

"Now meet my sister Lily," Laurie said, guiding us in another direction. Lily turned around at the sound of her name and offered me a big, welcoming smile. "Lily, this is Claire Stewart and Grayson Wills."

"It's a pleasure to meet you both. I've got to say, Claire, when Laurie told me you were a quilter, I looked you up online so I could check out your quilts." I couldn't believe how much Laurie and Lily looked alike.

"Oh, that's right. You're the one who owns Lily Girl's Quilts and Antiques in Augusta."

She nodded. "I only sell antique quilts, but I love all kinds of quilts. Do you remember the Hill area in St. Louis?"

"Of course!" I replied. "It's where you get the best Italian food around."

"Well, I lived there before moving to Augusta to open my shop. There are benefits to being single, despite Loretta's efforts to fix up Laurie and me." They all chuckled.

"There's nothing wrong with that," I added. "Are there still a lot of wineries in Augusta?"

"More than I can count these days," Lily answered. "You probably know that Missouri is known for the Norton grape. Next time you come home, we'll have to visit a few wineries."

"That sounds like fun," Grayson responded. "We both appreciate good wine, don't we Claire?"

Chapter 100

"Unfortunately, Lynn had to cancel at the last minute," Laurie told us. "She filed for divorce, and things are a bit crazy now, so she felt she couldn't take the time. We hope she gets through this okay."

"I'm sorry to hear that," I responded. "I was looking forward to talking to her about her art gallery."

"She wanted to meet you as well," Laurie noted. "Her marriage has had its ups and downs, and I think she's ready to move on." I nodded. "She told me to tell you that she, too, looked at your website and admires your work. You may want to contact her if you're interested in having some of your art in her gallery."

"Oh, I will indeed," I responded.

"So, poor Bill here is the only guy in the bunch," Grayson noted with humor.

"You got that right," Bill responded. "It's a challenge with these ladies who want to go, go, go. I had a good nap today while they shopped." Grayson chuckled.

"Bill knows he can't get a word in when we sisters are together," Loretta admitted. "We're all about food and shopping. I should visit Laurie here more often. I think we'll come back another day before everyone goes home. By the way, I'm the quilter of the family. Laurie told me all about the outdoor quilt show you did here in Fish Creek. I wish I could have seen it. Laurie said the show was good for her shop."

"The show has its challenges, but Main Street is perfect for the venue," I said.

"Claire, the Alexanders just arrived," Grayson noted. "Would you like to join me in greeting them?"

"Please excuse us for a bit," I said to the group. "We invited a couple from Borna, Missouri, to join us tonight. They just closed on some property in Sturgeon Bay."

"We look forward to meeting them," Lily said. "I'm familiar with that area in East Perry where all the little German towns are located."

"Yes, and I want Kate to tell you all about her guest house."

We finally got around to saying hello to Kate and Cole as they were removing their coats.

"Congrats, you two," I said. "Grayson told me the closing went well." Both nodded and smiled.

"Claire, you're going to have to take Kate off my hands," Cole complained. "She's talking nonstop about all her plans for the place." We all chuckled.

"I can understand," I said, nodding. "I'd be doing the same thing."

Grayson added, "I'll let Claire tell you a little more about the Rosenthal family here tonight. They have Missouri roots and are anxious to meet you."

"You'll love them," I said with excitement. "You met Laurie at her shop Trinkets when you were here the last time, remember?" Kate nodded with a smile.

Chapter 101

The harpist started playing, and everyone slowly found their assigned seat. Grayson had his arm around me as we sat down and whispered how hungry he was.

Laurie had placed us at the end of the long dining table with Cole and Kate. On one side of me was Grayson, and on the other was Lily. The chatter was loud while everyone was ordering their drinks. From what I could tell, almost everyone was drinking wine. When the head server finally got our attention, he listed the specials of the evening. Grayson was excited about the blue cheese crusted filet. I went for a seafood combo. When we finished placing our orders, Laurie stood up at the other end of the table to get our attention.

"Welcome, family and friends," she began with a nervous voice. This is our grand finale to a wonderful day. Claire, Grayson, Kate, and Cole, thank you for joining us at our traditional dinner. I took the liberty of ordering a variety of appetizers for us. We appreciate having a place like the White Gull Inn to accommodate our large group and serve such delicious food." Everyone agreed.

"I believe everyone has met the Alexanders by now, so I want to personally thank the Rosenthals for letting us crash their party," Grayson announced. "The Alexanders are here to celebrate their closing on a piece of Door County property today, so I'd like to make the first toast to them. Welcome to Door County, Kate and Cole!" Everyone cheered and congratulated them.

Next, Bill stood to extend his good wishes and thank Laurie for getting everyone together. He talked about what a blessing it was to have this time to gather with family and announced he'd just learned he was expecting another grandchild. Everyone cheered.

"So, with the season at hand, I'd like to wish everyone a merry Christmas, including those who could not be with us this evening."

Everyone cheered, "Hear, hear." I nervously stood up next.

"It's a pleasure to be with all of you this evening. I think we can toast the state of Missouri for bringing us together."

Everyone laughed and cheered, "To Missouri!"

"Well done, Miss Stewart," Grayson said, squeezing my hand when I sat down.

No one else made a toast, but the conversation that flowed felt like we were one big, happy family. The Rosenthals encouraged Grayson and me to come to St. Louis so I could bring my work to Lynn's gallery and then travel on to Augusta where Lily had her shop. Loretta continued to have questions about our quilt show and said she'd plan to return to Door County when we had another one. I briefly told Loretta that after the disaster last year, I wasn't sure there would be another one, especially outdoors. She told me she was sorry to hear that. Lily mentioned that she was hoping to persuade Lynn to move to Augusta after the divorce, but Lynn was more attached to the Hill.

"Grayson," Loretta called to get his attention. "You don't have any eligible men friends for my sisters Lily and Laurie, do you?" she teased. "Oh, and now Lynn, too!" Grayson blushed and grinned.

"I think they all seem pretty happy with the freedom of being single. And Lynn, for sure, will need a taste of single life," Grayson responded.

"I'll keep them in mind," I said with a smile.

I could tell Laurie was pleased with how everything was going. She was especially happy when Kate told her she'd be in to purchase some things for their new home in Sturgeon Bay.

Bill, Cole, and Grayson discussed real estate in Door County, which was right up their alley.

Many were too full for dessert despite the fact that the inn was known for its cherry pie. After everyone finished eating, Bill stood and invited the group to join him in the lobby for an after-dinner drink. Grayson offered to order us a glass of amaretto on ice, but I passed. I was ready for some quiet time with him.

"How about we take off to your place and make a fire?" Grayson whispered. I nodded. He could read my mind.

Chapter 102

We headed to get our coats. We said goodbye to each of the Rosenthals and then walked out with Cole and Kate. They had such a great time being welcomed to Door County. Cole said they'd be heading home tomorrow so they could spend Christmas with their family.

"I'm excited to see my son and his wife coming in from New York," Kate noted with a smile.

"Just wait when they can come visit you in Door County," I reminded her.

"I can't wait to tell them every detail," Kate added.

We finally had a moment to ourselves when we got back to the car. Grayson took me in his arms and gave me a warm embrace and a long kiss.

"I'm freezing. Let's get home to that fire," I said after another kiss.

"Well, it's getting a little steamy in here." I blushed.

We traveled the short distance to the cabin. While Grayson made a fire, I put on some coffee.

We started chatting about what a wonderful family the Rosenthals were and how having the annual get-together at Christmas was really special. I reminded him they had a half-sister, Ellen, who lived in Paducah, Kentucky.

"I bet that's a story," Grayson paused.

"Laurie had told Cher that it was through their father's affair. I give them credit for accepting her."

"Yes, I could see how it would be easy to resent her."

"It says a lot about how sweet they all are. Here's some coffee to get you warmed up."

"Thanks, sweetie. Come sit here on the floor by the fire."

"I'd love to," I said as I threw more pillows on the floor. "I have a couple of gifts for you, but I'm a bit embarrassed. You're hard to buy for."

"Well, let me be the judge of that."

I put the two packages in front of him. He opened the Green Bay Packers throw first.

"Claire, this is really nice. I could use one of these. Thanks, honey!" I smiled.

"The next one isn't much, but it's handmade, and it reminded me of you. Perhaps this would be nice to have in your office." He quickly tore off the paper.

"Claire, this is incredible. This is the kind of sailboat my dad once had. Just look at the detail. Where did you find this?"

"At the Christkindlmarkt in Sister Bay. I was going to save it for your birthday, but my Packers throw seemed so inadequate. I didn't know about your dad's boat."

"I'll think of him every time I look at this boat. I'm glad you enclosed the artist's card. This is the perfect gift for me, Claire. I'm going to put it on my desk. You're truly something."

"You really like it?"

He nodded. "You always think of something personal. I wish I had a knack for that. I'm afraid I went the safe route of buying jewelry again."

"I love jewelry. Do you like what I wore tonight?"

He grinned and nodded. "I noticed every inch of you tonight."

He then got up and took something out of his overcoat pocket. I didn't see him bring in any gifts, so I was puzzled. I felt awkward waiting.

"I guess I should ask you something first to make sure this is appropriate," he said.

"What's wrong? You know I'll love anything you pick out."

"Claire, look at me," he instructed.

"I want you to be my wife, and I'm making an official proposal to you." I felt stunned. What did he just say? Could this be happening again? "You're a wonderful woman, and I want you in my life every day until we take our last breaths."

"Um, you want me to marry you?"

He nodded and came closer. "Will you marry me, Claire Stewart?"

"Yes. Yes! Yes!" He grinned and looked surprised.

With my answer, he lifted me up and twirled me around. Off the ground. I couldn't believe his strength and what was really happening. We were both laughing aloud. When he finally put me down, he opened the little box that had a large center diamond surrounded by tiny pearls. It was stunning and absolutely the perfect ring for me.

"I had to add the pearls," he gushed as he put the ring on my finger.

"I love it! I absolutely love it!" I shouted. "I'm engaged!"

"Funny, so am I!" Grayson followed. "Now what?"

Chapter 103

We held each other tight as we looked at my hand where the diamond ring fit perfectly. Could this really be happening? We got comfortable again as we sipped our coffee and stared into the fire.

"How long have you been thinking about this?" I asked to break the silence.

"Since I first saw you walking into the Blue Horse," he joked with a grin.

"Oh, you flatter me. You know this brings up many other questions about our future."

He nodded. "I know, and we'll address them together. For now, let's just enjoy the moment."

He was right. That's what engagements were for. We'd committed to becoming husband and wife, and our plans would evolve around that. I'd waited for an engagement with Austen, but it never came. We were a couple going nowhere. It's actually a blessing that God never answered that prayer. As I stared at Grayson's handsome face, I gave him credit for asking me to marry him a second time after I'd turned him down last year on New Year's Eve.

"Do you think Kelly has any idea this is happening?"

"Yes, I think she does. And I feel pretty confident about her approval."

"Well, no one will be happier for us than my mom. Every mother wants to know someone is going to love her child forever and ever."

"That's exactly what I plan to do. I think we're both old enough to know what we want for the rest of our lives."

"I worry about telling Cher tomorrow because she's been feeling so down. She misses Ericka so much, and I don't know how I can help her through that grief. She's a bit disappointed in Carl also. She'd like more out of the relationship than he's offering."

"I think you have Cher pegged wrong. She loves you enough that she'd want you to be happy. Her happiness will come, and you'll be there for her."

"I hope so."

It was late when Grayson left. What an evening. From all the fun at the White Gull Inn to the proposal, I couldn't wipe the smile off my face. I was engaged, and it felt so right. When he'd asked me before, it caught me off guard. I wasn't ready then. *We* weren't ready then. But we'd grown a lot as a couple in the past year. I was getting married to the best man I knew. Lying in bed that night, I thanked God for giving me such a good, kind man who loved me. Then I drifted into a peaceful sleep.

The next morning, I lay there still smiling. Then I remembered it was Christmas Eve. As a kid, I remember waking up Mom and Dad early on December 25 because I was so excited about Santa. This year, Santa's gift came early. I looked at the beautiful ring on my finger. Pearls and a center diamond. It was absolutely perfect. But more than the ring, I loved what it symbolized: a lifetime with Grayson Wills. I wondered what he was thinking this morning. Was he as happy as I was? Had he already told Kelly our news?

I put on my robe and told myself that this Christmas Eve morning had to be special. After all, I may not be in this cute little cabin next year. The thought of that made me rather sad. This was home.

Puff was ready to eat. She was part of my life and would soon be part of Grayson's. I wondered if he realized that.

I decided to have one of Anna's pastries I'd frozen after her open house. A sweet morning called for a sweet breakfast. I'd call Mom when I finished eating to share my good news. I wondered if she and Bill were up.

Cher interrupted my thoughts with a text.

[Cher]
Merry Christmas Eve! I'm looking forward to dinner tonight. Love you, Claire Bear.

[Claire]
Merry Christmas Eve to you, too! See you tonight! Love you back, Cher Bear.

I'd share my news with her tonight. I got back to giving Mom a call.

"Well, how nice of you to call this morning," her sweet voice said. I could just picture her at the breakfast table.

"It's Christmas Eve, and I'm feeling a bit homesick," I confessed. "How are you guys?"

"Well, Bill is a little under the weather, so we may not get to church tonight, but we'll see."

"Oh, I hope you can. Mom, I have something to tell you."

"Go ahead, sweetie. I'm waiting," she answered.

"Grayson asked me to marry him last night." There was a pause. "Did you hear me, Mom?"

"I hope I heard you right, Claire. Did you say yes? I worry about you sometimes."

I chuckled. "I said yes three times!"

"Oh, honey. Wait till I tell Bill. Grayson is a wonderful man who will always treat you well."

"I think so, too. You should see the diamond ring he gave me! I'll send you a photo. He even thought to add pearls around the diamond since he knows how much I love them."

"That's so special. Congratulations, honey. I'm so happy for you."

Chapter 104

We chatted for another ten minutes. She had many questions about where we'd live, when the wedding would be, and more that I couldn't answer yet. We discussed Cher coming for dinner and how the evening went with the Rosenthals. I finally hung up and noticed I had an email come in from Marta. It read:

Merry Christmas, Quilters of the Door. I hope you're all well and finding time to quilt in this busy season. We have a lot to celebrate at our January meeting. Anna is getting married to a nice man from Germany, and Olivia is now the manager of Barn Door Quilts. I'm sure by our meeting time, there may be other noteworthy news. I sent a thank-you note to the Chans for inviting us to their wonderful Christmas party. I look forward to seeing you at our next quilt club, but until then, I wish you a happy New Year.

Marta was so sweet to keep us informed. I'd have my own news to share at our next meeting. Maybe Cher and I would have a plan for the next quilt show by then, too.

Before I dressed for the evening, I did some prep work on my sweet potatoes and green beans for my dinner with Cher. Suddenly, my cell rang.

"Merry Christmas!" two cheerful voices called out. It was Carole and Linda. "We're at the coffee shop and wanted you to know we were thinking of you."

"How sweet! I just talked to Mom. I guess all of you are trying to make me homesick."

"We are," they joked.

"So, are you ready for Christmas?" Carole asked.

"Yes, I am. Cher is coming to dinner tonight, and tomorrow I'll be with Grayson. I do have some news for you." There was silence.

"Is it what we think?"

"I said yes three times!" They screamed into the phone. "I keep pinching myself to make sure it's real. Of course, Mom is elated."

"So, when?" Linda asked with excitement.

"We don't know yet. I'm curious about what his daughter has to say about it."

We chatted for about fifteen more minutes, but I finally said goodbye and wished them a happy New Year.

At three, Grayson called.

"Have you changed your mind?" I joked.

"No, have you?" I chuckled.

"I just wanted to tell you that I told Kelly our news. She gave me a hug and said she was glad I was happy. She didn't act like it was a big deal at all."

"Well, that's a relief."

"I'm planning dinner for us tomorrow night around five o'clock. Would you like me to come get you?"

"That's not necessary. I'll see you there."

"Tell Cher I said hello, and enjoy your dinner."

"I will."

I took a deep breath knowing I didn't have to worry about Kelly. The house smelled divine with the turkey breast now in the oven. I wanted to call Michael and tell him about the engagement before Cher arrived.

"Hey, Claire. Glad you called. Jon and I were going to call and wish you a merry Christmas, so let me put you on speaker."

"Hi, Jon. I called to give you both some good news. Your sister is engaged to Grayson Wills!"

I had to move the phone away from my ear a little from all their whistles and cheers. I burst into laughter.

"Congrats, Sis!" Michael said. "Grayson is a stand-up guy, and I had hoped this would happen."

"You're a great pair," Jon agreed.

"Thank you. I'm glad he didn't give up on me when I told him no the first time. I guess I just needed some time. I envision the four of us hanging out a lot in the future. Hey, have a great trip to Colorado."

"We will. Happy New Year from both of us," Michael cheered. "We love you."

"I love you, too!"

I took another deep breath, pleased that those who were closest to me now knew my news. Then I thought of Cher. I could only hope she'd be happy for me, too.

Chapter 105

I'd just taken my turkey out of the oven to rest when I heard Cher at the door.

"Merry Christmas, Claire Bear." Her arms were full, so I'd have to wait to give her a hug.

"The same to you, Cher Bear."

"Give me your great-smelling bread pudding, and go warm yourself by the fire."

"Oh, this place smells like home."

"It's making me hungry. It's been a while since I cooked a big meal like this. I still have to do the gravy, but if you'll pour some wine, we can eat in a few minutes."

"Did you learn to make gravy from your mom?"

"I guess so. I saw her go through the motions anyway. I hope I have enough juice to do this, so don't watch." Cher chuckled and got out some wine.

Cher seemed to be in a good mood, which I was happy about. Still, I wasn't sure when I should tell her about being engaged. I didn't want her mood to change for the worse.

I lit the candles I'd set out on the table. So far, everything was turning out just as I'd hoped. Even the gravy. The two of us chatted about the big dinner party at the White Gull Inn and the good fortune with the Alexanders closing on their property. I was about to tell her about the evening Grayson and I had shared, but she interrupted.

"Carl and I worked till we closed, and then he suggested we have dinner at the Whistling Swan. That was a surprise. I didn't know if that was an afterthought or what. Maybe he felt like he had to feed me after a long day."

"Well, how did it go? Did he give you a gift by chance?" She nodded.

"He gave me a really generous bonus—even more than last year. Of course, that made me feel like I've been doing a respectable job there. He seemed to really like my gift, so all and all, it was a very pleasant evening. The real surprise was when he walked me to the car after dinner."

"Surprise? What happened?"

"He kissed me on the lips and told me he'd fallen in love with me. I couldn't believe my ears when he used the *L* word."

"Oh my goodness, Cher!"

"I know. It was so unexpected."

"I'm so happy for you! And here you've been so worried that Carl wasn't interested in you at all anymore. This is a merry Christmas indeed!"

Cher burst into laughter. "It really is. I left that boulder I've been carrying on my shoulder right there in the parking lot."

"So, I'm curious. Did you tell him you loved him, too?"

"Of course, I did!"

"Sounds like the two of you are moving in the same direction now. That's absolutely wonderful. Knowing your news, I have a little something of my own to share." I showed her my ring, and her eyes grew twice their normal size.

"Claire, it can't be!" she said in disbelief. "You're not joking, are you?"

"I'm engaged and said yes three times to his proposal!"

Cher got out of her chair and came over to give me a big hug. We both had tears in our eyes.

We took our glasses of wine over to the fireplace, where we decided to have our bread pudding.

"Forget the dishes. Let's open our presents."

Cher and I had several gifts for each other. She especially loved Rachael's barn quilts that I gave her for her living room. We giggled and laughed like schoolchildren until we started making toasts and Ericka's name came up. It was time to call it a night by then. It was midnight, and I was partied out and ready for bed. I'd clean up my messy kitchen tomorrow.

Morning came quickly. I didn't remember ever feeling this happy on Christmas morning. Cher's news about Carl enhanced my own joy about being engaged. There was so much to look forward to.

I ignored my messy kitchen for now. I wanted to enjoy my coffee and play with Puff first. She seemed to like the couple of toys I bought her. She even carried one under the tree to enjoy.

As I drank my coffee, I checked my phone for messages. Foster had sent a text asking me where I'd be next year at this time. If he only knew that I may be Mrs. Wills by then. Another Christmas wish came from George.

I looked out the window, and the threat of snow was upon us again. Snow wasn't my favorite ordinarily, but having it on Christmas was nice. I cleaned up the kitchen and looked forward to my evening with Kelly and Grayson. By two o'clock, I was sleepy and indulged in a short nap.

It was time to dress for a casual, yet festive Christmas dinner with my future husband. I chose my white sweater with scattered pearls that Austen had given me several years ago. In my ears, I wore my grandmother's pearl earrings. I looked down at my left ring finger and admired my favorite pearls of all.

I checked the weather again and said a quick prayer that the snow wouldn't start till I arrived at Grayson's. I put Kelly's wrapped painting by the front door so I wouldn't forget it. I sure hoped she'd like it. Paintings of people and pets are so personal. At least she'd appreciate the thought.

Chapter 106

I saw a call from Rachael come in and realized I hadn't told her my big news.

"Merry Christmas from Harry and me!"

"The same to you! You caught me just as I was heading out the door for dinner at Grayson's."

"Oh, I won't keep you then. I just wanted you to know we missed you at our Christmas Eve party this year. Did you and Cher have a good evening?"

"Yes, we really did. I also have big news to share with you."

"Pray tell," she joked.

"Grayson and I are engaged!" Screaming followed on the other end.

"Oh, Claire! A big congrats from Harry and me! We knew it would happen eventually."

"Thanks! I don't have much more to tell other than that my ring is fabulous. I'll be out to help with inventory soon and can tell you all about it."

"You've really made my Christmas, Claire Stewart."

Rachael's reaction put a smile on my face all the way to Grayson's.

I saw a car parked in front of the house that I wasn't familiar with. I grabbed Kelly's painting from the back seat and went to the door.

"Merry Christmas, sweetheart!" he greeted, kissing me on the cheek.

"Come on in. Kelly's in the kitchen helping the chef prepare dinner."

"Oh, I could have brought something."

"It was Kelly's suggestion that we ask Chef Mark to prepare dinner for us. We use him at the office for various things. Relax and give me your coat. I'll tell Kelly you're here."

I nervously paced the living room, pausing to look again at all the beautiful decorations on their tree.

"Hey, Merry Christmas, Claire," Kelly said as she came around the corner.

"You too, Kelly," I replied. "I like your new haircut, and you look mighty cute in that Christmas apron." She smiled.

"Well, I'm not much help in the kitchen, but I love watching Mark. I can tell you that dinner will be delicious."

"I can't wait."

"Dad told me you two are engaged. I'm happy for you." I smiled, not knowing what to say. I knew Grayson was watching us.

"Thanks, Kelly," I said, giving her a hug. "That means a lot coming from you."

"To be honest, it's a relief knowing someone is going to look after my dad," she joked, looking at Grayson. "Someone has to know that I'm not around. He's happy around you, and that makes me happy."

"Hey, let's not get too sentimental here," Grayson interrupted. "Claire, would you like some of my famous eggnog?"

"I'd love some," I nodded.

Things felt natural and easy between the three of us. It was certainly a lot different than my experience here last Christmas when Kelly was so moody. So much had changed since then. Kelly had accepted me as part of their life.

It wasn't long before Mark came out of the kitchen and announced that dinner was ready. Grayson introduced the young man with a glowing background, and then Mark recited the evening's menu. First we'd have butternut squash followed by a cranberry molded salad. Cornish hens, mushroom risotto, and maple-glazed Brussels sprouts would follow that.

Each course was beautifully garnished and tasted delicious. Kelly dominated much of the conversation talking about college. I was a bit surprised she hadn't asked any questions about our upcoming wedding or future living arrangements.

Mark served our dessert, crème brûlée, in a gorgeous crystal dish with a touch of holly for the season. I could only hope that our marriage would inherit the services of Chef Mark. After we had some after-dinner coffee, Kelly suggested we move into the living room to open gifts.

"I think it's time to see what Santa brought," Kelly said with humor.

We got up as instructed. On my way, I poked my head in the kitchen to thank Mark for the wonderful meal he'd provided.

"Congrats on your engagement," Mark said.

"Thanks," I replied, blushing. "It's been a special Christmas for sure."

I joined Grayson on the couch.

"Here, Claire. This gift is from me," Kelly said, presenting me with a rather large box.

"Thanks so much, Kelly," I said as I put the box on my lap.

I opened up two cute sweatshirts. One was from her college, and the other was a Green Bay sweatshirt. I gave her a big hug and told her I had a gift for her as well.

Kelly eagerly opened my gift, tearing the paper and throwing it aside.

"Spot? No way! You painted my Spot?" she asked with disbelief. I wasn't quite sure what her reaction meant. "How did you do this, Claire? He looks so adorable. I absolutely love this!"

I sighed with relief. "You really like it, Kelly? I was worried."

"I do. It looks just like him!"

"I couldn't agree more," Grayson chimed in.

"This painting is going back to the dorm with me," she announced.

"Great idea," Grayson agreed.

Chapter 107

"Dad showed me his gifts from you, Claire," Kelly revealed. "They're both pretty cool."

"Thanks, but did you see what your dad gave me?" I lifted my hand.

"It's pretty," she said, smiling casually. "Do you like it?"

"Yes, very much," I said, looking directly at Grayson.

"Dad, this last little gift is for me, right?" Kelly asked with anticipation.

"That's right," Grayson answered.

"Is this what I think it is?" she teased.

"Go to the garage and see for yourself," he instructed with a smile.

"Oh, Dad!" she squealed as she ran out the door.

"Kelly's been wanting a Smart car, and I refused to get her one till I saw how she did with a less expensive car. She's proven that she's responsible."

"That's very generous," I said, thinking back to my own first car: a clunker that died on me once a month and had a dent in the left fender.

Moments later, Kelly came rushing in the house to give her dad a big hug.

"You even got the color right. I have to make some phone calls. Claire, you'll have to excuse me."

With that, she took off for her room.

"Well, Mr. Wills, you seem to have made the two women in your life very happy this Christmas."

Grayson came to sit by me with a big grin on his face.

"That was my goal. You've certainly made mine happy."

"Look, honey!" I said, jumping up to go to the window. "We're having a white Christmas!"

"Let's go to the porch where we can watch it fall on the lake and trees," Grayson suggested as he took my hand.

We stood admiring the magic of snowfall on Christmas Day. At that very moment, we needed no words. I rested my head against his and closed my eyes briefly to appreciate the quiet around us. We'd figure out our future together. The most important thing is that we'd do it side by side, just like this. After a few minutes, Grayson opened the sliding doors that led to the patio. We stepped outside, hand in hand, giggling as the snow covered our hair.

"How about this Christmas surprise?" Grayson asked as he kissed my wet face.

"The best surprises in my life have been right here in Door County," I told him. "Merry Christmas, Mr. Wills."

WHITE GULL INN'S
Apple Dumplings with Brandy Cream Sauce

Yields 6 dumplings.

Dumplings:

3 frozen puff pastry sheets (9-inch × 9-inch), thawed

6 medium tart baking apples, cored and peeled

⅓ cup granulated sugar

⅓ cup chopped pecans

2 tablespoons butter, softened

Milk to brush with

Brandy cream sauce:

½ cup brown sugar

2 tablespoons butter

½ cup heavy whipping cream

1½ tablespoons brandy

A dash of cinnamon

Preheat the oven to 375 degrees.

Lay out sheets of pastry. Trim a 2-inch strip from one side of each sheet of pastry to form 9 × 7-inch rectangles. Set trimmed strips aside. Cut each rectangle in half to create six 4½ × 7-inch rectangles. Place an apple in the center of each rectangle. In a small bowl, stir together the sugar, pecans, and butter. Stuff 1½ tablespoons of that mixture in the center of each apple. Fold the pastry up around each apple, sealing the seams well and twisting the top to create a stem. If desired, decorate apples with leaf shapes cut from the trimmed pastry, and press those onto the dumplings. Place the dumplings on a baking sheet. Brush them with milk and bake for 35–45 minutes until the apples are fork tender and the pastry is golden brown.

While the apples are baking, combine the brown sugar, butter, cream, brandy, and cinnamon in a heavy saucepan. Cook over medium heat, stirring often, for 3–4 minutes or until the mixture comes to a boil. Serve the sauce over the warm dumplings.

Thanks to the White Gull Inn in Fish Creek, Wisconsin, for serving such a delicious breakfast and for sharing this recipe with us.

Author's Note

It's time to say goodbye to my beloved characters in Door County, Wisconsin. Bidding farewell to this series is just as hard as it was when I wrapped up the Colebridge series, the East Perry County series, and the Wine Country series.

In this last novel, I wanted to address your questions about the characters in my other series. I knew there was a way to do so because Anne (Colebridge series), Kate (East Perry County series), and Lily (Wine series) had all been to Door County. I hope you won't be disappointed with the new information this book presents.

Read more about Anne (Brown) Fletcher and Rev. Fletcher in the Colebridge series, which takes place in Saint Charles, Missouri.

Read about Kate (Myer) and Cole Alexander in the East Perry County series, which takes place in the German communities of Missouri.

Read about Lily Rosenthal and her sisters, Loretta, Lynn, and Laurie, in the Wine Country series, which primarily takes place in Augusta, Missouri.

I loved hearing from so many of you over the years. You inspired me to keep writing as I carried the responsibility of these characters on paper.

Thank you to all who made my research and visits to Door County so enjoyable.

Writing continues to be my passion, so I'll continue to write each day and see what comes next. Writing, as well as reading, can take you anywhere you want to go. Thanks for taking my journeys with me. I knew you were here beside me.

Much love,

—*Ann Hazelwood*

READER'S GUIDE:
Christmas Surprises at the Door

by Ann Hazelwood

1. A theme is a central idea or message that a book explores. Love is a theme in this book. Can you think of some others? What are the themes of your own life?

2. How does the setting of Door County affect the story the author is telling? If Door County were a character, what would its personality traits be?

3. Do you see Foster's persistence with Claire as charming and romantic or obsessive and harassing? Have you been in a similar situation? How did you handle it, and do you agree with the way Claire did?

4. Did Claire's answer to Grayson's proposal surprise you? What was different for her this time? What might their future obstacles include?

5. This is the last book in the Door County series. Who were your favorite and least favorite characters and why?

About the Author

Ann Hazelwood is a former shop owner and native of Saint Charles, Missouri. She has always adored quilting and is a certified quilt appraiser. She's the author of the wildly successful Colebridge Community series and considers writing one of her greatest passions. She has also published the Wine Country Quilt series and East Perry County series in addition to this Door County Quilts series.

booksonthings.com

Cozy up with more quilting mysteries from Ann Hazelwood...

WINE COUNTRY QUILT SERIES

After quitting her boring editing job, aspiring writer Lily Rosenthal isn't sure what to do next. Her two biggest joys in life are collecting antique quilts and frequenting the area's beautiful wine country. The murder of a friend results in Lily acquiring the inventory of a local antique store. Murder, quilts, and vineyards serve as the inspiration as Lily embarks on a journey filled with laughs, loss, and red-and-white quilts.

THE DOOR COUNTY QUILT SERIES

Meet Claire Stewart, a new resident of Door County, Wisconsin. Claire is a watercolor quilt artist and joins a prestigious small quilting club when her best friend moves away. As she grows more comfortable after escaping a bad relationship, new ideas and surprises abound as friendships, quilting, and her love life all change for the better.

Want more? Visit us online at ctpub.com